CATHERINE MEDE

# Finding Faith

A RACING HARTS Novel

*Racing Harts: Finding Faith*

*Publisher: Flying Kiwi Press*


*The smell of burning rubber, racing fuel and the adrenaline rush of watching racing of any kind is fun any time of the day. Wearing all of the protective gear on a motorcycle is the best option for keeping all of your skin intact. Never wear shorts or t-shirt when riding a motorbike!*



*ISBN 978-1-0670901-5-9 epub*

*ISBN 978-1-0670901-6-6 PDF*

*ISBN 978-1-0670901-7-3 - paperback*

*Dedication*

*To all the women who want to do more than watch the motorsports.*

# chapter one

Faith

I twisted on my seat, braked, changed down gears. Throwing my weight to the right, pulling the bike over with me. I straightened up, accelerated, gear change up, accelerate. Corner coming, brake, changed down again, weight to the left, the right, then the left again. The bike followed my every move. I followed the track, each tight corner, wide bend and chicane that it threw at me. I was so in the zone.

So, when I got tapped on the shoulder. I squealed and sat up on my bike.

The screen in front of me froze, then CRASH ZONE flashed twice before the screen went blank.

A moment later, a message in bold lit up the screen. CRASH DETECTED

I took off my helmet and shook my hair out. It wasn't long, but long enough to get static when I removed my helmet, making it cling to my head. I turned to see who'd interrupted my concentration and was surprised to see a drop-dead gorgeous guy standing there. Dark hair flopped over his forehead, his fingers hooked through the belt loops of his jean shorts. A big cheeky grin stretched over his clean-shaven face, and his brown eyes sparkled. That smile could melt the Antarctic ice in five seconds flat.

Warmth flooded through my body as I gazed at this Adonis standing in front of me.

"How'd you get in here?" I asked, looking around. We were alone in my gazebo at the Taupō Motorsport Park, in the pits of the racing track.

"Security." His voice washed over me like a warm summer wave. He indicated towards them with a thumb over his shoulder and blasted me with a beautiful megawatt smile. I couldn't help but grin back, even though I was still pissed at being interrupted. Security could be a bit slack at local motorcycle events. But still, I expected more from them.

"They're not there?" I asked.

He shrugged, which made me feel a little insecure. I got off the bike and put my helmet on the ground, keeping the bike between us.

"Nice set-up you have," he said, looking at the screen and the bike that was hooked up to it.

"Where I practice," I told him.

He nodded, a piece of hair falling onto his face which he immediately flicked back. His hair was maybe the same length as my own on top, but shorter up the back. I pushed a hand through my own, feeling self-conscious under the scrutiny of his gaze. His white shirt was kind of tucked into his shorts, but it was pulled out a little on one side. He wore no jewellery, his ring finger bare, but I told myself off for noticing that.

I didn't have time for a relationship.

"I enjoyed watching you race last year," he said.

"Oh? You a fan?" I asked, tightening the arms of the overalls that were tied at my waist. I pulled on my white cotton singlet top, wondering why I felt so hot all of a sudden.

"Yeah, you could say that." He grinned, and my heart fluttered again.

"Cool, well, I have a picture around here somewhere I can sign for you."

"That would be awesome, thanks." A small flush covered his cheeks. It was kind of cute. I mean, he was about the same age as me.

I turned and went over to one of the tool-trays and pulled open a drawer. There were postcard-sized pictures of me in my racing livery, holding my helmet, grinning at the camera. My racing number, seventy-seven in the background. I scrounged around for a pen.

"What's your name?" I asked him.

"Cole," he replied.

"Cole," I said as I wrote it down on the postcard. *To Cole, nice to meet you, Faith x.* I walked over and handed it to him. Our hands touched as he took it, and it felt like an electric shock through my body. He looked at the picture then back up at me.

"Appreciate that. Thank you," he said, waving the card at me.

"No problem. Now, we better find security so we can get you back to where you need to be," I said, walking out of the tent. There was more activity going on out the back of the track, where mechanics and computer specialists hooked bikes up and diagnosed problems, and riders and managers discussed strategies. I nodded to my mechanic who gave me a funny look. I rolled my eyes as I moved Cole back towards the security gate.

"Cole? Cole!" I heard from behind me. I turned to see Nigel Kinsey waving at the guy beside me. I looked at him and then back at the visitor. "You know him?"

"Yeah, I do."

My muscles tensed, suddenly not so keen on my visitor.

"He's my manager."

"Manager?" My voice pitched higher, and he looked sharply at me. Ignoring him, I marched back to my gazebo.

Cole was a fellow competitor? And Nigel Kinsey was his manager?

Bastard! I thought.

How could Nigel Kinsey have done that to me? I growled as I shut the doors on the gazebo to have some privacy and quiet to concentrate. I couldn't let the anger take over. I'd spent years racing against Nigel Kinsey, always coming second to his first. When he retired at the end of last year, I thought this would be my year, but Nigel was still involved in racing? Gah!

I climbed on the bike and restarted the practice ride. I had to make sure that I nailed every corner, got my acceleration and braking so precise that I would be the fastest on this track. I'd raced here in Taupō before. I knew the track like the back of my hand, but I needed to know it better, be faster than my competitors. This year, I wanted to win. I was sick of coming second. I deserved to win!

My focus was so intent on the track and bike that I didn't hear Sara, my computer tech, until she came into my peripheral vision. I switched off the simulation and sat up, removing my helmet.

"You alright?" she asked, her brows creased in concern.

"Yeah, why?"

"You've been in here for over an hour."

I looked at my watch. I hadn't even been aware that it had been so long since I'd escorted Cole from my tent and started back on the simulator.

"Just got my head too far into the game," I said, smiling. My heart rate was calmer after the training. This was what relaxed me: speed and high risk. The riskier the better.

"Ready for your race then?" Sara asked, grinning at me.

"Hell yeah!" I said, raising my hand. She high-fived me back as I climbed off the simulator and we headed out of the tent together.

# chapter two

## Cole

I sat on my bike in my livery of blue, silver and black. Bike Number eighty-six. Second from the back. Being my first year racing in the Superbike class, I had to start from the back. But that was okay, I knew I could work my way through the pack. On the start line, I had my helmet on, listening to Dad chatter to the crew.

"Now, Cole. Take it easy, watch those lights, be ready to go."

"Yip."

I was too focused on the lights, and the bike up the front with the red, orange and black livery. Faith. Oh my goodness, Faith. What a name. I'd always watched her racing against Dad, and I knew that she was a determined and focused racer, but I couldn't believe her reaction when I said I knew Nigel Kinsey. She stormed off, like I had the plague!

Dad retired from racing last year, mostly because of age, but diabetes was starting to slow him up too. He's well into his fifties now, and he'd had too many spills off his bike. He has a permanent limp from damage to his right leg.

The beeps of the lights caught my attention. They were counting down. I let my clutch out a little, and started revving the bike. Flashing red, pause, then Green.

I dropped the clutch and the bike shot forwards. I weaved around the two slower riders in front of me and easily moved up into sixth position. The corners were tricky and deceptive. I'm pleased Dad brought me here to practice in the off-season. Otherwise I wouldn't have known the track.

Left, left, right, straight, chicane, left, right, hard right.

The world whizzed by in a blur of movement of light. I only focused on the track in front of me and the riders I would have to overtake. I had to keep my head in the game. Look for the opportunities to overtake when I could.

We hit the long straight and I saw it, I dropped a gear, weaved around the rider and slotted in front of him in time for the right-hand turn. I felt his front wheel nudge my back one as I tucked into the corner. I accelerated out of the turn and shot ahead. He couldn't keep up. Racing was all about using your gears and less about braking. Braking can cause all sorts of issues, gear changes are more predictable. I was now in fifth, and I could see the next rider take the corner, but he took it too wide, he got the speed wobbles and the bike tipped, spewing the rider off as the bike skidded into the tyre guard rail. I managed to zip around the downed rider and avoid my own downfall, but his loss was my gain. Fourth.

I rode the track hard and fast, trying to gain ground on number three. I could see him, and I was gaining, but not fast enough.

"Slow it down there, speedy, your fuel consumption is too high."

"I'm in fourth. I'm going for third," I said.

"You have enough laps to take it, save your energy and strength," the old man said.

I didn't want to, though. I wanted third. My first year racing at this level. Dad wouldn't let me race with him, didn't want me beating him, I think, and I wondered if perhaps I was getting close to his track record.

"You have five laps to go, don't waste your fuel now," he growled.

I tried to shut out the voice in my ear.

"Just work on getting closer. You don't have to win every race. Not at this stage, anyway," Dad said.

"Don't I? But didn't you have to win every one of yours?"

There was silence on the other end. I knew about the rivalry he had with Faith. He hated the fact that a woman beat him on the track occasionally. She was good, I love watching her ride, the way the bike flowed underneath her as if it was an extension of her. She held those corners so tight and clean, it was never messy or over-calculated.

I slowly gained on the third motorcycle. I took my time to assess the rider and their faults, and I knew that undertaking on a corner, while risky, was a worthwhile manoeuvre because they took them wide.

I undertook him, and the poor rider just about sat bolt upright on his bike with the fright I gave him, but he recovered and was soon chasing me down, but I had the upper hand.

I crossed the line for the last lap. I wasn't going to get second, so I had to hold on for third, which wasn't a bad placing for my first ride of the Superbike championship on the track. And for starting at the back.

I followed the track, catching glimpses of the number two bike, which was yellow and black like a wasp, but it wasn't Faith. She must have been right out the front. I came around the corner to the checkered flag, and she was already pulling into the pits. She got off her bike with cheers from her team. A well-deserved win for her. I pulled up alongside her team and pulled off my helmet.

"Well done, Faith, good race." I gave her my biggest grin because she'd done well. Her happiness seemed to lose a little of its brightness as soon as she saw me. Her sultry mouth dropped into a thin line.

"Thanks," she muttered and turned her back on me. I shrugged. I could only do my best.

I rode down to our trailer and pit and stopped the bike. Dad was already waiting for me, and I knew the lecture before I even got off the bike.

"You need to have patience. You could've gotten at least second if you hadn't flown off so fast."

"It wasn't an endurance race, Dad. We only had ten laps. I got third, aren't you happy for me?"

"You could have gotten first if you'd followed my rules."

"Which are?"

"Take your time, watch your opposition, find their weakness."

"I did. Third place, I got to third place, that's points on the board, Dad."

"Fourth place is points on the board too," he said.

"And did you see Faith win?" I couldn't help grinning. I hadn't seen her cross the line, but she won, which is great to see for our first race of the season.

Dad turned away and muttered something. I didn't really care. I got off the bike and let the mechanic set it up for the next race. New tyres, more fuel, check the brakes, brake fluid, all that stuff. I had to sit back and watch as the next two categories had their races. We raced again at one that afternoon. I didn't mind. Something to eat and some meditation before I got onto my next race, provided Dad didn't want to chat more.

# chapter three

Faith

"And then, the second race, I won again, but the third race…" I rolled my eyes.

"What? What happened?" Hope asked.

"That upstart Cole won."

"Who is Cole again?" Grace asked.

"Nigel's prodigy."

"Nigel Kinsey? The one that has won every championship for the last three years?" Hope looked confused.

"That exact one."

"I thought he'd retired?" Grace asked.

"He has, but he's obviously mentoring Cole and on his team."

"Did Cole race last year in your class?"

"No, the class under us."

"Then you have a chance this year." Hope said.

I deflated a little. I would like to say that I had a really good chance, but with Nigel Kinsey, there was a chance that I wouldn't.

I sat back on the couch, hugging the cushion to my chest, both of my sisters sitting on the large couch opposite me. I was home for the week, before the next race the following weekend at the Manfield track in Fielding. I stared out the window at the large vista before me. We owned all that land. We run a vineyard which sponsored most of our racing, because Hope and Grace raced too. Hope was into sprint cars and wanted to head overseas to race, while Grace raced rally cars and called Riley Hayden, the international rally champion as a friend. I was the freak who liked two wheels in our family.

"Earth to Faith," Grace said, waving her hand in front of my face. I tuned back into my sisters. Hope was gushing over something.

"Is this Cole?" she asked, holding her phone out towards me. I looked at the picture with Cole Blythe smiling back at me. I felt a jolt of excitement as I looked at the gorgeous man, leaning against a fence post, his riding leathers unzipped to reveal a small dusting of chest hair. I hadn't seen it under his shirt that day. There was just enough to run your fingers through…His eyes were sparkling as he smirked at the camera, aware of just how good-looking he was. His hair, highlighted by the sun, flopped over his forehead in a boyish way.

"Yip, that's him," I said, trying to keep my voice from sounding dreamy.

"He's quite handsome. When is your next race?" Hope asked.

"Never you mind," I said, feeling a shaft of annoyance flitter through me at the thought of her chasing after Cole. Yes, he was good-looking, and that smile, it made me weak at the knees just thinking about it. I smiled a little bit too.

"I think someone is falling in lust," Grace sung as she got up from the couch. I took a swing at her as she walked by, but she tucked her butt in before I could smack it. I wasn't falling in lust. Or love. I couldn't fall in love. What was love? Sure, our Aunt and Uncle showered us with love and attention, but there was little love between them. The fights they had about who was spoiling us the most, and all the little things. I used to just hide out in my room and read. As I got older, I learned how to do yoga and practiced breathing, which helped to keep me calm. But I think I'll need more than yoga and meditation to keep me from flying after Cole..

"So, what's happening on the vineyard?" I asked.

Grace, the managing director carried a glass of water back to the couch area within her office, in the main building on the site. "The grapes are ripening up nicely. Provided we don't have too much rain, we should see a great crop this year."

Hope nodded and added,"Last year's harvest has been bottled and ready to be put down for the next year. It tastes superb, and I can't wait to sell it.

"Awesome, so I can start looking at the overseas market to sell our wine then?" I asked.

"Have you heard from England?" Hope asked.

"Yes, Tony has been in touch and is keen to get his hands on our pinot gris. I told him it wouldn't be ready until next year, but that didn't worry him. He has just the person to send it to. Some guy named Roger Hartley? I think that's his name. He's going to set up a meeting for me after New Year's."

"Fabulous.," Grace said. And with that, the work meeting was concluded.

I got up and headed out to my own unit. We all lived in the vineyard. We shared the lounge kitchen, which also doubled as a restaurant in the summer season, and during the winter, it was our home away from home. We each had a villa which had a small kitchen, bathroom, two bedrooms, once of which I'd turned into my office. I did marketing, Grace managed the winery and Hope was the winemaker. It suited us all, we were each single and happy on our own.

Our aunt and uncle left the vineyard operations to us when they retired. They were somewhere in the North Island in their campervan making the most of their retirement. We'd worked enough with them to understand how everything worked, and we'd all studied at university to get degrees: Grace in Management, me in Marketing, and Hope in Viticulture with a master's in Wine Science.

Hope had travelled to Italy and learned how to make wine and refined her skills in France before she came home. She was the youngest internationally acclaimed winemaker in New Zealand. Something we liked to remind her of. Every time she talked about racing in the United States, we reminded her that there weren't many award-winning wine growers over there. She always says there is, but we like to tease her.

The windows of my villa were open to catch any breeze that might go through. It was December, the hottest time of the year in New Zealand, and it looked like it was going to be a long, hot growing season.

I sat down at my desk and started sending out emails, getting my day started at seven thirty in the morning. Yeah, we liked to get up early to work.

I also had to get ready for my next race the following weekend in Fielding at the Manfield track. It was one of my favourite tracks, but with Cole Blythe racing, I had to make sure I was at the top of my game.

# chapter four

## Cole

I was sanding down the front fender of a 1932 Cadillac Sports Coupe I was turning into a ratrod. I liked the lines and the styling of the car, which looked like something Al Capone once drove, and I wanted to keep it all authentic, except for the throaty V8 motor that I'd ordered to put into it. It would look like an old-fashioned gangster car with a deep, maroon colour with a hint of glitter through the paintwork.

It was what I did. I was a panel beater and spray painter. My mates' cars all looked amazing. But my Caddy was still a project, even after eight years. I'd started when I was twenty. Dad bought it for me after he saw me drooling over it, and I've loved it ever since. It sits in the back of my workshop, and when I get the opportunity, I work on it. And this week was a great time to sand off the original paint and see what the body looked like. Fortunately, there seemed to be little rust in it and not much filler. I liked the smooth curves; they were feminine.

Unfortunately, my mind kept drifting off to Faith and her curves, which were accentuated when she wore her racing overalls. Especially when she tied the arms just below her waist…Mmm, delicious.

"Hey," Dad said. I looked up to see him entering the workshop.

"Hi." I put down my sanding block and brushed the dust off my hands.

Dad leaned on the chassis and folded his arms across his chest."How's she coming along?"

"Good, just making sure she's all smooth," I said, running my hands along her clean lines once again. I found a rough patch and mentally made a note to check that out later.

"How long until you paint her?"

"Couple of weeks away, I think."

Dad nodded his head. I could see him critically eyeing the work I'd done, but he wasn't a panel beater, so he wouldn't know if I was doing it right or not. No doubt I was doing it wrong in Dad's eyes.

"Ready for Manfield?" Dad asked.

I nodded. I'd been in the gym every day after work building up my strength and stamina. It can be hard work fighting those g-forces when on the bike.

"You must be on top of your game this weekend. We need to get ahead of that woman." He said the words with such venom.

"What do you have against Faith?"

"I have nothing against Faith," Dad said, but he wasn't looking at me; he was clearing dirt from under his nails, something he did when he was avoiding the question.

"She's an amazing racer."

"She shouldn't be racing. There should be a separate class for women."

Misogynistic bastard, I thought. Faith was an amazingly talented rider.

"You just need to get on top of that leaderboard."

Dad's fidgeting had me a little worried. It wasn't like him to be antsy. And against a woman? He'd won the last three years, so I don't know what his problem was. Would it be so bad if Faith won the championship this year?

"I reckon she'll win this year."

"Not if I have anything to do with it," Dad grumbled. "You need to be winning all of your races from now on."

"That won't be possible," I said.

"You need to be better than your best. You need to win."

"What would it matter if she won?" I pushed.

Dad walked around the car, seeming to inspect it, before he headed out the door towards me.

"How's your mum?" he asked, changing the subject.

His tone made the hair stand up on the back of my neck.

"She's good."

"Gotten over her problems yet?"

I nearly snorted. He was the problem. It had taken every ounce of strength and courage for Mum to leave Dad.

"Pick you up Thursday lunchtime?" Dad asked.

We would be driving up with the bike trailer from Christchurch. It was a long trip, but worth it in the end. We were taking a late ferry to Wellington, then driving up to Fielding. Friday to set up, racing Saturday and Sunday.

"Yip, sounds good."

"See you Thursday," Dad said as he walked away.

I went back to sanding the rough patch I'd found, using my hand every now and again to check the smoothness of the panel.

"Was that your Dad?" Mum came into the workshop with her handbag slung over her shoulder.

I sighed. "Yes."

"How is he?"

"He's fine. Wanted to know if you were over your problems yet."

Mum barked out a laugh.

"I know," I said.

She wrung her hands. Their split had been anything but amicable. Dad had worn her down over the years. And because of his attitude, she now avoided him like the plague. Still too much hurt there, I guess.

"I've paid some bills, written up a couple of quotes, and now I'm off to lunch."

"Oh, okay," I said, kissing her cheek before she left the workshop. I stood there, watching her walk away, pleased that she'd left Dad. How she'd managed to stick it out for so long was beyond me.

I shook my head as I picked up my sanding block and worked along from the rough spot. I ran my entire hand over the area, closing my eyes to feel if the curve was smooth enough. I felt for any differences in surface height. She was smoother than I expected. Perfect.

Ready for paint.

I removed the front fender from the stand and put it on the back wall with all the other finished pieces that were ready to be cleaned and painted.

I couldn't wait to get them in the spray booth and paint them up.

# chapter five

## Faith

The trailer was parked, the gazebo was up, and I was ready to go. The only problem was, it was Friday. Racing didn't start until tomorrow. I'd been avoiding Cole, but I kept looking out for him too. His dark hair, the cheeky smile; I wanted to catch a glimpse of him.

I got the bike set up with Geoff and Sara, and we worked out what problems may arise. The bike had been running well, and there wasn't anything that really needed doing, but there were always tweaks that could be made.

After lunch, we were left to our own devices. Sara and I decided to go into Fielding. It was a small North Island town, just outside of Palmerston North, where Hope often raced her Sprint Cars. There wasn't much to Fielding, but I liked to go and visit places while I was there. We were staying at a local campground anyway, so why not spend some money in the town too.

We found a little cafe and sat down to have a coffee after a round of shopping. Sara had managed to find some Christmas pressies for her nieces and nephews. I only had Hope and Grace to buy for; I already had presents for my team. They were the best, and I liked to make sure they knew it.

"So how's everyone at home?" Sara asked. She's been my best friend since college. She went on to study Computer Science at uni, while I studied Business and Marketing. When she finished, she approached me about my racing, and I realised that she could be quite useful because bikes were becoming more computerised. Not only that, she was able to produce these amazing simulations of the tracks that would help me prepare for the races.

"They're good. Hope is off racing soon, Grace has this season off. But she's gearing up for the next one."

"And work?"

"Work is good." I grinned. I loved my job at the vineyard. We all worked so well together, it was nice to be able to work as a team.

"How's your family?" I asked. Sara had six brothers and two sisters, and she was the youngest. And as such, at twenty-four, they were pressuring her to find a special someone. But she hadn't yet. I think that was why she liked hanging out with me, I didn't have that kind of expectation. And I wasn't in a hurry either.

She rolled her eyes. "Usual stuff. Arguments already over where we are going for Christmas and who is bringing what. I just pick up Mum and Dad and take them wherever we're told." She smiled. She loved her family, but having so many siblings was hard, and even harder when most of them had offspring. She had more nieces and nephews than fingers on her hands!

"I'll be pleased when the silly season is over."

"Girl, I feel you," I said, giving her a sympathetic look. When my aunt and uncle were here, there were constant arguments about what to have for Christmas dinner. Us girls were pleased when they left us to it. Now, we have Christmas dinner at home, and we have cold meat and salads. No hot meals or stress about getting turkeys and lamb cooked in time. With the large industrial kitchen we had, and Michel, the chef who catered for the visitors, we just had cold cuts for Christmas Day and Boxing Day. Then Michel was back at work creating his wonderful meals again.

"Don't look now, but someone is watching you," Sara said.

"Where?" I asked, turning my head to look out the window. Cole stood there, a big grin on his face as he waved to me. I gave him a half-hearted smile and waved back, turning back with bug eyes to look at Sara. She laughed at me. Actually laughed at me.

"What? He's cute?" she said.

"He's also Nigel Kinsey's prodigy."

"What's that got to do with the price of fish?" Sara said, waving a foam-covered spoon as she spoke.

I stared at her again. What was she talking about?

"Nigel? The one who did everything he could to stop me from riding for the last three seasons?"

"Nigel isn't racing any more. So what if Nigel got a new rider. He's new, he's racing from the back. When did he last beat you?"

"Last race in Taupō."

"*Pfft*" She flicked her fingers as if dismissing my words.

My whole argument against Cole was that Nigel was his manager, but it didn't mean he was misogynistic like Nigel.

But I needed to focus on my racing career. I wouldn't make it to Formula One motorcycle racing if I fell in love. Where would I fit a relationship into my busy schedule?

Back at the track, I had my overalls on, and was leaning over my bike talking to Mike, my manager. He's the one that makes sure I keep my mind on the track when I'm racing. He doesn't need to navigate my every move like most managers, but he's pretty good at knowing when I need a pep talk.

He also likes to do the final checks of the bike before I race, so, like me and Geoff, he knows mechanics.

"You doing okay there, Faith?"

"Yeah, I'm good."

"Those last three races were phenomenal. Keep up that performance and you should win the championship this year."

"That's what I'm aiming for," I said.

"Good thing Nigel retired."

I heaved a sigh. Mike understood my frustrations over Nigel's performances and constant queries to the race committee about my racing. Each time we got a call from the committee, Mike assured me that we were fine, and that next year would be our year. This year might be the one.

"Yeah, less stress from that quarter, except from Cole."

"I don't think you need to worry about him. Just keep an eye out for Ken Montgomery and Tyrone. They're the up-and-comers this year."

Ken had been racing for years and had been relatively stagnant in his racing until last year, when he and I were fighting it out for second place. He got there in the end, but by one point. Tyrone was a new racer, rookie last year, but placed fourth only a few points behind me. Mike was right, they were the ones to look out for.

"I see you have some fans already," he said, nodding over towards the fence. I turned to see Cole, a big grin on his face. My cheeks heated as I realised I'd been bending over the bike, with my ass waving around in the air. I turned back to Mike, mortified, and he chuckled at my discomfit. "And now he's coming over."

I wanted to run away and hide, but a part of me wanted to stand up to him.

Taking deep breaths I listened to Mike clear his throat as Cole got closer.

"Hey, Cole."

"Hey, Mike, Faith. How you guys doing?"

"Good thanks," Mike responded. "Racing in Formula Two this year? Big step up."

"Yeah, but I'm enjoying it so far."

I was still trying to tame the heat in my face.

Cole turned to me. "Saw you in town earlier."

"Yeah, saw you too," I said, wondering where this was going.

"Where you staying?" he asked.

"Campground,"

"Same, got anything organised for tea? Would you like to go and grab a burger somewhere?"

"Burgers aren't my thing," I said, daring Mike to say otherwise. He hid a grin as he seemed hyperfocused on the chain on the bike.

"Pasta? I know the perfect place."

"That's sounds great, otherwise she'd just be eating with us," Mike said.

I opened my mouth to object, but Cole grinned.

"Great, I'll pick you up at seven?"

I went to say that I was unavailable when Mike said, "Perfect. I'll make sure she's ready."

"And I'll make sure she's home by eleven, Dad," Cole said, winking and pointing his finger at Mike.

He walked away, tucking his hands in his pockets as he did.

"What? How? What just happened?"

"You've got a dinner date tonight," Mike said, grinning at me.

"But I don't want to go out tonight."

"And now you sound like a whiney teenager," Mike said.

I put my hands on my hips and pouted, aware that now I looked like a petulent kid.

"Go out and enjoy yourself. Otherwise you'll only be sitting on that simulator, and we all know that you don't need that much practice. Besides, we're finished here. Let's go back and have a drink, aye?"

He rocked the bike off its stand and wheeled it into the trailer where he put it onto another stand. He locked the trailer tailgate up, and we headed back to the campground.

# chapter six

Cole

I couldn't help the skip in my step as I went over to the cabin where Faith and her crew were staying. They didn't have a bus like we did, and we were parked up in the caravan area, but that didn't worry me. I was taking Faith out for a meal. I knocked on the door which she opened. She smiled as I said hello, then pushed me out of the way as she shut the door behind her.

"Embarrassed to be seen with me?" I asked, grinning like an idiot.

"No, not at all, but Mike has been teasing me since he set me up for our d—dinner." It sounded like she'd been about to say date.

I smiled, then noticed that she was wearing a dress. I hadn't seen her in a dress before. I'd only ever seen her in overalls, or shorts, or trousers. Her legs were long and lean and seemed to go on forever. They were tanned, along with her arms. Her blonde hair had that fluffy appearance of having recently been washed. Her hazel eyes flashed with alarm at my staring at her.

"Am I overdressed?"

"No, not at all, I was admiring your…dress," I stumbled. I wanted to say legs, but it was way too early for that sort of talk. But her legs were amazing.

"Thanks. So where are we going?"

"Follow me," I said, leading her over to my car. She burst out laughing as I opened up the door to a small blue Smart Fortwo.

"What? It fits perfectly inside the bus!" I said, laughing along with her. It wasn't my choice of car; Dad had used it for years. But when we sometimes had to pick up parts or fuel, we needed something other than driving the bus all over town once we'd parked up.

"Do we need to breathe in when we get inside?"

"Don't do that, the walls might implode on us!" I said, making her laugh more. She was so beautiful when she smiled, and her laughter was a bright happy sound. Not forced like some people.

I drove us from the campground to a nearby hotel. It was always my favourite place to visit when I came to Fielding.

"Stockyards?" she asked, reading the name on the building.

"Yeah, sorry, no pasta, but they do nice food."

"It's a pub."

"Yeah, why, do you want to have an intimate meal?"

Her cheeks flared red, and I could feel the heat from them. "N-no," she stammered. We got out of the car, and she followed me into the bar. It was a busy night, being Friday. We ordered a lemon lime and bitters for her and a pint of the house craft beer for me.

"Do you not want a wine?"

"Not on a first date," she said.

"Is this a date?" I grinned. Her cheeks flamed again, and I laughed. "Sorry, just teasing you."

We found a small table to sit at and took our time perusing the menu. It made my mouth water just thinking about the burgers here. I wondered what she would have, probably chicken?

"What do you do when you're not racing?" I asked her.

She leaned on the table, stirring her drink with the straw."My sisters and I work on a vineyard. I'm the marketing person. I sell our wine."

"Oh, and here I was thinking you didn't drink wine." I smiled at her.

"I do drink it, but I have so much of it at work that I prefer spirits to wine."

"Really? Let me guess, vodka, no…um…" I studied her, narrowing my eyes, making her smile. "I think you're a brandy girl."

"Nope, neither. I like a good whiskey."

"Wouldn't have picked you for whiskey. Which is your favourite?"

"Too many to choose from. You like whiskey?"

"Love it. Prefer Scottish to Canadian, and won't touch American."

"What? No bourbon?" She acted shocked and I laughed.

"No, Scottish or nothing. Though I do like an Irish whiskey."

"Fair enough. What about you? What do you do for a living?"

"Spraypainter." I waited for her expression to drop, but it didn't.

"Mum owns a panelbeaters and spraypainters, so I manage the place for her. I can panelbeat, but prefer to paint things."

"Wow, didn't have you pegged as a blue-collar boy. I thought you'd be an executive or something."

"Nope, always preferred working with my hands."

I saw a small flush appear on her cheeks at that comment, and she looked down at the napkin she was fiddling with.

"I'm also working on doing up a 1932 Cadillac Sports Coupe, you know, like one of those mafia-style cars." She nodded. "It's in pieces at the moment as I'm not far off painting it."

"When do you fit that in?"

"When it's not busy at the shop. Which isn't very often."

"Where is your shop?" she asked.

"In Christchurch."

"So, you from Christchurch?"

"Born and raised, how about you?"

"Nelson, never moved, never been overseas."

"Cool." There was an awkward pause while we flitted glances at each other, waiting for the other to speak.

"What got you into racing?" I finally asked.

"My aunt and uncle got all of us into kart racing. We did alright at it, too, but I preferred two wheels, so I got into trail-riding. But I had too much aggression, so my aunt and uncle got me into motorcycle racing. Helped me blow off steam, and I worked my way through the ranks. Until I got to Formula Two, and I've been stuck there…"

Her words petered out. I thought she was going to say something else, but she didn't.

"What about you?" she asked.

"Same, except Dad started me out in minibike racing when I could barely walk. I liked speed, so I went through the ranks too."

Her eyes lit up a little, like I understood her better.

"And now Nigel is your manager coach?"

"Nigel can be an ass, but he's well-meaning."

"Do you know, the first year I started in Superbike racing, he complained to the governing body about me? Wanted to know why I was allowed to race and not in a women's class." She sighed. "He's pretty much protested every win I managed to make against him. Nigel is a misogynistic bastard," she said under her breath.

"Yeah, well, that too," I admitted. Her eyebrows rose at my comments.

"Look, Nigel's not perfect, but he's been a great coach."

Nothing I could say would sway Faith's opinion of Dad. He was a hard man, but he was fair, and I hadn't seen him do anything against Faith, or any of the other riders and teams for that matter. But I didn't understand why he had a thing against Faith in particular. Was it because she was a girl racing in a male-dominated field? That was what Faith seemed to think.

"Shall we order something to eat?" I asked, hoping the change of subject would help lift the sullen mood.

"Sounds good," she said.

"So what are you having?" I asked, wondering if I would be correct.

"Steak, big juicy steak, with salad, no fries."

I was surprised. But I couldn't help but smile. I liked her more and more.

After we ate, I patted my stomach which felt like it was twice as big as it once was.

"I'll need to go to the gym twice when I get back," Faith said, "but that was really nice."

"You go to the gym too?"

"And I do yoga to keep myself flexible."

"I do too. Gym builds the muscle and yoga gives me flexibility."

Another thing in common. I couldn't help but smile at her.

"What's that goofy grin for?" she asked, with an equally silly grin on her face.

"I was just thinking how we have so much in common."

She was silent for a bit. "I guess."

She glanced at her watch. "I need to get going, I like to have an early night before racing."

"I do too," I replied, feeling warmth flood through my body. I really liked this girl, and I couldn't help but think that we were made for each other.

If only I could convince her of that.

# chapter seven

## Faith

I sat at the back of the grid, my motorcycle revving beneath me. I focused on the first corner, watching the lights with my peripheral vision. My mind was two corners ahead as the light turned green. I dropped my clutch, and my bike shot forwards. I weaved around the riders who were slower on their take-off. Cole was up ahead somewhere, but I had to focus on my ride, not his.

It took a while for me to get to sleep last night. I lay on my back with a silly grin, just thinking over our conversation. He was into restoring cars, and I had a vague idea of what the Cadillac looked like. The way his hands moved as he talked about it, like he was touching the lines of the car.

"Focus, Faith," Mike said into my earphones.

"Thanks," I muttered, realising that my first line on the corner was off. I brought the bike back up and kept my attention on the track. Five laps until I finished, I had to focus on getting up the front, which shouldn't take too much.

"Focus." I used the word as a mantra as I zipped around the corner and braked for the next one, accelerating out. I focused on my breathing, keeping it even and calm. I passed three riders all clumped up together and made my way into fourth. I hadn't passed Cole yet, so he had to be in the top three.

"Focus. Breathe in, breathe out." There was a long space between me and the next rider, and I wasn't sure I would catch them, but they somehow mucked up the corner, and I cut in. I sped up hard and caught up with second place, which was Cole. Warmth flooded my system as I thought about him.

"Focus, breathe in, breathe out." I concentrated hard, looking for a gap, and I found it just as the straight with the checkered flag came into view. I floored it, hoping my bike would handle it, and I flew past Cole just before the checkered flag. I came in second, one place ahead of him. My heart raced as I slowed my bike and pulled into the pits. I had a ridiculous smile on my face as I took off my helmet.

"Beat ya," I said as Cole rode past. He didn't have his helmet off, but he nodded as I did a silly dance beside my bike. I felt exhilarated, like I did every time I finished a race, and it felt more so, I think because I didn't have the stress of Nigel and the pressure to beat him. I only had to focus on points, and with each race, my points climbed.

"Settle, Petal," Mike said, grinning at me.

"Racing is starting to feel better this year," I said.

"Because you're beating your boyfriend?"

It felt like a bucket of ice had been poured over me. "He's not my boyfriend," I said, fists clenched at my side.

"Sorry, I didn't mean to upset you. Good race; the bike went well; you were awesome." Mike tried to placate me, but he'd already upset me more than he realised.

I strode off to the gazebo, looking for water to hydrate before I hit the simulator.

"Great race," came a voice behind me. My heart thrilled, but I turned to stare at Cole.

"It was a race," I replied, keeping my face neutral.

"Hey, what happened? You were celebrating out there." He pointed outside. I sighed.

"Sorry, personal stuff," I said, trying to hide my awkwardness. His face was serious, and he looked worried, his eyebrows high over his soft brown eyes. His dark hair flopped over his forehead. He pushed it back.

"Okay, I'll leave you to it then." He backed out of the tent, stopped, like he was going to come back in, but then he walked away.

I put my hand on my forehead and leaned on the table. What an idiot. What was going on with me? I liked Cole; he was fun, and I enjoyed his company. Yet if someone suggested he was my boyfriend, I freaked out. But I also knew that I couldn't let myself fall for anyone, let alone Cole. Love wasn't something that was pretty or kind. It was argumentative, and bitchy, and just ugly to look at.

I took a deep breath and went into simple yoga vinyasa to calm my nerves and steady my thoughts. Anything to stop the mental mess going on in my brain. Not what I need when I'm trying to stay focused on racing. At least the next race, I would be starting at the front of the grid and not at the back. I don't mind starting at the back, as it gave me an opportunity to chase down opponents, but starting at the front, I didn't get caught up in any clutter; my mind could be clear, and stay clear. Here's hoping.

I got down into a cobra pose, staying for a couple of breaths, feeling the stretch in my back and neck. I came up into downward dog, one of my favourite poses, and stretched out my hamstrings and thighs. I slowly stood up in a salutation, breathing out as I finished up.

Yes, that felt a lot better.

I closed my eyes and took another couple of slow, deep breaths.

Nice.

Easy.

Calm.

Relaxed.

Ready to race.

Focused.

I took a drink of water and then went out to check on my bike.

They'd changed the tyres, and fueled it up. Nothing else needed to be done to it.

I waited for the call to line up on the dummy grid. I sat on my bike, staring ahead, focused.

I felt a tap on my shoulder. Then a thumbs-up from Cole. He was right beside me. My heart jumped, and I had to breathe really deep to calm it down again. I gave him the thumbs-up, too, and smiled through my helmet, though I couldn't see him in his. I presumed he was smiling. I had my visor down; it helped me focus, and then I didn't forget to put it down once I got out onto the grid and ready to race.

This race was important. I was currently ten points ahead. I needed this one to really push me into the top zone.

We rode out to the grid once the track had cleared from the previous race. I sat in pole position, Cole beside me. I focused on the lights, but I could feel heat from beside me, from him. It wasn't really there, but I knew that he was there.

I breathed.

Focus.

Breath.

Focus.

Green light. Shit. I was a split-second late, and Cole burst out in front of me. How had I missed that? I spent the entire race berating myself and trying to catch up with him, but he had every corner tied up so tight, I couldn't slip through. And the more I tried, the more flustered I got. And then mistakes happened. I pushed myself and didn't brake early enough, and the bike slid out from underneath me. A bloody rookie mistake, and the bike and I tumbled down the track and into a wall. I cursed as I waited a second before getting up. Only my pride was bruised. I wanted to throw my helmet at the ground, but such a show of unsportsmanlike behaviour wasn't a good look. I was angry at myself, not Cole or any other competitor. Race officials ran over to me. I shook them off once I was on my feet and went over to the bike. Someone picked it up, and I could see the livery scuffed up the left-hand side. I was gutted. It was the first time in years that I'd dropped my bike, and I hated seeing the fairings scuffed and scratched.

Mike raced over and put his arm around me as I removed my helmet. "You okay?"

"Yeah, just pissed at myself."

"Okay, we'll talk back at the pits."

"Yip," I nodded, then walked off the track, waving as the crowd cheered. I tried to smile, but the adrenaline was wearing off, and I wanted to cry. I headed over to the track vehicle, which took me to the ambulance for a check-up. I knew I was alright, other than a bruised ego and a few physical bruises as well. They checked me over, checked my vision. They wanted me to take off my leathers, which were pretty scuffed and banged up, but I had little on underneath. I told them I was fine and walked back to the pits.

Cole was there to greet me.

"You okay? You vanished from my vision, and I freaked. What happened?"

"I fucked up," I muttered.

He reached out to touch me, but I backed away. He dropped his hand.

"I can't," I said, looking up at him. His brown eyes were wide with concern and something else, but I couldn't look him in the eye, so I dropped my head, moved around him and headed to my trailer. I needed to get out of these racing overalls, check out what I wouldn't let the ambulance officers see, and get into new ones. Hopefully, the bike was good enough to race in the last race.

Mike had the bike up on the stand, and Geoff was stripping off the fairings. The exhaust was dented and looked awful all scuffed up. "You okay?" he asked as I passed.

"Yip," I said and kept walking. Sara was in the trailer and had some jeans and a T-shirt laid out for me.

"No, the other leathers," I said.

"Are you sure?"

"Yes, I know I'm fine," I snapped. I was sick of everyone asking me if I was alright. I was upright, and walking. The adrenaline was gone, and I was shaking.

"Sorry," I said as I sat down on the chair. She passed me a bottle of water, which had some glucose mixed in.

"I know," she said quietly, moving around and getting my new leathers out. I would need to order another set. I liked to have a couple up my sleeve, just in case.

"What happened out there?" she asked.

"I fucked up."

"I know that, but what happened?"

I sighed. I was thinking about Cole and trying to get past him, but I couldn't.

"Where were you?" Mike asked.

"Trying to find a way through?" But I knew that wasn't what he wanted.

"Nope."

"I was trying to find a gap."

"Nope."

"I was," I argued.

"Nope, you had your head in the clouds. You heard nothing I said over the intercom, did you?"

I thought hard, but I didn't recall hearing anything over the intercom. I shook my head.

Mike reached out and touched my hand. "It's okay. You were trying to find a flaw, you should've just sat back and let the race go; you were in second. Now you have a DNF on the board. It's the only one this year, okay?"

I felt the jostle of the trailer as Mike left. I put my head in my hands, feeling sorry for myself. I didn't have my head in the game. If that continued, I would blow this year's championship.

Sara tapped my shoulder, and I moved forwards for her to undo the zip on my shoulder. She slid it down my front, and I shuffled my arms out of the suit. I had on a singlet top, and wore bicycle shorts underneath, and after a few minutes,

Sara had my boots off and the entire suit removed. She dropped it on the floor. I picked it up, looking at the damage.

The back was all padded up, but the leather had worn through to the resin plastic boning underneath. The padding on the butt and legs were scuffed and not far off having let go, so I was lucky. I stood up and looked in the mirror. I had some red marks, which might turn into bruises, on my thighs and backs of my legs, but other than that, I was fine. I climbed into my new overalls. They were stiff and made noises. They smelt of polished leather, a fresh scent, not of oil, exhaust fumes and sweat like my old pair.

They were tight compared to my other overalls, which were well-worn. I looked over my boots, and other than a chunk out of one heel, they were fine. I pulled them on and did them up. The overalls sat at my waist, feeling awkward as they didn't fall like the other ones did. I thanked Sara and left the trailer and headed over to Geoff.

"How is she?" I asked.

"She'll go another race, but we need to do some serious work on her, not to mention new fairings."

"I'm sorry," I said to him.

"I hope you said that to your bike and not me." He grinned. I smiled back but didn't feel as confident.

I had to get back on the bike and race once more.

# chapter eight

## Cole

I'd seen Faith's livery in my peripheral vision, and then she was gone. I thought she was going to overtake me. One minute she was there; the next, *poof.* I'd had to keep racing. The orange light flashed up, so I slowed my pace, the others behind me catching up quickly.

"What happened to Faith?" I heard Steve, my mechanic, ask through the headset.

I heard chuckling. "The idiot fell off her bike," Dad responded.

"What?" Steve asked. He sounded as incredulous as I felt about my father's laughter.

I couldn't believe he'd found it funny.

Surely he was laughing at something else.

By the time I came around the corner, Faith and her bike were gone. As soon as I finished the race, I dumped my bike in the pit and ran back to her trailer. She was just coming back from the ambulance.

"You okay? You vanished, and I freaked. What happened?" I reached out to touch her, to comfort her and to reassure myself that she was okay.

"I fucked up," she muttered, leaning out of reach, which stabbed at my heart. I let my hand drop.

"I can't," she said, shaking her head. She looked at the ground and walked away. What did she mean by *she can't*? I wanted to chase after her, but I didn't. I let her walk off. Maybe she just needed time.

I went back to the pits and saw Dad. He was gloating over how I'd won the race to another official.

"Faith is okay," I said to Dad.

"Huh?" he responded. He didn't really care.

"What did Faith ever do to you?"

"She's a girl. Women shouldn't be racing motorbikes."

"But she does, and she's good at it."

"Really? She canned off today. That's a sign that she should quit."

I stood there, slack-jawed.

"How many times did you fall off your bike?" I asked, pointing at his knee.

"My racing has nothing to do with that," he muttered.

I couldn't believe what I was hearing. My father was being a dick. I shook my head and went back to the trailer. I needed to calm down. I put music into my headphones and started doing some aggressive yoga poses. Anything to keep the demons at bay.

After an hour, I heard the call-up for the third and final race. I hoped Faith would be there, but I wasn't entirely sure.

I lined up on the dummy grid, ready for the call-up. I looked around, but couldn't see Faith or her livery anywhere. I hoped that her bike was okay. It looked pretty banged up, but then some of it would just be scratches from skimming over the ground. It didn't look out of alignment or anything like that.

The last of the contestants from the previous race left the track, and we filed out onto the grid. I had pole position. I couldn't see Faith at the back of the pack, but I hoped she was there. I just had to race to the best of my abilities. If I won this round, then Faith and I would be tied for first place. That was if she didn't race. I hoped she did..

I brought my attention to the lights, watching them flicker then go green, and I was off. I focused hard on the track and stayed out the front. I refused to look behind me, instead, just looking at the corners and making judgments about directions and movements as I needed them.

The race was over in no time. I popped up from my crouched racing position as soon as I crossed the start-finish line, looking to see who was behind me. Someone else came second, but it looked like Faith came third. I whooped, not only for me, but for her. She deserved to get in the top three, and if she'd been racing from the back again, she sure did know her stuff to get ahead of the rest of the pack. When there were ten bikes racing, making it to first was incredible, so third wasn't to be sneezed at.

I slowed down and rode into the pits beside her, trying to catch her eye, but she wouldn't look at me, instead pulling into her mechanics bay and riding the bike into the trailer. I wondered if she was staying tonight, like we were, or heading back to Nelson. I hoped she was staying, I knew of another bar we could have a meal at.

There would be racing here tomorrow, too, but would she be staying or packing up? I kept an eye on their mechanics bay as I helped put the bike away for the night and got changed out of my racing gear. As soon as we'd finished, I headed down to see Faith.

"Hey, Faith," I called out as soon as I was close enough. She didn't look happy, and I couldn't blame her.

I ran up to her. "How you feeling?"

She looked at the ground. "I'm okay, a little sore."

"Want to go out for dinner tonight?"

"No."

"Okay, I know a place that does massage. Let me book you in there."

"No, thanks."

I wasn't taking no for an answer. I reached out and gently took her chin, lifting it so that she looked at me.

"You'll actually enjoy the massage, and I won't be giving it." I grinned.

"Thanks for the offer, but I need an early night."

"Tomorrow you'll be stiff and sore. You planning on racing tomorrow?"

"Yes," she said.

"Then you'll need this therapy. Please, it will help. Goodness knows how many times I've done it. It does work."

She sighed heavily, and I gave her the puppy dog eyes. "You'll feel better for it, I can guarantee it."

"So if I feel worse…"

"Since I'm paying it won't even cost you a cent."

"I'm putting this on you if I do feel worse, I'll know that you've stitched me up."

"I wouldn't do that to you." I let go of her face, resisting the urge to kiss her lips, which were still pouting at me, but I'd got an agreement.

“You ready to go?” I asked.

She looked at the crew around her. Her mechanic and manager grinned at her.

“Yes, she’s ready.” Sara said, and with that, she had no choice.

While she grabbed her jacket and purse, I made a quick call to the Thai massage place I knew here and booked us in. When Faith came out, her jacket slung over her shoulder, she followed me to my smart car. She cracked a rare smile again at seeing it.

“I know, but it works,” I said.

She was silent the entire trip, but I knew she would be. I stopped the car and we both got out. I opened the door to the massage rooms and entered with her.

“You’re not going to watch me get a massage are you?”

“No, getting my own, in a separate room,” I said when I saw the look of apprehension on her face. I introduced her to Kimi and Kimi gave her instructions. She had to sit in the sauna for five minutes, then get into the plunge pool, and back into the sauna for five more minutes. Then into the massage room. It was a cross between sports therapy massage and Thai massage.

I smiled as I left her to it.

I had my own massage to get on with.

# chapter nine

Faith

The sauna was too hot, the plunge pool too cold, and then back into the sauna for five more minutes. Any longer, and I think I would have boiled from the heat. But when I lay down to have that massage, I swear I drifted off into another land. All those taut muscles relaxed, and though I didn't get a deep tissue massage, the therapist manipulated and stretched the muscles. When I finally finished, Cole was waiting out front for me. I sat and had tea that the lady gave me, and I felt so relaxed and boneless.

"Pretty good, aye." Cole smiled at me.

I couldn't respond; it was taking all of my time to hold the delicate cup in my hand and sip it. I nodded, but it felt like my head would come off. I'd never felt so relaxed before, and all those muscles that had hit the ground and been twisted and grated, were now relaxed and free. I wasn't sure I'd be so free-moving in the morning, though. I finished my drink, and Cole helped me out to the car. He seated me in the passenger seat and even did up the seatbelt for me. I was in a dreamlike state, almost out of body.

I don't remember the drive back to the cabin, or being carried to bed, because that is the only way I could've got there.

I woke up fully clothed, and more awake than I'd ever been in my entire life. There was a little tenderness in my muscles, but no damage from the fall yesterday. Kimi, the massage therapist, had magic fingers.

"Feeling okay?" Mike asked.

"Yeah," I said, feeling surprised. I felt okay. You'd never have guessed I'd had a crash yesterday. I mean, ambulance visit and everything. I'd be sore today, but I was going to ride no matter what, just to keep points on the board. Today, I knew I could win.

"How's the bike, Geoff?"

"Your bike is made of titanium; it takes more than a spill to damage her," he said. I knew he was kidding; thank goodness for decent tyre walls.

Sara was the only one who looked dubious. "You sure you're okay to race?"

"I feel great. In fact, I've never felt this good after a crash before. I seriously need to get massages more often." I swung my arms around, twisted my spine and squatted a few times to show her I had a full range of movement.

"Did she do magic on you?" Sara asked, squinting her eyes at me. I laughed, of course it looked like it. It certainly felt like it.

This time, I focused on my races, keeping up with the riders, not pushing my bike, because I knew it needed some work.

Pushing it would only make things fail faster. Still, I maintained my position in second on the championship board behind Ken.

I knew that any aches or pains from yesterday's tumble would manifest late in the afternoon. There was a little muscle ache, nothing that paracetamol and ibuprofen couldn't deal with. I didn't see Cole before we left, having packed up immediately before the last race, so we could just put the bike in the back and go. Which we did. And we didn't run into them in Wellington at the ferry terminal either. I was a little disappointed, but I also kept reminding myself that I didn't need anyone in my life. Love wasn't fun. It was complicated. My life was busy enough without complicated. I could do friends, but I had a feeling Cole wanted more than that.

We arrived back in Nelson early—very early Monday morning. We split off to our individual homes; Geoff took the bike to his to work on, Sara headed off to her place, Mike to Brightwater, and I headed out to mine. I crawled into bed as the sun rose into the sky, leaving a note on my door not to disturb me. We all did that after we'd been racing, especially if we travelled all night to get home. Most of us still had day jobs keeping the money coming in so we could afford to keep racing.

I woke up mid-afternoon. It was late. Normally I allow myself until lunchtime, but I knew my body needed all the rest I could get. I headed up to the office to catch up with Hope and Grace, and the chef Michel. I wanted something to eat, and Michel air-kissed my cheek as I came into the kitchen. He was tidying up after the afternoon rush and getting ready to head home. He whipped me up a quick sandwich, which tasted like heaven, because he cooked with so many herbs and spices. The chicken salad sandwich had zing and flavour. I had to sit down and appreciate the taste.

That is where Grace found me, sitting at the bar in the kitchen.

"How was the weekend?"

"Rough, I came off my bike."

She winced and rubbed my back. It ached a little but not like it probably should have.

"It's alright. I got a massage afterwards, and it's all good, apart from a small niggle." I rocked from side to side to try and free up that small area that pulled when I leaned the wrong way.

"Massage?" Her eyebrow quirked up, which made me smile.

"Yeah, Cole—"

"Cole, aye? You ran into him again?"

"Yes, I did. We had dinner—"

"You went on a date!"

"Will you stop interrupting me? No, it wasn't a date. We had dinner together."

"Sounds like a date to me."

"It wasn't," I grumped. It wasn't a date! "And when I fell off, Cole organised a massage for me."

"Cole massaged you?"

"No! Will you stop twisting my words?"

Grace laughed as she pulled out a stool to sit down. "I'm just teasing you."

"Well, don't. You know I don't like it. And I'm not dating Cole."

"Why not?"

"Why should I?"

"You could use a good man in your life."

I stared at her open-mouthed. "So could you and Hope, but you don't see me rubbing that in your face." My eyebrows were so low over my eyes I was having trouble seeing her.

"You bite so hard!" she laughed.

"Will you stop it?"

"No."

I took a bite of my sandwich so that I wouldn't have to talk to her and ignored her attempts to wind me up further.

"So how's things with you?" I asked.

"Yeah, good. Quiet. Can't wait to get racing again."

I grinned at her. We all raced; it was in our blood, I guess.

"Oh yeah, Aunt Dill and Uncle Chives will be here in a couple of days. They're staying for Christmas," Grace announced, rolling her eyes.

I groaned. I loved them both dearly, but not the bickering that they always did. It drove me nuts. If you love someone, why do you constantly argue with them?

"I'll have to get out for some long walks, I guess," I said.

Grace nudged me and grinned. "I'm with you."

# chapter ten

Cole

The drive back to Christchurch was long. So damned long. We left on Monday because we knew it would be a slow drive. Down to Wellington, nearly three hours on the ferry, then a four-hour drive to Christchurch.

The whole time, I wished I'd gotten Faith's phone number. I could probably get it, but I wanted to get it from her, not just blow up her phone with texts or calls. If she's anything like me, I don't answer the phone for numbers I don't know.

I stood on the deck of the ferry, watching the beautiful native bush of the Sounds go by. It was peaceful here, restful even. Might have to look at taking some time off and coming up this way, see if I can hire a bach in the Sounds. I liked quiet. I really wasn't a big-city boy, even though I lived in Christchurch. Since the earthquakes, it had been a lot quieter than it used to be. It has grown again, but people are wary. When you live through those sorts of terrifying moments, you develop a wariness of any ground movements or rumbling sounds. Many nights I've woken up in cold sweats because thunder has made me think it's another big quake.

Dad found me on the deck. He was looking very pleased with himself. "What's up?" I asked.

"Not much, just working out the strategies for the next few races."

"We have a six-week break, Dad."

"You can't slack off just because it's Christmas."

"You always took a break over Christmas when you raced."

"Three weeks. After that, I was back on the bike or at the gym. You can't let that girl beat you."

"*That girl* has a name."

"I don't care. Women shouldn't be racing."

"Does the fact that she's actually good at it got anything to do with your negativity?"

"Good at it? She fell off her bike."

I wanted to wipe the smirk off his face. "She had an accident. Everyone does."

"Not me. I never fell off."

I raised my eyebrow at him because I knew he was lying.

"I never fell off when it mattered, let's put it that way."

I rolled my eyes.

"Don't you roll your eyes at me."

"I'm not a kid any more; I'm twenty-eight."

"I'm still your dad," he said, side hugging me. I let him squeeze me and took a breath in when he let go.

"Okay, so I'll hit the gym every day. I do anyway." I said. "And I will ride next weekend, and then after New Year, okay?"

"Deal," he said, and still smiling, as he wandered off.

I stared out at the calm waters of the Sounds, once more thinking it would be more peaceful to live here, without Dad's constant criticism.

The drive to Christchurch was quiet. I could've driven the Smart Car, but it fitted in the trailer with the bike, and it saved on fuel to only run one vehicle. Dad and I said little, but then we had Steven, the mechanic and computer specialist, in the car too. Thankfully. Steven had talked about the win and the points I scored. I was fourth on the table. Even though Faith had fallen off her bike in her second race on the first day, she was still second in points. And it bugged Dad that Faith was ahead of me. I really didn't get what his problem was with her.

I couldn't wait to get home and away from the negative atmosphere that seemed to suck the energy out of the car. Then it was only two weeks until Christmas, which was going to be with Mum and my brother at ours before heading over to Dad's. I already wasn't looking forward to it. But I had work to do in the meantime, about a week's worth of work before I could shut up the workshop for the three weeks over the holiday period.

We always shut down, and often we would head away for the summer, heading north to Kaiteriteri, but since we were teenagers and the arguments Mum and Dad used to have while away on holiday, we haven't done it. But this year, I got a site at Kaiteriteri Motor Camp for ten days after Christmas, taking in the New Year. I'd even scored tickets for us for the concert at the Hart Valley vineyard to listen to

LabSix. I was looking forward to letting my hair down and relaxing away from the family drama.

When Dad dropped me off at home, I walked through the door to a wonderful aroma drifting through the house.

"Hey, Mum," I called out. Yeah, I lived with my mum. I own the house, and when she and Dad split, I let her move in. Strangely, it hadn't cramped my style, or hers, and we both got along well.

"Hey, Cole. Good trip?"

I dropped my bag in the hallway outside my bedroom door, and headed into the open-plan kitchen lounge area, then took a seat at the breakfast bar. Mum put down her wine glass, opened the fridge and pulled out a beer for me. I opened it and slugged down a big mouthful. On a hot day, a cold beer tastes so much better.

"Yeah, had a win," I told her.

"Good work," She said, picking up her wine glass and tapping it against my bottle.

"Smells good." I nodded towards the oven.

"Yeah, roast chicken for tea, with salad and garlic potatoes."

"Mum, you're the best."

"Worked hard at it my entire life." She smiled and tipped her glass to me as a salute. I nodded my beer bottle at her and took a swig myself.

"How was work today?" I owned the panel beaters, and Mum kept her finger on the pulse of the business for me.

"No dramas, work's coming in, everyone wants it done yesterday."

I laughed. Every year, everyone wanted their repairs done before Christmas, yet it wasn't always possible.

"Met the new insurance assessor from Premium Insurance. Pretty hot," Mum said, fanning herself with her free hand.

"Mum!" I said.

"What? He's closer to my age; in fact, I think he's older than I am."

"Oh?"

"Yeah, quite the character, and a bit of a flirt."

"Are you okay with going out with him?"

"Who said anything about going out with him?" She shrugged, but the grin on her face told me she was interested. It was nice to see Mum finally getting over Dad.

About time, really. Mum and Dad separated about a year ago. Mum left Dad after having had enough of the negativity. I can't say I blame her. Dad had always put her down and told her she wasn't good at anything.

To prove him wrong, she looked for a job, but because of her age, couldn't get one, so I gave her a job at the shop, and she started making her own money. She was great with the customers, young and old, and I think she finally got the courage to tell him she was leaving.

I didn't mind her living with me. We both did the chores around the house, so it wasn't just Mum doing everything. We alternated cooking every night, except Friday, which was get-yourself-sorted night, because that was when I went out with the boys.

Mum living here suited us both. And Dad really didn't care, because he could still keep tabs on her through me, which is the part I didn't like.

"Did you see that girl you like?"

"Faith, yeah, took her out for tea on Friday night, and got her a massage on Saturday because she fell off her bike."

Mum winced. I knew she would; she's that type of empathetic person.

"Is she okay?"

"Yeah, hurt pride more than anything. She was racing again on Sunday."

"Did you get her number?"

I hung my head and picked at the label on my beer. "No, they took off early on Sunday. I didn't have time to."

I felt Mum pat my shoulder. "Don't worry, love. You'll snag her." I smiled, but didn't lift my head.

I sometimes wonder if I would.

# chapter eleven

Faith

Aunt Dill and Uncle Chives turned up with their motorhome, which was a caravan on steroids. They parked it out the back of the gardener's shed, out of sight of the restaurant, because their arguing could be vicious sometimes. The farther away from the clientele, the better.

We spent a few days decorating the restaurant, and Grace had instructed the gardeners about preparing the outdoor auditorium for the New Year's Eve concert we put on every year. We gave the raised money to a local charity, Caring4Kids, because we wanted to make sure that all New Zealand children had food and clothes. This year I'd lined up one of the best New Zealand bands on the scene at the moment, LabSix, which the young people were really into, but they also provided great songs for the older generation as well. A week before Christmas, we had nearly sold all the tickets. I was looking forward to talking to the band and listening to their music.

After the restaurant closed in the evenings, we would get together in the main lounge area and stare at the overlarge Christmas tree we dragged in every year. We'd first planted it in a large pot about five years ago, when tehe tiny seedling looked funny in the pot. Now it touched the roof, so it was well over three metres tall. It might have to be trimmed for next year. Another job for the gardeners.

Sales had been steady up to Christmas. Hope had been off racing and was looking forward to a couple of weeks off. Grace doesn't start until February, so she was up to her neck in business and getting things sorted for the Christmas party we planned for the Caring4Kids cause. Presents already sat under the tree from generous people who donated them, or money for them. They were practical gifts, like pencils and paper, felt-tip pens. We didn't believe in over-the-top toys like remote control cars or dolls. They would be nice, but Caring4Kids is about lifting children out of poverty. We received tablets one year from one agency, which were loaded up with books and educational games, which went down a treat. But we never accepted cell phones. We wanted these kids to learn, not be addicted to social media.

Every day ticked down to Christmas, and I'd avoided Aunt Dill and Uncle Chives. Tonight, however, wasn't one of those times.

"Hello, darling," Aunt Dill drawled as she came in, flowing light silk caftan over the top of white linen trousers, and white hair coiffed to within an inch of its life. She was drowning in perfume, which, while pleasant, was overwhelming with the amount she used. She floated rather than walked. Aunt Dill enveloped me in a hug, and swirls of fabric and her perfume curled around me. I had to resist the urge to sneeze.

"Hello, Aunt," I said as I stepped back. Uncle Chives stepped into my space. My nose still tingled, and I had to resist the urge to rub it.

"Hello, Faith. She get's up my nose too," he said as I stepped out of his embrace.

"I do not," Aunt protested, waving her hands around trying to dismiss him. She wandered off to look for my sisters.

Uncle Chives rolled his eyes and then turned to me. "How are you doing, chickadee?"

We called him Uncle Chives, but his name was Charles. And as I couldn't say that when we first moved in, I called him Chives, and it stuck, with all of us girls. He was the nearest thing I had to a dad, so I was close to him.

"Good, busy getting things sorted for the dinner tonight and the concert next week. Sales are good."

"How's your love life?" he asked, a genuine smile on his face. He wasn't asking to be facetious. He wanted all of us girls to be happy and in love.

"It's non-existent."

"Oh, we need to find you a nice young man." He patted my shoulder as we moved towards the lounge.

"I'm quite happy on my own," I replied.

"I know, but there's nothing like having the love of your life with you." He looked over at Aunt Dill with a wistful look on his face.

I stared at him, wondering what he was talking about. He and Aunt Dill were always bickering and arguing with each other. It was so hard sometimes not to hear them. I often left the room so I wouldn't have to put up with it.

We came to the lounge where Grace and Hope were, along with Aunt Dill.

"Doesn't everything look lovely?" Aunt Dill said, opening her arms wide to encompass the room with the Christmas tree and the presents, the tables with votive candles on them all set ready for the children and their parents who were coming.

"Very ordered and organised," Uncle Chives said.

"What do you mean by that?" Aunt Dill put her hands on her hips and squared off with Uncle Chives.

"Nothing at all, my dear. I just mean that the girls have everything ready to go."

"And I don't?"

"You do sometimes."

"Sometimes? I'm always organised!"

"Unless we're trying to leave for something, then you have to tidy the lounge, check your face in the mirror, check your clothes, put on more perfume—"

I zoned out and started backing out of the lounge area. I didn't need to listen to this. Grace and Hope were rolling their eyes with smiles on their faces. I don't know how they coped. Aunt Dill and Uncle Chives always picked on each other.

I got to the kitchen and caught up with Michel.

"You okay?" he asked, side-hugging me.

"Yeah, family."

He continued to move around the kitchen, prepping food and getting everything organised. "But they love you, and that is all that matters," he said in his French accent.

"Anything I can help with?" I asked, choosing to ignore his comment.

"Thought you'd never ask. Can you sort out that salad?" he asked, nodding over towards four large iceberg lettuces, tomatoes, carrots, mint, croutons and other various bits and pieces. Pleased to be of service, I wrapped an apron around my waist and washed my hands.

An hour later, the salads, along with dressings, were ready. The roasted chickens, fries, potatoes, roasted kumara, cooked carrots, beans, peas, broccoli and garlic bread were on the tables ready for the kids to dig in. The adults hung back, watching the children enjoy the feast. The adults would get food, too, they just waited for the children to get their fill first. Leftovers would be divvied up and sent home with the families.

Icecream sundaes followed, then we presented the children with their gifts, and sent them home with food in their tummies and new clothes, drawing tools and school stationery for the next year.

I helped tidy up the kitchen and washed dishes as my sisters farewelled the guests. It had been another successful night, one we always enjoyed doing for the local children. We had our favourites, who nearly always turned up year after year, and the vineyard had even set up a few with scholarships for going on from college to university or polytechnic, to get them out of the poverty trap. It was something we all felt so passionate about because we had been fortunate, but there were kids at our school who were less so. We wanted to do something for them, so when we were old enough, we started fundraising by selling grape skins for compost; we clambered around underneath neighbouring sheep yards and scraped out sheep poo to sell. Aunt Dill and Uncle Chives then matched, dollar for dollar, what we raised, and we donated it all to a local charity.

The concert was the biggest event on our calendar, and the one that I looked forward to. Even though there were so many people there, I could get lost in the music and the crowd and blend in, and people wouldn't see me as the owner of the vineyard or the racer chick.

I was just plain Faith, who liked to have a dance.

# chapter twelve

Cole

You'd think with all the driving around the countryside I do for racing, that I would be sick of travelling over the summer holidays, but there is something idyllic about driving up to Kaiteriteri, where the sands are golden, the water is refreshing, and the campground is full of people. I forgot how many damned people they crammed into this place.

After finding our spot and setting up the caravan and awning, my brother, Reuben, and his wife, Cheryl, and I sat down for a well-earned beer. It was two days before New Year, and it was just pumping. Teenage girls in skimpy swimwear meandered past, much to Cheryl's chagrin. She still had a fantastic body, just a little more filled out in a truly sexy way. My brother never minded. He barely saw the skinny teenagers because he was staring at Cheryl so much.

Ah, love, it must be grand if you can get it. Which got me thinking about Faith. I knew I wasn't in love with her, but given half the chance, I could be. We were interested in similar things, like going to the gym and yoga, which was a good start. We hadn't tackled movies or books, but they were next on the list of things to ask her. I was counting down the days until I would see her again, which would be at the next race meet, Christchurch, in sixteen days' time. I knew where I would take her out for our next meal together—my local. In the meantime, I had to be patient, and keep thinking about her, with her blonde hair, and those flashing hazel eyes. They could be ice-cold, or warm as the Tasman Bay when she smiled, which she really didn't do often enough.

"We're heading out for a swim. You coming?"

"Nah, bro, I'm good," I said as I pulled my shades down and leaned back on my lounger. I would just do some chick-watching while I waited for them to get back.

Two days later, we were parking up at the Hart Valley Vineyard, tickets in hand to see LabSix. They were one of the best New Zealand bands at the moment, and I couldn't wait to see them. It would be the second time I've seen them live, and their music just rocks. We were decked out in our summer gear: shorts, T-shirts, sandals. It was a no-alcohol event, which seemed weird on a vineyard, but then, it was a fundraiser for Caring4Kids, so there would be lots of teenagers there to see them, I guess. The vineyard was gorgeous, set in amongst native bush, with little pockets of views across the vineyard. People were moving around us towards the amphitheatre that they had purpose-built on the land. We'd never been here before, but once we rounded the corner, it was a view to behold. They cut the amphitheater into a hill, curving it towards the stage at the bottom. It was a terraced grassy slope that everyone could sit on, with chairs or blankets. People were already basking in the late afternoon sun with their picnic baskets, enjoying a meal before the main event. A couple of local bands were warming up the crowd before LabSix would come out.

I was right about the teenagers, so many kids there, but it was great to see. There were as many adults as older generations too. LabSix were popular with all the age groups. With their sultry jazzy tones and the reggae beat, they showcased our very own New Zealand culture in their songs.

We found the area that we were to be seated in and set up our chairs before cracking open some lemonades and a cheeseboard that Cheryl had somehow arranged. The atmosphere in the place was just amazing, and I wondered if this was the vineyard that Faith worked on, but surely she would've mentioned the concert if she had. A twist in my chest made me aware of just how much I missed her. We were still at the getting to know each other stage, but I wanted to get to know her so much more.

Every time I saw a blonde head, I would think it was her until they turned around and they had a ponytail, or extremely short hair. Faith had hers in a bob style. And there were so many shades of blonde.

But then my heart gave a lurch. There, up by the stage, was someone who had the body shape and the hair colour, and a similar style to Faith. Surely it wasn't?

"Excuse me," I said as I got up, and without taking my eyes off the mysterious woman, I walked through the crowd. As I got closer to the stage, the woman moved, and although she had a similar gait, I was pretty sure it wasn't Faith until she turned side-on to me. It had to be her. I followed until I caught up and tapped her shoulder. The woman turned around. It wasn't Faith, but damn, she looked so much like her.

"Sorry, I thought you were someone else."

"No worries." The woman smiled as she turned and headed backstage. I stared after her, because she was so like Faith.

Disappointed, I turned back to the area where my brother and sister-in-law were sitting.

"Did you find the toilets?" Cheryl asked.

"No, thought I saw someone I knew. It wasn't her."

"We're a long way from home, bro; it would be a miracle to see someone we knew here."

I nodded, but I was so sure it was Faith, and she looked so like her, except the woman had freckles across her nose, and her hair was more strawberry blonde.

Ten minutes later, the young woman stood on the stage, introducing herself as Grace Hart.

"Hart…" I was pretty sure that was Faith's last name, wasn't her team Racing Hearts? Maybe it was Racing *Harts*?

"My family and I would like to thank you all for coming today. First, some housekeeping. We are under fire restrictions at the moment, so refrain from lighting a fire. As this is a smokefree venue, you shouldn't need to light up a cigarette. We are also vapefree, so put those things back in your pocket. This is an alcohol-free event, but that doesn't mean it is fun-free.

"If there is an earthquake or a fire, please leave the amphitheatre by the nearest exit, and meet on the other side of the cellar restaurant. There is a clear open field there; it will be big enough to keep everyone safe and away from buildings.

"If you get peckish, there are food caravans set up outside the amphitheatre. Most of them have EFTPOS with them, some will accept cash.

"Toilets are on the left and right, outside of the theatre itself. Please be kind to those who also have to use them." There were smatterings of chuckles around the auditorium.

"Right, tonight, we have LabSix to play for us and to rock your world. In the meantime, please put your hands together for two local bands. The first is Candotoo, and after them is Wednesday's Child. Hope you enjoy your evening."

Cheers went up from the crowd as the blonde left the stage and Candotoo came onto the stage. They were a cover band, but they sounded alright. Lots of kids got up to dance, and the evening started off well.

I kept catching sight of the blonde, and the next time I saw her, she was with another blondie, who also looked like Faith, but I was fairly certain it wasn't.

But what were the chances of Grace, the hostess, having the same last name as Faith?

# chapter thirteen

Faith

The two local bands had played, and Hope finally got up on stage to introduce LabSix. The crowd cheered, and when the band struck the first few chords, the crowd screamed in recognition. I watched from the sidelines, amused as people sang along. As it got darker, the dance floor really got going, and that was when I felt most at home, dancing my legs off. I got out there and threw my hands in the air, nodded my head to the rhythm, and then I started jumping up and down. It was exhilarating because I could zone everyone else out. I was in my own world.

Occasionally I would bang into someone, and I'd turn to apologise, only to have them dance along with me, but mostly it was me in my world.

I could do this all night, but I needed a drink.

"You're getting into that," Grace said.

"Why do you think I asked them here?" I grinned.

"Our little bookworm is a closet nightclub dancer," Hope said. I stuck my tongue out at her and then took a long swig from my bottle. I was soaked in sweat, but I really didn't care; I was feeling fine. It was dark; lights flickered over the dance floor and mosh pit, throwing an unnatural light on people, making them look like they were in stop-motion animation. Then the light pattern would change.

"Come dance with me." I tried to drag Grace and Hope out with me. Grace gave a half-hearted attempt before smiling and walking away. Hope jumped up and down with me for a couple of songs, before she disappeared into the dancers as well, probably heading off to get away from me. I laughed.

Someone banged into my back. I turned, and my heart skipped a beat.

"What are you doing here?" I asked.

Cole grinned. "Doing the same thing as you, dancing," he said. And he was, he was swaying to the music, and air drumming with his hands. I laughed and joined in. My heart soared at sharing this moment with a friend.

Friend? Did I consider Cole a friend? Yes, he was just a male friend.

We danced, all body movements, bopping along with the band. When they finished their first set, it was still an hour before midnight. Cole took my hand and dragged me towards the amphitheatre.

"Where are we going?" I asked as he dragged me through the crowds.

"Taking you to meet my family."

"Wait, what?" I stopped. He turned and looked at me.

"I'm here with my brother and sister-in-law. I'd like to introduce you."

My heart rate slowed. I wasn't ready, or in a fit state, to meet anybody, let alone members of Cole's family. Cole tugged my hand and pulled me forwards. Soon we were with two people sitting in chairs on the terraces.

"This is my brother Rueben and his wife, Cheryl. Rueben, Cheryl, this is my fellow Superbike competitor and friend, Faith."

I waved my hand awkwardly. "Hi." Then tucked it behind my back.

"So, you're the one," his brother said, winking at me.

I looked between Rueben and Cole, who had a hand behind his neck.

"The one?" What had Cole been telling them?

"The one that keeps beating his arse—in racing." Rueben grinned.

"Yip, I'm whipping his arse on the track," I said, smiling wickedly at Cole.

There was an awkward silence, where we all looked at each other. Cheryl kept staring at me, with a broad smile on her face.

"It's a great concert," Cheryl finally spoke.

"They're an awesome band."

"And a fantastic cause too." Cheryl said.

I smiled as I relaxed a bit more. "It's a cause close to our hearts."

"So you own this place?" Cheryl asked, circling her arm around.

"Not exactly; we run it for a trust."

"Wow, you must be rich," Rueben said.

My face flushed as my mouth went dry. I swallowed. "I wouldn't put it that way. We don't make a lot of money from it. It's a company, so we pay tax like everyone else. It's not just my sisters and me either; there is also my aunt and uncle."

I always felt uncomfortable when people talked about us being rich. "I like to think that we're comfortable, and all the excess money goes to charities that we support. We like to give back to the community." And then I felt I'd said too much. The heat lingered in my face as I fidgeted with my fingers.

"It was lovely to meet you, Faith. We've heard so much about you," Cheryl said.

My head popped up. "You have?" Why would Cole talk about me?

"Okay, let's get our space on the dance floor again," Cole said as he pushed me away from his laughing brother and sister-in-law.

"They seem nice," I said, for lack of anything else to say.

"Yeah, I'm close with Rueben. We're camping at Kaiteriteri at the moment for a few days."

"Are you? It's a beautiful spot when it's not crazy busy."

"You could say that again." Cole kept grinning at me, which was a little disconcerting.

"Hey, can I get your phone number? So…" He reached a hand up behind his neck again as he ducked his head down. "I can call you before I head home, catch up, maybe for a coffee?" He pulled his phone from his pocket and unlocked the screen.

"Yeah, I think I can do that." I waited until he got to the contacts screen and took the phone from him. I typed in my name and number.

"Done," I said.

He waved the phone at me. "Thanks," he said as he tucked it back in his pocket. Something about his awkwardness made a brief twinge happen in my chest. It was sweet how he seemed confident one minute, and awkward as a teenager the next.

Chords struck from the band, and the next set started. It would stop again just before midnight for the countdown, then the band would play until one o'clock, before we shut the party down.

But until then, Cole and I danced like there was no one else there, whooping it up, waving our arms around, jumping and enjoying ourselves.It was a couple of minutes to midnight; the band was just playing the final chords of their song and a countdown clock appeared behind them. There was a mumble in the crowd, and as the clock counted down, people shouted out the numbers.

"Five!"

Cole grabbed my hand, and I let him take it.

"Four!" Cole squeezed my hand.

"Three!" I turned and grinned at him, all hyped up on dancing energy.

"Two!" I jumped up and down.

"One!" He pulled me into his arms.

I didn't hear the next words as his mouth came down on mine and the world melted away. His kiss was searing and hot, and his tongue touched my lips. I opened my mouth, and then...oh man, this was so panty-melting hot. I felt myself melt into his arms, and he pulled me tighter against him, as if trying to fuse our bodies together with the heat. The kiss ended naturally, and I looked up into his eyes, mesmerised by the kiss, his warmth, his eyes, which sparkled but seemed to glow with something else, even in the night's darkness.

He grinned, then bent to kiss me again, and I let him. It was a magical moment where my bones just disappeared, and I wanted to lean into him and let him support me.

The music started up, and I realised the crowd around us was cheering. I felt my cheeks grow hot, and I ducked my head. I grabbed his hand and pulled him away from the dance floor.

But the spell had broken, and I felt like I'd betrayed myself.

I'm not meant to fall in love, but I think I might have just done that.

# chapter fourteen

Cole

You couldn't wipe the smile off my face. I'd kissed Faith, and she'd responded. After midnight, we spent the last hour of the concert just cuddling each other, until she had to leave and bid everyone good-night. She talked with the band, thanking them, and I didn't get to say goodbye, but I had her number, and I rang her the following day.

"Hello, Faith speaking."

"Hi," I said. I heard her sigh.

"Hello," but it sounded like she was grinning.

"Sleep well?"

"Yeah, and you?"

"Not too bad."

There was quiet on the other end of the phone.

"What are you up to?" I asked.

"Nothing much, just lying in bed."

"Did I wake you?"

"No, not at all! I've been awake for a while, just being lazy."

I chuckled, because Faith didn't strike me as lazy. "Busy day today?"

"No, not really?"

"Work?"

"No."

"Wanna catch up?"

There was silence at the other end of the phone. It continued, and I bit my lip, wondering if she was going to turn me down. I could hear rustling on the phone line. "Yeah, I can do that."

My heart lifted in my chest, and I thought it was going to take flight.

"I'll come and get you," I said.

"No, I'll meet you," she said. I could hear the jingling of keys and was curious what kind of car she drove.

"Okay, I'll meet you outside the campground, and I can direct you to the caravan."

"How about I pick you up and take you over to Marahau?"

"Where's Marahau?"

"Over the hill."

"Okay, I'll see you soon."

Nearly an hour later, I was already antsy as I waited for her outside the campground. There were so many people and vehicles and no car parks; it was complete chaos in the small holiday hamlet. I was nervous that she wouldn't turn up.

But she did. I saw her grinning face as she swerved her pink RAV4 to a stop in front of me. I smiled at her and couldn't stop.

"Hi," I said as I opened the door and got in. I leaned over and kissed her. She moved the car as soon as I sat back because we were in the main line of traffic. I put my belt on as we continued up the hill and started swerving around the corners, climbing higher away from buildings and into native bush.

"Love the car," I finally said.

"Thought you would." She kept her eyes on the road, which I appreciated.

I couldn't help but notice the short shorts she was wearing and the bright red tank top. She looked sporty and summery. A cap with the Racing Harts logo covered her blonde hair. I wanted to reach over and rest my hand on her leg, but I didn't know how she'd react, so I kept my hands to myself.

I didn't travel well if I wasn't driving, but she kept it slow and steady. Finally, we stopped climbing and headed down, and a small inlet opened up before us, and a sleepy little place, which was alive with tractors and boats, appeared before us. It was a beautiful place, and I loved it. We crawled behind a tractor towing a boat with kids and adults on it. The kids were waving and giggling as the boat bumped over the road. They turned off, but Faith kept driving through the little township. I wondered where we were going until she pulled up at a gateway and a large cafe.

"This is the start of the Abel Tasman Track," she said. "Feel like a walk?"

"I don't mind," I said, and we climbed out of the car. I walked around and I couldn't wait another moment. I took her in my arms, hugging her, kissing her on the mouth. Her cheeks flushed, which was rather cute, and she looked down when we stopped.

"You okay?"

"Yes, just not into PDA."

"PDA?"

"Public Displays of Affection."

I laughed. "Okay, I'll take it slow until you're used to it," I said. She ducked her head again as I took her hand.

"Hang on," she said. She walked to the boot of the car and pulled out a backpack.

"What's in there?"

"A secret, but you might want some water, which I have in here."

"Okay, I won't argue with that."

She locked the door, and I took her hand. She happily walked beside me as we headed off on the track.

"Are we walking all the way to Anchorage?" I asked.

"No, too late in the day, but there are lots of nice beaches along the way."

"Sounds good to me," I said. It was already early afternoon, and the sun was beating down, so hot. I was pleased I had my cap and sunglasses and was slathered in sunblock.

After what felt like an hour, we headed down a track and came out into a little bay. I looked around. The water was a turquoise blue, and the sand was golden. Nowhere else in New Zealand had I seen anything that looked so exotic. I turned to see Faith unpacking the backpack with a blanket and food.

"Wow, a picnic."

"I had to feed you once I made you walk so far," she said, handing me a bottle of water. I gratefully accepted. The water was ice cold and felt great as I drank it down.

I sat down on the mat and looked at the food that she'd provided. Crackers, brie, fruit relishes, small dinner buns, freshly buttered and still slightly warm, lettuce, chopped chicken, cherry tomatoes, cucumber, homemade mayo. It was a fair smorgasbord of delicious delights.

"Yum. Where do I start?" I asked, looking at the various foods.

"Wherever you like," she said, smiling at me. She pushed a strand of hair away from her eyes, the slight breeze tossing it back into her face. I leaned over and swept it behind her ear. Her cheeks reddened, something I loved to see. She looked down, then up at me through her eyelashes.

It was at that moment that I knew I'd lost my heart to her.

I picked up a cracker and spread some of the fruit relish on it and a slab of cheese. Instead of eating it, I offered it to her. She held the hair out of her face as she opened her mouth to accept my offering. Watching her lips close around the food made me feel hot inside, and my heart quickened its pace. I just wanted to throw her down on the blanket and kiss her senseless. I had to look away, so I made myself a bun with chicken, relish and some salad. The bun was slightly sweet, and with the chicken, it was like heaven in my mouth.

"Did you make this?"

"No, my skills don't extend to cooking, I'm afraid."

"You can't cook?"

"I can burn a boiled egg," she said, laughing.

I couldn't help but laugh with her. "Really? I'll have to cook for you, because I know how to."

"But are you any good?"

"My mum thinks so, and so far, Rueben and Cheryl haven't died."

That set her off again, and we giggled along together.

"I'm actually not too bad. I cook a mean steak," I said, remembering that she loved steak.

"I'll have to try it sometime." She helped herself to a bun and salad.

We ate in silence, and when we'd finished and packed the leftovers, I pulled Faith over towards me and we snuggled up together in the sand, watching the gentle waves break on the golden beach.

This moment would imprint on my mind as probably one of the best days ever.

# chapter fifteen

Faith

The day at the beach was lovely, and I wanted to keep Cole with me, despite my conflicting feelings about him. Dad left us kids because he didn't love us; aunt and uncle argued all the time, but I couldn't stop this warm, fuzzy feeling inside. I knew it would hurt eventually, and maybe I could still have some fun before I ended it. He was only up here for a couple more days. Perhaps I could send him home and get on with my life.

He got out of the car reluctantly after giving me a kiss on the cheek. He promised to call me later, and I drove home, still trying to work out if I was doing the right thing or not. Was I strong enough to say goodbye at the end of this and keep him at arm's distance while I was racing?

"How was your day?" Hope asked as I got out of my car.

"It was nice. How was yours?"

"Not anywhere near as much fun as yours." She grinned.

I felt my cheeks flush as I pulled the backpack out and took it into the kitchen, emptying the containers into the sink and rinsing them, more to avoid questions than anything.

Hope followed me in and picked up a tea towel. No getting away from it then.

"Did you have a good picnic?"

"Yes, the food was lovely, thanks to Michel."

"You're going to have to learn how to cook," Hope said.

"Not while we have Michel here, I don't."

"What if he leaves?"

"We pay him too much to leave."

"True."

There was a pause as I washed the containers and put them on the bench for Hope to dry.

"So how was Cole?"

"How do you know I was out with Cole?"

"You wouldn't take a picnic like that for Sara," she pointed out, and she was right. Maybe I needed to do this with Sara too. But they knew I wasn't good at lying.

"Cole was good."

"Oh, so where did you take him?"

"Out on the Abel Tasman."

"Wow, did he manage that?"

"He goes to the gym, so of course he's fit enough to cope, besides it was all flat."

"When are you seeing him again?"

"I don't know." I wasn't lying. It was probably tomorrow, but I didn't know what time at this stage.

"Do you like him?" Hope suddenly went serious.

I looked at her before I replied."He's a friend."

"I didn't ask if he was a friend, I asked if you liked him."

My cheeks went hot. "I like him as a friend."

"You know, it's okay to fall in love, don't you?"

"Yeah," I said, but I didn't feel it.

"Mum and Dad loved each other so much." Her eyes went dreamy as she remembered our parents. She had the advantage of actually remembering them. I was five when Mum died. And all I remember is Aunt Dill and Uncle Chives. Dad apparently couldn't cope with us, so he gave us to Dill, his sister. They'd never had kids of their own and took us in with open arms. They showed us all the love we needed, but they weren't exactly role models for love. And if Dad loved us, why did he give us up? And where is he now? I didn't say any of this.

"I want to have what they had, how they smiled at each other all the time. Mum and Dad would touch whenever they could. It was so romantic," Hope continued.

"Hmm," I said.

"What? You don't want that?"

"I don't know what I want, but I know I don't want to be bickering and arguing every day," I said.

"Aunt Dill and Uncle Chives love each other; it's what they do."

"That isn't love; that's something else," I replied.

"It's not what I want either, but they are still together."

"They should just divorce; they'd be happier."

"It takes many things to make one happy. Perhaps arguing is their way of appreciating each other."

I raised my eyebrows at her.

"Okay, it isn't ideal. But what about Cole? Is there anything there? A spark? A desire to spend time with him?"

Oh, there was definitely that, but I didn't want to be drawn into anything at this stage.

"We're just friends," I said as I wiped down the bench and walked away, leaving her to finish drying off the dishes.

My phone dinged as I walked to my villa. I checked; it was Cole. I smiled as I read his message:

*Hi, really enjoyed my day, dinner tonight?*

I was tempted…But I needed an early night after last night's concert.

*Not tonight, having an early night. Catch up tomorrow?*

My phone rang as I got into my unit. I put my car keys on the wooden table by the door and answered the phone as I plopped down on my couch.

"Hey."

"I miss you already," Cole said.

"I miss me too," I replied, making Cole laugh. I wouldn't encourage his feelings because he was going back to Christchurch. Once we were back racing, then I had to focus on the championship.

"Let me take you to lunch tomorrow, then."

"Where do you want to go?" I asked.

"Where's a good place to go?"

I knew just the place. "I'll pick you up at ten thirty. I'll book a table for us. Just a word of warning, it isn't cheap."

"I'll get some money from my mum to pay then." He laughed.

"You'll probably need a loan from the bank," I said.

"I'll manage, I'm sure. Will you show me around while I'm up this way?"

"We're going to Nelson so I know of some places you'd probably like."

"Sounds like a plan." There was silence on the phone. "What are you doing?"

"Sitting on my couch, talking to some guy on the phone." I laughed.

"Is he good-looking? Is he worth it?"

"I don't know. Kind of sleazy, really." I smiled at teasing him.

Cole laughed. "As long as he has a good heart."

"I don't know about that. He's rather brash."

"Brash? What makes you say that?"

"He came up to me when I was training and scared the living daylights out of me, and then, he didn't tell me he was racing for Nigel Kinsey."

"Did he forget to tell you he's Nigel Kinsey's son?"

"What?!" I spluttered. How had I not put that connection together?

There was a moment of silence. "Yeah, Nigel's my dad."

"Oh-kay," I said slowly. Nigel Kinsey's son! "But your last name is Blythe?"

"That's Mum's last name. My older brother is Kinsey, I'm Blythe to continue Mum's family name. But it shouldn't make any difference, that Nigel's my dad, should it?"

"Um, yeah, it does."

There was a pause. "Why?"

"Because your dad hates me."

"He doesn't hate you," he said, but didn't say it with much conviction.

"He did everything he could to sabotage my last three racing seasons, often going to the council to protest my wins, to stop me getting points."

There was quiet on the other end of the phone.

"Look, I don't know why he didn't like me. I presumed it was because I was a woman racing with the big boys. He did everything he could to keep me from racing."

"I don't know either, but I'm not like my dad; you should know that by now."

It was my turn to be quiet. He certainly hadn't tried to protest my races and had congratulated me on my wins. Cole had arranged for a massage after my crash. He wasn't anything like his dad.

I begrudgingly agreed.

"We still on tomorrow?" he asked, worry pinching his voice.

I sighed. "Yeah, we're still on."

"Great!" Relief flooded his voice. "Can't wait to see you again."

"Okay," I replied. "See you tomorrow."

I hung up before he could reply. My mind went crazy. Cole was Nigel Kingsey's son.

My conflicted feelings kicked into overdrive. All the more reason to put distance between us.

# chapter sixteen

Cole

It got closer to ten thirty, and I felt like I had a mouthful of cotton balls. My heart was racing, and I started pacing. I wasn't sure whether Faith was going to turn up.

"Relax, bro, she'll come."

"I'm not sure. She didn't realise that Nigel is our dad."

"And her problem is?"

"Dad doesn't like her, doesn't like her racing and doesn't want her winning."

"Why not?"

"I don't know; he's really anti-Faith. You know what Dad's like."

Rueben and Cheryl both nodded. I think it's part of the reason Cheryl doesn't come to any family dinners at Dad's, not that he has many.

"And why won't she turn up today?" Cheryl asked.

"She's only just found out."

"Okay. But she will turn up."

"Are you sure?"

I looked at them. They didn't know Faith like I did.

A car tooted, and I looked over. It was Faith. I breathed out, smiled at Rueben and waved at him as I ran towards Faith's car. I climbed in, relieved to see her.

"Hi," I said breathlessly.

"Hi," she leaned towards me and kissed me on the cheek.

I felt a smile spread across my face, and relief relaxed my knotted stomach as she moved the car into drive and headed out of the caravan park. We drove in silence out of Kaiteriteri, but as we got through Motueka, I broke the silence.

"How's your morning?"

"It was busy, so I needed to get some work done."

"And pay the band."

She smiled. "Yes, and pay the band."

"They did an amazing job. It was a great night."

"It was, we raised a lot of money for Caring4Kids."

"That's great."

"We think so."

As we started driving out of Motueka, we lapsed into silence again.

But I felt like I needed to address the elephant in the car.

"Look, you might not like my dad, but I'm nothing like him."

"I know," she replied, concentrating on driving.

"My dad can be an asshole to me too. I just wanted you to know."

"I get it."

"Do you? What is it between you and Dad?"

"I don't know. It first became an issue with him when I got competitive and won races. I guess he just doesn't like women riders."

I thought back over my family life with Dad. He'd derided Mum constantly until she finally left him. He talked down to most women, including Cheryl, who just let it wash off her. She's stood her ground with him, but it hasn't stopped him from making cutting remarks.

"You might be right. I don't think he likes women. Mum left him about two years ago, and she moved in with me."

"You live with your mum?" A smile curled up the corners of her lips.

"No, Mum lives with me," I said. "There's a difference."

"Is there?"

I laughed. "Of course! But, having Mum as a flatmate is pretty cool. We take turns cooking, and cleaning. Mum has her social circle, so she get's out and about; it's not like she's always at home. She works as my office manager."

"You're close with your mum?"

"Yeah, I am. What about your mum? You close with her?"

Faith's smile fell, and I could tell I'd touched a nerve by the slight twitch under her eye.

"Mum died when I was little. We moved in with Aunt Dill and Uncle Chives when I was five because Dad couldn't handle us girls."

"Do you see your dad much?"

"I haven't seen or heard from him since he ditched us." She said the words through gritted teeth."It's why I don't believe in love and relationships; no one in my family has happy relationships."

"No one? What about Aunt Dill and Uncle Chicken?" That made her laugh.

"Uncle Chives. They argue and bicker all the time. It's not healthy."

"But you know what a healthy relationship looks like?"

"It doesn't look like arguing and bickering or abandoning those you love when they need you the most."

"I won't abandon you," I said.

She looked at me out of the corner of her eye. "That's because I won't be in a relationship with you."

"You can't live your life not loving someone. You love your sisters. You love your aunt and uncle; you loved your mum and dad at one point."

"But that's different."

"Why is it different? What's different about that?"

"They're family. You can have arguments with them, and you stop talking, but you talk to them again once you've cooled down."

"Your aunt and uncle are still together."

"Only by the grace of God," she said, rolling her eyes.

"You can have arguments with someone you love and still love them. You can be angry with them, but still love them. It doesn't mean that you can't love them."

"My dad didn't."

"Was he angry with you?"

"No, he just couldn't live with us kids any more after Mum died."

"Have you ever asked him why he left you guys? Maybe it was because he hurt so much."

"Then why didn't he come and get us once he'd sorted it out?"

"Maybe he hasn't sorted it out. Maybe he's still sad, and even more so now because he's left it so long without being in contact with you girls."

"Do you know my dad? Did he send you?" She narrowed her eyes, shooting me a side glance.

"No, just throwing ideas out there. Playing devil's advocate. Maybe he's sad and lonely and needs you girls to reach out to him."

"Or maybe he just wants to be left alone. Or he's dead," she snapped.

"I see this is a tender subject. I'm sorry. I didn't mean—"

"Let's just drop it, aye, before you spoil a decent day more than you already have."

I shut up and sat back in my seat, staring out the window as we approached Richmond. I wish I had said nothing, but then I hadn't known. How was I supposed to know? I haven't looked her up on the internet to find out all about Faith Hart. Maybe I should have.

"I'm sorry," I said as we drove through the lights, wondering how we were going to have a nicer day from here onwards. I didn't want to talk about racing, because it's the holidays, and racing would begin again soon enough.

Talking about her family was off-limits. Perhaps music and other sports might be suitable conversation pieces. Or the weather.

"Wow, the weather is stunning at the moment," I said.

"Yes, great for the grapes."

"How long have you guys been running the vineyard?

"I started once I got back from uni."

"What did you study?"

"Bachelor of Business Studies and Marketing."

"Cool."

"What about you? You study, or just go straight into spray painting?"

"I did a Bachelor of Arts. But I couldn't stand being in an office."

"Wow, a BA. Any specific subject?"

"Psychology."

"Really?" Her voice pitched, like she didn't believe me.

"Really."

Her silence filled the car, and she was probably thinking back over our conversation about her dad.

"I wasn't analysing you earlier."

"I wasn't thinking that."

"What were you thinking?"

"That you're a strange man. You studied, but prefer a blue-collar job. You're a motorcycle racer, yet you drive a little Smart Car.

"Hey, that has nothing to do with my masculinity," I said.

She laughed. "I never said it did."

"Well, you're a woman who races motorcycles, and probably knows her way around one mechanically too."

"Can strip and put a motor back together in a couple of days."

"Very impressive."

She'd parked the car, and we were sitting along the port, looking out over the harbour.

"We're here." She said, nodding to a shed over the water. It looked like nothing more than a rickety wooden shed.

"It was a boat shed once, hence, Boat Shed Cafe. But they have the best menu in town, if a little pricey."

"Will the building hold up?"

"It survived a couple of cyclones. I think it can hold you and your ego up." She snickered, and her cheeks flushed pink. I had to laugh at her. She was cute when she was laughing.

# chapter seventeen

Faith

We got a seat with a view out over the harbour. It was a beautiful sunny day, with very few clouds in the sky. The water was calm, and there was a gentle sea breeze. The plastic walls wafted in and out as the breeze moved around the outdoor area.

He sat staring at the water below us through the cracks in the decking.

"Don't drop your phone or wallet." I said. He pulled them out of his pocket and put them firmly on the table.

"Nope, not planning on it."

"This is one of my favourite restaurants."

"Does it stock your wine?"

"Yes, it does."

"Then I'm going to try one. Which do you recommend?"

"The pinot gris was nice last year."

The waiter turned up just as we were talking about it.

"May I take your drink order?"

Cole looked over at me.

"Two Hart Valley pinot gris, thanks," I said.

"Are you ready to order your meals?"

"Not just yet," I replied, opening up my menu.

"Wow, this place has quite the menu," Cole said as his eyes flicked over the page several times. "I don't know what to choose!"

"I'm having the risotto, but the market fish is nice as well."

"What was the fish of the day?"

"Gurnard, I think."

"Hmm, might be the answer," he said, closing up his menu. The waiter arrived back with the two glasses of wine. We ordered our meals, and then I sat back and watched as Cole picked up his glass of wine, swirling it, then sniffing it. He swirled and sniffed several times before taking a sip. I watched a drop of condensation bead down over his fingers holding the stem.

"Did it look like I knew what I was doing?" he asked, smiling at me.

"Nope, just looked like you were doing something you thought you should do."

He laughed, and the sound warmed my insides. He was so comfortable to be around. I didn't feel intimidated or aggravated by him, but then, he was an intelligent man. He was a spray painter, but he was clever, especially if he'd gone to uni. Knowing he had some formal education made him more relatable somehow.

"You ever been fishing?" I asked.

"Hmm," he nodded his head from side to side. "Once or twice. I get seasick. What about you?"

"I love fishing, but I don't do it enough."

"You don't mind the motion of the boat?"

"Nope."

"The up and down, side to side, forwards and back…" The grin on his face made me smile.

"Seasickness doesn't bother me."

"Lucky you," he said, taking a sip of wine. "This is actually quite nice."

"Describe it to me." I sat forwards to see what he would say. I picked up my wine and had a sip too.

"Smooth…Crisp…smells like…like…grapes."

I laughed. "Yes, well, that's a given. What else."

"It's not a dry wine."

"Pinot gris tends not to be."

"Really. Okay."

"Do you normally drink wine?"

He grinned. "No, beer, but I like this. It isn't sweet."

"Another good descriptor, yes."

"Do you make the wine?"

"No, not at all. In fact, as long as I can drink it, I don't care how it's made."

"What? You're making me describe the wine to you, sounding all official-like, and you don't make the wine."

I grinned back at him. "I never said I made the wine, I market it. So, I need to know what flavours to put down and aroma's etc. Hope is the winemaker."

"Okay, I'll let you off with that one."

I couldn't help smiling when I was around him. He lifted my soul up inside, and I felt warm when I was around him. What was this feeling? Surely it wasn't love.

I twirled the wine, watching it move up the side of the glass.

"What are you thinking?"

I felt my face go red as I was caught up in my thoughts.

"Nothing, just watching the wine in the glass." My throat felt like it was tightening as I spoke, but I got the words out.

He stared at me for a while before reaching out his hand and touching mine. It felt like an electric shock went up my arm, and I jolted, pulling away from him. There was a brief flare of hurt on his face.

"Sorry, electric shock." It sounded lame, even to my ears. I put my hand down in the hopes he might try to take it again, but he didn't, leaving me feeling disappointed and hurt. Why had I jerked my hand away, such an idiot thing to do?

After the meal, I took him up to the top of Princes Drive to the lookout. I pointed out where Kaiteriteri and Motueka were, and where, approximately, Hart Valley was. He leaned against the railing and looked back at me.

"You are amazing, you know that?"

I felt my face heat again as I looked away from him. I heard him stand and felt his hand on my face, turning it towards him. "You are amazing."

"No, I'm not."

"You are," he said, leaning in closer. My heart raced. I could feel his breath on my face, and I closed my eyes. His lips were soft and warm. I leaned into his kiss, feeling warmth flood through me. I stepped closer and embraced him, pulling him towards myself. I sighed, and I felt him smile against my lips. He ended the kiss, leaned back and looked at me. I saw him through a haze of lust, and I wanted him so badly. Part of me was relieved that we were in a public place, but another part of me also regretted that we wouldn't be able to continue this on, as by the time we got into the car and back to my place, the feeling would have gone.

My cheeks flushed again, just as he leaned in to kiss me, his hands cupping my face. Once more I was lost in the feelings that swam around my body, through my blood, my nerves, my muscles. I even felt it in my bones. The intensity of the feeling of the two of us, holding each other, wanting each other.

A car tooted behind us, and cheers followed, which made me step back. I didn't do PDA. How had I managed to be suckered into kissing him in public? The sound of the city filled my ears, and I knew we were so exposed. I stepped back again, putting space between us. The hurt in Cole's eyes cut, but I didn't know what else to do.

"It's my last day tomorrow; would you give me a tour of the vineyard?" he asked.

I hesitated. I really wanted to show him, but Aunt Dill and Uncle Chives were there, still bickering, and my sisters…

"I…I…"

"It's okay, I understand," he said. He put his hands in his pockets and headed back to the car. I followed him and got in.

"Here's the thing. My sisters give me a hard time about not having a guy. They've been hounding me since they saw us dancing together to meet you. But…I want to keep you to myself." My explanation sounded dumb even to my ears.

"I get it," Cole said, putting his seatbelt on.

"You don't. You see, they tease me mercilessly. I can't take it if I introduce you to them, and then the teasing will get worse."

"Why do they tease you?"

"Probably because I react."

"So, don't react."

I just gave him the side-eye. He didn't know what it was like living with my sisters. Never mind introducing him to Aunt Dill and Uncle Chives, I mean…it would show him just how dysfunctional our family really is.

I started the car. The drive back to Kaiteriteri was done in silence, other than the radio playing softly in the background.

He got out of the car as soon as I pulled up outside the camp. "I'll call later," he said, and closed the door. No kiss, no hug, no goodbye.

Pain sliced through my heart as I waved goodbye, forcing a smile on my face.

Which was stupid, because I wasn't in love with Cole.

# chapter eighteen

Cole

"Just go," Rueben said.

"But she was so hesitant," I replied.

"She responds when you kiss her?"

"Yes."

"She likes you. Just do it," Cheryl said.

"Would you guys come with me?"

"Are you kidding? No!" my bro said.

I'd spoken with Faith last night after our lacklustre goodbye. I'd been despondent after our date and wondered why she didn't want me to visit her place. I'd already been there, and her excuse about her sisters was lame. My brother teased me all the time; I just gave it right back.

So, I bit the bullet and drove out.

I arrived and parked in the car park, my heart pounding in my chest, wondering if I had done the right thing. I couldn't see her car around, so I went into the large building which was the cellar and the restaurant all rolled into one. It was like walking into what I imagined a Swiss chalet would look like. All wooden timber, large beams, large windows with a view out over the vineyard for as far as the eye could see.

The mountains framed the background. It was cool inside, despite the summer heat.

"Can I help you?" A tall, blonde, with freckles over her cheeks and a mole above her lip. The one I thought was Faith when I first saw her at the LabSix concert..

"Yes, I'm here to see Faith," I said.

"Do you have an appointment?" the girl asked with a beautiful wide smile.

"Ah, no, I don't," I said, tucking my thumbs into the belt loops on my shorts.

"Never mind, I'll call her. Who can I say is calling?"

"Cole."

"Ah, so you're the famous Cole."

"The one and only," I said, curious why I was 'the famous Cole'.

"She keeps you to herself," she said, her eyes travelling up and down my body.

"She's worried about being teased by her sisters," I said.

"Hi, I'm Grace, her older sister." She held out a hand to me, and I shook it firmly. Grace had a firm grip herself, which was nice, because often women had such limp handshakes.

"And yes, we tease her, because she's such an ice queen around men, but," she turns her head to the side, "you're different."

"Thanks?" I said, wondering what she meant by that.

She smiled again. "I'll let her know you're here," she said and disappeared behind a desk. She picked up the phone, and I couldn't help overhearing Grace tell Faith that she had a visitor, but didn't say who it was. Obviously, Faith wanted to know because Grace turned her back on me and said it was 'some cute guy'. I could imagine Faith rolling her eyes.

"She'll be over in a moment," Grace said, smirking. "Would you like a drink?"

"No, I'm good, thanks."

She stood beside me in awkward silence, and I wondered why she was hanging around. Probably wanted to tease Faith more. Now I understood why Faith had been reluctant to have me here, and I regretted putting her through that situation now. But it was too late; I was here.

I heard a door open behind me, and the clopping of sandals on the stone floor.

"Cole!"

I turned around and gave her my most brilliant smile."Hi, Faith."

"What are you doing here?" She looked from me to her sister, a horrified look on her face. I glanced at Grace, who looked rather too smug.

"You're nasty," I said to Grace, who grinned at me.

"I know." She turned and wandered off, leaving me with Faith, who was wringing her hands.

"I understand now; my brother isn't anywhere near as bad as that."

"What did she say to you?"

"Nothing other than you're the ice queen."

Faith frowned and crossed her arms over her chest.

"I already knew that," I said, crossing the distance between us and tapping her on the nose with my finger. Her frown turned into a slight smile before her lips curved into the most tantalising smile I'd ever seen. I kissed her on the lips.

"Keep it seemly; this is a family-friendly space," another voice echoed behind us. Faith grabbed my arm, and we went back the way she'd come before I could turn around and see who the other speaker was, but I presumed it was another sister.

She marched me out the door, down a covered walkway to a small house off to the left of the main building. She opened the door onto a lounge area. Her own private space.

"This is my place," she said, waving her arm around. The lounge area opened into a dining and kitchen area. The kitchen looked out onto a private garden with a lawn that sloped down onto a large pond.

"Wow, this is really cool," I said, looking around. The artwork on the walls was beautiful, a large photograph of a beach scene at sunset or sunrise. The other wall had a photo of the three girls and two other people who must be her aunt and uncle.

"The bedroom," she said, opening a door and closing it before I had time to have a proper look. I moved past her and opened the door. The room had muted green walls and a dark green feature wall. It matched the outside with the lawn and the patio that was framed by star jasmine, the scent floating in through the open doors. The double doors opened up to the same view as the kitchen, of the pond and the lawn. Her bed was queen-sized, with a bright yellow duvet and a dark green comforter. Thousands of pillows were on the bed. I raised my eyebrows, but she just smiled.

"This is the bathroom," she said. This had to be my favourite room. It was a deep burgundy colour, and opened onto a large private garden, complete with a fountain pond, even filled with fish. The garden enclosed the entire space and included native bush, ferns and the water feature. Dappled light shone down into the area. The bathroom itself comprised a shower, a bathtub set right in front of the window, and a toilet. The space mesmerised me. It was amazing and so unusual.

"This is…wow," was all I could say.

"Yeah, it's home," she said. The last room was probably a spare bedroom, but she had it set up as an office, and there was paperwork everywhere.

"I hope your workshop doesn't look like that," I said.

"Workshop?"

"Where you work on your bike."

"My mechanic has that covered. I don't keep my bike here."

"Why not?"

"It's safer with my mechanic." She shrugged.

My bike was in my workshop. My mechanic, Steve, came and worked on it there.

"It needs a bit of work since Fielding," she said, giving me a knowing look. I nodded, because yes, I remember her coming off her bike. It had scared me.

I took her hand and pulled her back towards her bedroom. "So, this is your room?" I asked as I sat down on her bed.

"Real smooth, Cole." She remained standing as I lay down on her bed.

"This is really comfy," I said, adjusting my position, throwing pillows off it as I did.

"Cole!" she giggled.

"Come on, let's try snuggling on it," I said.

"No, I got up and made it. Now I'll have to make it again."

I grabbed her and tugged her down to me, and she fell giggling into my arms.

"Now this feels nice," I said, pulling her into my body with my arm around her shoulder. I had her trapped between my legs as well. Her back pulled tightly into my chest. "Snuggly," I said, nuzzling her neck. She stilled as I found her secret spot, and her breathing changed from a breathless giggle to a deep sigh. I kissed it and nuzzled it some more, and she edged herself into my embrace.

"Feels nice, doesn't it?" I mumbled as I moved my mouth around, exploring her neck. My hands explored her arm as she arched into my body. What had started as a bit of a joke was turning into a serious turn-on, and I didn't want it to stop. She kept pushing into my groin, which was reacting to show her exactly what I was thinking, but she didn't stop, even though she would have felt it. I eased my hand off her arm and slowly inched my way towards her chest.

She twisted in my arms, turning over.

"I don't know if I want to do this," she said. Her eyes were looking at my mouth, and the next thing I knew, she's kissing me. Her tongue slipped between my lips. I turn us so that I am lying on top of her, deepening the kiss. When we stopped, we're breathless.

"We can stop," I said, looking at her through half closed eyes, and hoping she wouldn't.

She pushed my top off, her hands roaming all over my body, making it feel hot and cold all at the same time. I lower my face to hers and kiss her again. I pull on her top, and we stop kissing long enough to struggle to get it off over her head. She's wearing a lacy bra, fully padded, but the cups still outline her breasts. I want to pull the bra off and worship her properly, but I'm letting her take control and allowing her to set the pace. So far, she has called nothing off.

I kiss down her neck and around her chest, at the breasts that are peeking out over the bra, and down her belly. She groans as I sweep my fingers lightly over her skin. She still has her shorts on.

I get out of bed and take off my shorts, leaving me in my boxers. I lie down beside her, my hands feeling the curves of her body. So smooth, compared to a car body.

She blinks at me as she considers her next move, and I allow her the time. Again, I reach over and kiss her; her body smells like spring flowers and feels just as delicate. I let my fingers glide over her body. She gets off the bed and removes her shorts.

She has panties that match her bra, soft satiny fabric that clings to her hips, showing off her body. I groan as she sits straddling me and starts kissing me again.

She pushes up and reaches behind her back. The bra drops and her breasts are revealed as if by magic. The soft, smooth texture had my hands reaching for them, making the nipples tighten at my touch. She tipped her head back as I massaged them in my hands, feeling the weight. They are more than a handful, which I tease by pinching the nipples gently between my fingers.

She moans and leans down, her hair falling forwards as she rests on her arms above me. My eyes move to her face. She's sucking on her bottom lip; her eyes are closed as she concentrates on the sensations I'm creating within her.

She grinds against my groin, her wetness soaking through, and my cock strains at the material, wanting to find her inner warmth. I don't want to talk and spoil the moment, but I don't want her to feel pushed either, so I let her take the lead.

And she does.

# chapter nineteen

Faith

His touch is gentle; his hands are warm and soft. I gasp when he teases my nipples between his fingers. I can feel every nerve in my body responding and screaming at me to get a wriggle on and do something more. I grind against him, feeling him hard beneath me, and I want it. I've never wanted something more than I want him inside of me, right now.

I ease off my knickers, and when I move out of Cole's reach, he looks at me questioningly. I just reach down and pull his boxers off, and I see he's hard and ready for me. I'm ready for him too. I stroke him, making his head fall back onto the pillow as he groans. I reach into my bedside cabinet, making him look at why I've stopped. When he sees the condom in my hand, he understands. I tear the little package and pull the rubber down, hoping that it'll stretch and not strangulate his cock. With the condom on, I straddle him again. He reaches up and grabs hold of my arms. We're looking into each other's eyes, and I position his hardness at my entrance. He's waiting for me to go down slowly on him, but I'm wet, and it won't take much for it to slide inside, and

I'm right. I plunge down on him, making his eyes open wide and grab hold of me, stopping me from moving.

"Damn! Hold still!" he mutters as I squirm around on top of him, a grin on my face.

"Stop!" he implores, reaching around to smack my ass. I can't help it. The look on his face, between pleasure and pain.

I stop fidgeting and let him breathe. Which he does; a deep, steady breath. I can feel him twitching inside me, which is driving me just as crazy. My body hugs him tight, constricting his movement, but feeling every little twinge.

He blows out noisily. "That was intense."

"Are you ready?" I ask, cocking my head to one side.

"I was born ready." He gives me a sly smile.

I slowly ease up and allow myself to slide down onto him. We both groan at the sensation that causes, even with a barrier between us. I feel him twitch, and I use my muscles to grip onto him.

"Damn, sweet baby beetroot," he says.

I almost laugh, except I understand the sentiment, although I would've sworn and used more sacrilegious language.

I can feel the growing power within me, and I close my eyes, focusing on the sensation and the movement, the pull, tug, push, and suction and I feel myself breathe in, in until I can't take any more air into my lungs before tumbling into a body-wide orgasm of world shaking proportions. I quiver and shake, and every time he moves, it starts another wave of mind-numbing goodness. I hear him cry out and grunt, and then he, too, is shuddering and shaking beneath me, quivering every time I clench around him.

I collapse down onto him, and he envelopes me in his arms. I lie there, stunned and breathing hard. I'd brought myself to orgasm many times before, but that was so much more, even than with previous boyfriends.

"What's your secret?" he whispers.

"What?" I don't understand what he's asking.

"What makes you so good at giving orgasms?"

"I could ask you the same thing."

"That was the best I've ever had," he said.

"I bet you say that to all the girls."

"Meh," he said, making me giggle.

"That was incredibly intense," he went on. "I didn't think I would ever stop."

"Do you always talk about sex after you've had it?"

"Do you not?"

"No!"

"Why not? It's always good to compare notes. I might have areas you want me to improve."

I laughed again as I slide off him and lay down beside him. We both look up at the natural wood ceiling.

Silence filled the room as my heart rate finally settled. I didn't want it to. I wanted to experience that again, and again, and again, but I knew I couldn't go there. It was nice to know he was good at sex…

Argh, who was I kidding? He was great at sex. And my heart was warm and fuzzy, and I was falling for him, but I can't. I can't let myself be in love with him. Love wasn't fuzzy and warm; it was cold and prickly and full of arguments and death and people leaving when you needed them most. I tried to keep those thoughts at the front of my mind, but I couldn't when fingers started tracing invisible lines across my skin, making my nerves and body crave him again.

"We need to get up and moving, otherwise my sisters will wonder where we are."

"They know we're here, don't they?"

"I don't want them thinking I slept with you. Could you imagine that? I'd never hear the end of it." I got up and hunted around for my knickers and bra to put on. Cole stayed on the bed. When I looked over, there was a look of hurt on his face.

"Cole. They tease me mercilessly; the less they know, the better." I knew I was whining; I could hear it in my voice, but I had no other way of explaining it, plus, it was a good way to get him out of my bed. Which would now smell like him.

I shuffled into my shorts and blouse. He was sitting on the edge of the bed, looking stunned and dazed.

"Coffee?" I asked him.

"Yeah," he said, and I headed into my kitchen to make a pot of coffee. He wandered out a few minutes later. He put his arms around me from behind, and I snuggled into him.

"You run hot and cold like a tap," he said.

"I know. It's the way I am," I said, trying to keep my own emotions in check. I wanted to just turn in his arms and be swallowed up by the warm fuzzies his kisses and embraces gave me, but I couldn't allow myself to fall for him.

We had our coffee sitting on the patio outside the kitchen, watching the ducks on the pond, and enjoying the sun on our faces.

"Want to have a look around the vineyard?"

"Won't that make your sister's suspicious?" I heard the hardness in his tone, but refused to give in to it.

"Not as much as not appearing at all from here," I said, taking his cup inside.

I slipped my trainers on, and we headed off, walking around the large estate.

# chapter twenty

Cole

My mind whirled as I drove my car back to Kaiteriteri. It had been a strange experience to witness Faith within her own family environment. She seemed on edge and kept me pretty much at arm's length, unless we were in her villa. Even the abrupt change after sex felt…weird.

I met Grace, who seemed nice. She kept giving Faith sidelong glances. No doubt she wound Faith up mercilessly after I left, and I felt bad about that.

Faith was uncomfortable with her siblings teasing her. Why? It's normally just a little give and take with family, but it's like she doesn't feel comfortable admitting anything within her family or else they would pester her about it. Rueben and I wound each other up all the time. Why was it different for Faith and her sisters?

I got back to the caravan, grabbed a beer from the fridge and settled in.

"We weren't expecting you back before tomorrow," Cheryl said, grinning at me.

"Yeah, well, plans change," I mumbled.

"What happened?"

"I don't really know. It was going so well, but then, it was like someone turned the tap and suddenly she was Miss Ice Queen again."

Cheryl nodded. "How many sisters does she have?"

"Two."

"She's the youngest?"

"Yip."

"I'm guessing she finds it hard to show emotion around her family, especially towards those outside of the family unit. The sisters are tight?"

"I think so; they work together for the family business."

"Faith probably struggles to show her emotions because of something from her childhood," Cheryl said. "Something happened when she was young."

I knew exactly what she was talking about. "How do you know?"

"I don't; I'm just making some assumptions based on what you're saying. But she obviously has some childhood trauma, and she finds it hard to express herself, probably not just to you, but to her sisters too."

"Yeah, you're right." But then he hadn't told his brother he loved him since he last got drunk, a couple of days before Christmas. It was the only time he told people how much he cared about them.

"Give her some space." Cheryl sighed.

"We're heading home tomorrow, so how much more space do you recommend?" I snapped and instantly regretted it. "Sorry."

"It's okay. What I meant was, let her come to you."

"Yeah." I proceeded to my bed and fell face down on it. The sex had been amazing, mind-blowing, and yet…How had she detached so quickly? It's like she's two different people. Relaxed Faith around me, and uptight Faith around her family. I didn't like it. I preferred relaxed Faith. I wanted to be with her, but if she couldn't be relaxed around her family…

I didn't do games. I'm not a complicated person. I don't want to deal with complicated issues, which is what that was.

"Hey, bro," my brother said, interrupting my thoughts.

"Yeah."

"Wanna go for a beer, you know, last hurrah and all that stuff?"

"Why not?"

After an evening of laughing, drinking and pizza, I felt more relaxed, probably too relaxed. Faith texted me to say she'd had a fun day, which I responded to. Told her we were heading home early in the morning. I was tucking myself into bed, determined to stop the world from spinning, when my phone rang.

"What time are you leaving?"

"Early, early," I said, slurring slightly.

"Have you been drinking?"

"Yip, pizza and beer, baby."

"Oh, okay. Well, I hope you have a safe drive home."

"We will, leaving about six  in the morning."

"Sure your head will cope with that?"

"Probably not, but that's what greasy burgers are for."

"Urgh."

I giggled."Sleep well, my ice queen." I shut my eyes, thinking I'd made a monumental mistake.

"Good-night, Cole. Sleep well. Keep in touch, aye."

"I will, sweetheart. Good-night."

I hung up without further delay. I closed my eyes, my phone resting on my chest, and fell asleep.

The next morning, the alarm went off at 4:00 a.m. I shut it off and wondered who the idiot was that had set it for that time until I realised it was me. I stumbled out of bed and straight to the jug, which I switched on. Being on a hollow bench, it was loud, and eventually Cheryl and Rueben woke up too.

"Way to wake us up, bro," he groused as he ran a hand through his tousled hair.

Cheryl yawned loudly and stretched her arms above her head."What time do you call this?"

"Early enough to get packed up and on the road before everyone else does," I said, clanging coffee cups and slamming the fridge door.

"You okay?"

"Yip, just wanna get going," I replied.

We wasted no time downing our drinks and packing up the caravan. We'd packed up most of the stuff last night and loaded it into the truck. It was things like taking down the awning, stowing all the outside stuff inside, hooking up the caravan and we were out of there by six thirty in the morning.

"We stopping to say bye to Faith?" Cheryl asked.

"Said goodbye last night," I said as I climbed into the back seat of the truck.

"You sure?" Reuben asked.

"Yip." I hadn't looked at my phone since the alarm went off. I didn't want to look at my phone, but as we left Kaiteriteri and headed via the back roads to the Motueka Inland Highway, I saw there was a message.

*Hope you have safe travels today x*

*Thanks, already on the road x*

*Let me know when you get home* came up quickly on the phone.

*I will. Have fun*

*Work, work, work today*

*I start that tomorrow.*

*You've had a good break then*

*Yeah, was nice to catch up with you*

*I liked that. See you in Christchurch*

*That you will*

I wasn't sure what to make of the messages. She was so inconsistent, and I was still confused after yesterday. I wanted to get into something with her, but if she continued to hold me at arm's length, I wouldn't keep pushing.

She either wanted to go out with me or she didn't.

# chapter twenty-one

Faith

The bike looked fantastic. Geoff had done an amazing job, considering he'd arranged the parts just before Christmas. She looked beautiful, and I couldn't wait to get out on her and ride her hard. But I couldn't, so I had to use the simulator instead, and since Cole had left, I'd hit the gym and yoga mat as well. I needed it after all the food I'd eaten over the holiday period.

I hadn't heard from Cole since he'd returned to Christchurch, other than him letting me know he'd arrived. I'd been really busy at work, and while I thought about messaging him, by the time I got to bed, I'd forgotten. It had been two weeks since we last texted.

My heart lurched at the thought of losing him, but then I had to remind myself that I wasn't looking for a relationship. But what I had with him was something that made me feel warm inside. And the sex. Oh my, that was spectacular. I'm just not the person to tell him that. It felt awkward and strange and foreign, so I didn't. I'd send him a message tonight to see how he is.

Our next race was coming up in Christchurch at Ruapuna Raceway. I set the simulator up and climbed aboard. I had to remember every turn, corner, and chicane so I was ready for the race. And I had to be fit.

"Going okay?" Grace asked as she came into the games room. I stopped the simulator and stayed on my bike as she stood in front of me, leaning on the machine.

"Yip, all good."

"Heard from Cole?" she said with a cheeky grin.

"Nope."

"Oh, really? Cole gone cold?"

"Nope, I have."

Grace suddenly went serious. "What? Why? He's so lovely."

"I don't do relationships."

"But he's perfect."

"Then why do you guys tease me about him?"

"Because it's fun watching you blush. But that's not answering my question."

"Yes, I did. I don't do relationships."

"Bullshit. You have us; we're your sisters; we're in a relationship."

"That's different. I love you guys."

"Do you not love Cole?" Her hazel eyes burned into my soul, which made me squirm inside.

"I don't think so."

"What do you mean, you don't think so? You either know or you don't."

I shrugged. "I don't know. I don't know what love is."

"Aw, sweetie." She came around and hugged me while I sat on the bike. "Love is what we have." She moved her arms around to show she meant everyone within the complex.

"You're just my sisters, I love you."

"Do you feel warm inside when you're around us?"

"Maybe not warm fuzzies, but I love being around you guys."

"What about when Cole is around? You light up when you see him."

I felt myself blush. "Do I?"

"Yeah, you do; you smile, and your entire face gets lighter. Does he give you the warm fuzzies?"

I wouldn't admit to her that he did. "I enjoy his company; I like being around him."

"You're avoiding the question again." Grace frowned at me, which made me smile.

"Nope," I answered. "I can't be. I don't believe in love."

"Are we back on that dead horse again?"

"I honestly don't know what a healthy relationship looks like. Dad ran away. Aunt Dill and Uncle Chives…" I shrugged.

"Dad couldn't look after us after he lost Mum. He was too deep in his own grief."

"Then why haven't we seen or heard from him since?" I asked.

Grace looked down at her hands. "I don't know the answer to that, but I know he loved us very much."

"So much that he left us with his sister and brother-in-law, who argue all the time."

"It's just the way they show each other they care."

"That's bullshit, and you know it," I growled. Grace backed away.

"It's not bullshit. They love each other. Bickering is something they do."

"That isn't normal."

"How do you know it isn't normal?" Grace put her hands on her hips and frowned at me.

"Well, look at you and Lachlan."

"What about me and Lachlan?" Her scowl told me not to go there, but I did.

"You guys were perfect together, but you broke up with him."

"He broke up with me because he was going overseas," she hissed.

"Why didn't you go with him?" I put my hands on my hips, echoing her stance.

Her frown faded, and her whole demeanour changed.

"I didn't want to."

"You didn't want to. Because you don't believe in love either."

"I do. There is more to it than that. Come on, you can't bring Lachlan into this argument; this is about you, not me."

Hope burst into the room at that moment, her face red and her eyes stormy.

"What are you two arguing about? We can hear you out in the foyer."

I dropped my head as my throat thickened, and heat tingled in my face.

"Sorry," Grace and I said at the same time.

"What are you arguing about?" Hope pushed.

"Love," I replied.

"*Pfft*!" She walked out of the room.

"See, even she doesn't believe in love."

"She has her reasons," Grace spat back at me.

Had Hope been hurt in love? When? I didn't know about it.

But I know I never had. And I intended for it to stay that way. Besides, I needed to focus on winning the championship.

"You're just being a hard-nosed ice queen. If you don't sort your shit out, you'll lose Cole, and that would be a real shame." Grace marched across the room, and without a backwards glance, pushed her way through the door.

I sat on the bike, unsure whether I had won or lost that fight. All I knew was that she was probably closer to the truth than I really wanted to acknowledge. I liked Cole a lot. But I was afraid he would abandon me like Dad did, or that we would constantly argue like Aunt Dill and Uncle Chives. I couldn't cope with that; it did my head in just listening to them. Why did I feel this way? I was just too scared to commit because I didn't want to get hurt. Too much hurt had already scarred me. I didn't need any more.

But she was also right. If I didn't sort it out, I would lose Cole, and I liked him as a friend. Besides, he was great at sex.

I shook my head. What was I to do?

# chapter twenty-two

Cole

I slowed down my bike as I came past the start-finish line at the Ruapuna Raceway. I turned and came back to Dad, who held a stopwatch.

"Not good enough," he said as I flipped my visor up.

"What? That was the smoothest so far," I griped.

"Might have been the smoothest but wasn't the fastest. Go again."

"Dad, I've done way too many laps. I'm tired and thirsty."

"Then you won't win any races on Saturday." His brows lowered over his eyes.

"What if I don't want to win?"

"Then what am I wasting my time here for?" He dropped the stopwatch on the ground and walked away.

I sighed, hanging my head. Dad was the travel agent for guilt trips.

"Dad," I called out. He stopped, but didn't turn around. "Alright, I'll do one more lap, then I need to have a drink and something to eat."

Dad stood there for a minute, then turned around and picked up the stopwatch from the ground.

“Two more laps,” he said.

I snapped my visor back down and went back to the start line. He lifted his arm, and I took off. I rolled the bike to the left and right, through a chicane, and around some tight turns and back through the start-finish straight, and did it all again, focusing on the corners, feeling the bike move underneath me as I went through the turns. I slid past the start-finish and decelerated.

I turned the bike back towards Dad. He was shaking his head.

“Nope, was the second fastest, but not enough.”

I got off the bike, undid my helmet and took it off.

I picked up my bag from beside Dad and pulled out a chocolate bar and my drink bottle. I took a deep swig. It’s surprising how thirsty riding a bike can make you, or how much you can sweat in a leather riding suit.

I took another long sip from the bottle and sat it on top of the rail that Dad was standing next to.

“You need to memorise the track so it’s like second nature when you’re riding it.”

“I have.”

“You’re not riding like you have. You jerk up on some corners and don’t swing around properly. And you need to stop using your brakes so much.”

“I’m barely touching my brakes!” I said through a mouthful of chocolate bar.

“No, I can see the front of the bike dipping; you’re touching those.”

I shook my head. I hadn't been aware that I had. "Okay, I'll try to be more aware."

"What're you thinking about out there?" Dad asked.

"The bike, the track." Faith and the fact that I hadn't heard from her since I'd arrived back in Christchurch a week ago. I know that I'll see her this coming weekend, because she's racing, but I hadn't received so much as a text to say hi, how you going.

"Well, at least you've got your head in the right place."

I won't argue with him. And I wasn't going to message Faith either. If she couldn't contact me, what was the point? I just had to suck it up and keep going. And try harder to beat her, just like Dad wanted.

"You have to beat everyone this weekend. This is your home track. You can't take it for granted; you need to win here to really cement your place on the leaderboard. We can't let Faith win."

"Why not? If she's the better racer?"

"Better racer? She's a woman. On a bike. She doesn't deserve to win."

"Pardon?" My eyes open wide. I know we've had this argument before, but I want to get to the bottom of it. Is my father just a misogynist, or is there something else behind his hatred of Faith? Because that is what it is. Hate.

"Women don't race bikes. They stay at home and cook meals and keep houses tidy."

"We both know that is bullshit, Dad. Because Mum works for me, and you were alright with that."

"She was bringing in an extra income, how could I not be alright with that?"

"But you still expected her to keep the house clean, cook and look after you," I pointed out.

"Son, if you haven't worked out what the role of a woman is, then I feel sorry for you. You'll end up pussy-whipped in no time."

"Pussy-whipped?! How could you even say that?"

"Easily. Any man who runs around after a woman needs his head examined."

This conversation was taking a very dark turn, and I wasn't happy about that. I never realised that my father was such an old-fashioned, misogynistic bastard. My heart hammered in my chest as he continued to expound on the social place of women and their place in the world, which was pretty much under men. He wouldn't get anywhere with that attitude, but I couldn't change or adjust it for him. I just had to suck it up for now, and try to distance myself from him once this racing season was over. Once I got through this year, I could finance my own team, buy my own bike, and race without him being near me. But he was still my dad. Even if I didn't like the way he talked about women.

And I understood on a deeper level why Mum avoided him after she left him. She didn't need that kind of bullshit in her life. Mum had hidden a lot of Dad's views from us kids, and it's only now coming to light, especially since racing against Faith.

"I can't believe you just said that," I said kind of under my breath, but he heard.

"It's how I've lived my life."

"And how's that going for you?" I asked, heat crawling up my face, and my skin itched in my suit. My father looked suitably told off, but not repentant. I sighed as I swallowed what was left of the chocolate bar and pulled my helmet back on. The sooner I got a quicker time, the faster I could get out of his company, because my father had become someone I wasn't happy being around.

# chapter twenty-three

## Faith

Ruapuna!

One of my favourite tracks, and right now, I was in the lead, and I was flying. The curves and turns just flew by, the bike moving beneath me as I rounded the last corner onto the start-finish straight. I took the checkered flag and pumped a fist in the air in celebration. I slowed my bike as I went around the track for a final, slower lap and received applause until I came into the pit lane. I pulled up next to my crew, ecstatic with the win.

"Well done, champ," Mike said, patting my back. I got off the bike, pulled my helmet off, and raked my fingers through my hair.

"Who was second?" I asked.

"Cole," Sara said, smirking.

"Wahoo!" I fist-pumped again. I headed down the track to Cole's tent.

"Hey, Cole!" I called out. He looked up and semi-froze when he saw me. His face went stony as he gazed at me. Suddenly I felt awkward. Why was he acting this way?

"Congrats on second," I said, my fingers intertwining with each other.

"Yip, I'll get you next time," he said, even his voice was cold.

"Okay," I said. I stood for an awkward moment, but he turned away from me, so I walked back to my pit with a cold and sharp pain radiating through my chest. I thought we were friends. What happened?

I got back to my tent and grabbed a bottle of water, drinking it down in quick gulps.

"You okay?" Sara asked. "You look pale."

"I'm okay," I said, not wanting to share the panic that was building up inside of me. Had Cole got what he wanted and then…that's it? Was the sex not good enough? Was I not good enough?

Why am I thinking like this? I don't want to be in a relationship!

I drank down the water and got onto my simulator, because yoga wouldn't stop my mind from overthinking this whole thing. The simulator probably wouldn't either, but it would make me keep my balance on the bike.

I rode it for a solid hour, going around corner after corner, feeling the bike react underneath me, focusing on the feel of the bike, when the screen in front of me flicked off.

"Next race," Mike said as I looked up. I nodded, pulled my helmet on and went out to my bike. I watched down the pit lane as Cole got on his bike and headed off to the dummy grid. An icy hand gripped my heart and squeezed it. It stole the breath from my chest, and I had to take a deep breath to get it back.

“You alright?” Mike must have noticed my near panic attack.

“All good,” I smiled back at him. I started my bike and headed to the dummy grid. I was next to Cole. He looked up and nodded at me.

“Good luck,” I smiled at him and held up my fist. He fist bumped me, but didn’t look at me. Another squeeze had me blinking back tears.

“Now isn’t the time,” I told myself.

“What?” Mike asked through the headset.

“Talking to myself.” I dropped my visor and took a deep, even breath. I had to focus on the ride.

We were in the middle of the pack, so a good start would get me through the worst of it by the second or third corner, depending on which way the leaders went. Our bikes drew up to the start-finish line, and we watched the lights, waiting for them to flash green. When they did, I dropped my clutch and pulled on the accelerator, making my bike leap into the air. I had to slow down incrementally to get the front wheel back on the ground, but the inattention had cost me a chance to get out into the leading pack. No bother, at least I had something to focus on, rather than Cole.

I could see the leaders in front of me, and I slowly worked my way through the pack, gaining on the second-place getter. Cole was first, and I was determined to get him. I passed the second-place holder and was right on Cole’s rear wheel. I could easily overtake him, but there was only one lap left in the race, and it really wasn’t enough time to pull the overtaking manoeuvre. I followed behind him, and when we came onto the start-finish straight, I pulled up alongside him, and it was a photo finish. I knew because we were both leaning down over our fuel tanks, trying to get every inch of speed out of our machines. I decelerated and popped my head up, allowing the gears and brakes to slow me down.

"Nice work," Cole called as he rode past me in pit lane. I smiled. It was the first positive words he'd spoken to me. Maybe he was just having a bad day?

I got off my bike and went over to my phone to text him.

*You got up on the wrong side of the bed today?*

I watched as the dots on the screen moved.

*No*

*Then why the silent treatment?*

*Two weeks and no text, no phone call. You're clearly not interested*

Those words ripped through me.

*Sorry, there is no excuse for me not calling. But I always said I wasn't ready for a relationship, but I value your friendship.*

*What if I want something more?*

My heart stopped in my chest, because this time, he acknowledged he wanted a relationship rather than hinting at it. Even though I told him I wasn't interested. Maybe these feelings were something more.

*Sorry. I'm a self-centred ice queen* I wrote. I didn't hit send. I wasn't sure whether I should. I closed my eyes, took a deep breath, and pressed the button.

*Yes, ice queen is very much what you are.*

*Never promised to be anything else*

*You're right. You didn't. I don't know if I can do friendship. Especially not after...*

I nibbled my bottom lip. I knew what he meant. The sex had been…

*I get it. We could be friends with benefits*, I replied and winced as soon as I had sent it.

*Lol, yeah, nah*

*Can we catch up and have a meal after, talk things through?*

*Is there anything to talk through?*

*Maybe?*, I sent. My heart juddered in my chest, and a hollow feeling pulled at my stomach.

The dots cycled up and down, letting me know he was writing a response. Then they stopped. Then they started again and stopped. I couldn't stand the suspense, so I put my phone down and sighed. While part of me didn't want to start anything, another part of me knew I already had.

A hand landed on my shoulder, making me shriek with fright. I turned to see Sara grinning at me.

"Come on, spill," she said.

"There's nothing to spill."

"You've been acting weird since the first race. What's going on? What's up between you and Cole?"

I took a deep breath, debating whether or not to tell her, but she stood there, with her hands on her hips, and I couldn't keep anything from Sara.

"We slept together."

"What?!" Sara's face exploded into a big grin. "And you didn't tell me earlier? When did this happen?"

"*Shhh,*" I tried to hush her. "When he came up to Nelson over the holidays."

"He was up in Nelson over the holidays?" Her voice kept pitching higher.

"Are you going to parrot everything I say?"

"Well, I feel you've been keeping a lot from me." She grinned.

I looked down at my hands. "I probably have, sorry."

"So, start at the beginning," she said, sitting down on a foldout chair.

I took a seat next to her and told her about him turning up at the New Year's concert, and how we hung out just about every day afterwards.

"And was he good in bed?"

"Sara!" I felt my face go hot, and I looked around to see if anyone had overheard. I leaned in and whispered,"He was amazing."

"So, what's the problem now?"

"I didn't contact him for the next couple of weeks." The look on Sara's face was pretty much the same as the one I'd seen on Cole's.

"I was busy, and I kind of kept forgetting to call or text him."

"What? How could you do that? He's gorgeous."

"I…I didn't know what to do."

"You still don't?"

"I don't. He's been stonewalling me since I went down to his pit to congratulate him on him getting second."

"Well, I'm not surprised. You can't run hot and cold with a man, especially if you've slept with him."

"Yeah, well, I was trying to tell myself I felt nothing."

"And now you do?"

I looked down at my fingers and started fidgeting with the nails. "Maybe. I don't know. All I know is that it hurt when he shunned me. Like a 'knife through the heart' hurt."

“Oh, hun, that hit you in the feels. You’re in love.” Sara’s expression went all dreamy and I had to look away.

“Am I? But I’m scared.”

“Everyone is. But you can’t go into something like this and expect not to feel emotions, and you can’t expect the worst to happen either.”

I nodded, feeling contrite. I had so much to learn about relationships. I didn’t have the best examples around me.

“Thanks,” I muttered, and felt my heart plummet. I glanced at my phone, and there was a message from Cole. I was too nervous to look at it, but I did.

*The Bealey, 7pm* was on my phone. My heart leapt, and I felt a little easier, brighter, and the world wasn’t quite so nasty. I held my phone up to Sara and smiled.

“Go for it. What have you got to lose?” she asked.

My dignity, probably. At worst, my heart.

# chapter twenty-four

Cole

I arrived at the Bealey and wandered around the bar; it was a busy Saturday night. I found Faith hunched up in a corner, quietly nursing a lemon, lime and bitters.

I touched her shoulder, and she turned to see who it was; her face lighting up. She leaned in and kissed me on the cheek.

"Good to see you," she said. Her shoulders were tense, and there was a line in her forehead where she'd been frowning. I didn't know whether that was good or bad.

"So, what is there to talk about?" I asked. I cringed inwardly at how formal and cold I sounded. I saw her flinch, but tried to keep myself hardened. I liked this girl. I liked everything about her, but I didn't want to get hurt.

"I want to apologise, I'm a coward."

That struck me as odd. I kept my mouth shut and let her continue.

"I fear getting hurt, and I don't know what a healthy relationship looks like. I don't want to get into something where it won't work and I get hurt."

"We all get hurt somehow."

"I know, I've had that lecture." She held her glass with both hands, the moisture beading on the coaster underneath. I could imagine her sisters telling her what she should do.

"Look, I'm sorry. I should've texted you. I wanted to very much, but I…got busy. I'm such an idiot."

"An idiot and a coward. Wow, and she rides a motorcycle." I laugh. Faith looks up at me, her eyes brimming with tears. I take pity on her and hug her tight.

"Unless you take the step, you won't know what it's like to be in a relationship. Unless you let me in, you won't know how I can make you feel, how you can make me feel. We might never hurt each other; we might do it daily, but until you take that step, we'll never know. And I've made it very clear what I want."

"You have," she said, shrugging.

"And you've made it plain where you stand," I said.

"No, I haven't. Thing is, I like you. I enjoy being with you. I'm scared."

"Of course you are. Everyone is."

"I want to know you better," she said, a shy smile on her face.

"So, what does that mean? Speak English."

Her smile widened. "Okay, I'll be your girlfriend, and see how this goes. I want to take it slowly."

My heart levitated, and I'm sure it fist-pumped as well. I had to contain all my excitement within a smile, which split my face and made the muscles ache. "Okay, I can do that. And I will be your boyfriend."

"I feel like some love-struck teenager," she mumbled, her smile still clear though she tried to hide it by having a sip of her drink.

"Shall we get out of here?"

"And go where?"

"My place?" I shrugged, trying to make it seem like just a little thing.

"Okay." She put down her drink and picked up her shoulder bag. I took her hand, which she squeezed, and we left the pub.

Faith had taken a taxi to the Bealey, so I took her home in my car. Mum had cooked a meal, so there was enough for Faith too. I had hoped she would say yes, so Mum had made enough for all three of us.

"Mmm, what's that smell, smells delicious," she said as we entered the front door.

"Hello?" Mum called out.

"We're home," I yelled back. Mum came around the corner to meet us. "Hi, I'm Cindy, Cole's mum."

"Hi, I'm Faith." She held out her hand, but Mum pulled her into a hug.

She looked over Mum's shoulder at me, and I grinned back. They would be good friends, I could tell. Mum rarely hugged my girlfriends the first time she met them. I was relieved. I'd spoken to Mum a lot about Faith. I think she could relate to Faith not wanting to be in a relationship. For years, Mum wanted out of her marriage, but she didn't know how. Dad had fed her so many lies that she didn't know what was real and what wasn't.

"It's so nice to finally meet you," Mum said, directing her into the lounge room with her arm around her. "Cole has told me so much about you."

"Has he? It's not all bad, I hope," Faith said.

Mum laughed. "Not all of it, but then I wouldn't believe anything he told you either." She giggled. My mum giggled!

Faith looked at me and shrugged, but her smile was beautiful. It lit up her face, and her eyes sparkled.

"Dinner is ready when you kids are," Mum said.

"I'm hungry now," I replied, and Faith nodded.

"Riding does that to you, all that energy you use to keep that bike upright." Mum said. She linked arms with Faith and led her into the kitchen. I think I lost my girlfriend to my mum!

She sat Faith down at the table and went into the kitchen. "How was the racing today?"

"Good," Faith and I answered together. We looked at each other and smiled. "We both had a win each out there today."

"Okay, so you guys are equal on points."

"No, Faith is slightly ahead."

"Really?" Mum raised her eyebrows at me. She knew Dad would ride my ass for that.

"How long have you been racing?" she asked Faith.

"I was in karts when I was little, but preferred two wheels, so started on the bikes in my teens. I preferred fast to rugged, so ended up on the racetrack instead of on the trail rides."

"Can't say I blame you. Those bumps and hills can be quite painful."

"Not to mention bone-breaking. I broke my wrist once and decided it wasn't fast enough or flat enough, so as soon as my wrist healed, I was on the track. Been racing at this level for four years."

"Wow, you well and truly know Nigel then."

"Yes," Faith ground out through clenched teeth.

"Enough said. We try not to utter his name in this house," Mum said. We hadn't really made it a rule, but we preferred not to taint the peace of the house with his animosity, negativity and anger.

We ate dinner as we chatted about things. Faith and Mum really hit it off, and they laughed and giggled about many things. I couldn't believe how well they liked each other. I couldn't have hoped for better.

# chapter twenty-five

Faith

Cindy was lovely. I couldn't believe that she'd been married to Nigel. She was so friendly, bright and bubbly, and he was so…the opposite. We chatted about anything and everything, including Cole as a child, although I defended his honour and insisted she didn't show me childhood photos of him. Yet…

"It's getting late, I better head back," I said, looking at Cole and Cindy.

"You could stay the night. I have to be at the track in the morning too."

"But Sara and Mike are expecting me back at the camp."

"Just text them and tell them you had a better offer." Cole wriggled his eyebrows, and I couldn't help but smile at him.

I glanced over at Cindy.

"Don't look at me; you're his girlfriend. This is his house." She waved her hand at me and turned away, smiling.

"Okay," I said, almost shyly. It felt uncomfortable staying with his mum in the house, but as she said, it was his house, and we weren't teenagers.

"I'm tired though; it was a big day," I said.

"I'll show you to your room then," Cole replied. I looked at him and back at his mother.

"He's teasing you, unless you want to sleep in separate rooms." She laughed.

"I'm...ah..." I could feel the heat creeping up my face.

Cole laughed and stood up, holding his hand out to me. "Come on, I'll save you from further embarrassment. Goodnight, Mum," he said.

"Night, Cindy." I waved at her over my shoulder as Cole led me from the room. We walked down the hall to his room. It was large and light. Warm cream walls with a large picture window looking out over a field.

"The windows are tinted, so nobody can see in unless I turn the lights on," he said.

I walked over to the window. The field was extensive, with pockets of trees.

I felt Cole's hand on my waist. "It's no man's land. It won't be built out, so I decided this was a perfect place to have a large window." It was, there were walking tracks, but none close to the house. "Nice and private," he said, nuzzling my neck.

"We can't do this here, your Mum..." I tried to push him away, but he snickered.

"Mum's room is at the other end of the house. Mum won't hear anything, believe me."

I didn't believe him, but I liked the nuzzling. I turned in his arms, and his lips found mine. Soft and smooth, and his tongue urging me to open up. I did, and we kissed deeply for a few minutes. I relaxed into his arms and sighed. It felt safe, and good. And I liked it.

He walked us over to the bed, and we fell onto it. We continued kissing, and fumbling to remove clothes from each other. I pulled his top off and let my hands roam over his hard chest, before moving to his back. I felt the muscles flex and move under my touch. His hands found their way into my bra and fumbled with my breasts until I undid the clasp. Nothing is worse than having nipples pinched unnecessarily.

The kisses turned intense, and before I knew it, he was on top of me.

"Condom," I said, while trying not to break the mood. He nodded, and his lips left mine, making them feel cold and bruised. I watched as he leaned over and grabbed one out of a box and tore the wrapping. He eased off me and worked the rubber down his shaft. I shimmied out of my knickers, and lay down. He eased himself on top of me, his lips on my neck and breasts.

He reached down and guided himself to my opening, and then he slowly entered me.

His fullness stretched me, and I remembered the sensations that he aroused last time. I melted into the movements and enjoyed the rhythm we created. I felt the intensity build, and the climax washed over me in waves as I breathed hard, feeling my body tense and relax as the excitement slowly left my body. He came soon after, and we lay in each other's arms for a long time.

The sun had set, and with no light on in the bedroom, the purple, orange glow on the horizon lit the room in a romantic, hazy light.

"Hmm, I could stay here forever," Cole said, nuzzling into my neck again. It seemed to be his favourite place.

"I can't; I didn't bring any PJs with me."

"Who needs pyjamas?"

"What if I need to use the toilet during the night?"

"That's what the ensuite is for."

I looked around the room, but didn't see another door. He laughed at my confusion, then got up and slid a panel open. Behind was a bathroom that instantly lit up. He wandered in and I heard him moving about, and the toilet flushing before he came back out.

"All yours," he said as he sauntered back to bed naked. I had to admit that he had quite a nice body. Like me, he had to work out to control the bike when it's moving. We had to lift them up if they fell over, and those bikes were heavy.

Suddenly self-conscious, I got up and sprinted to the doorway, closing it behind me. I glimpsed myself in the mirror. My cheeks were flushed, my neck reddened with stubble rash, and my hair was mussed, but I looked happy. There were sparkles in my eyes that had been missing for a while. I relieved myself, and after sliding the door shut, sprinted back to the bed.

I slid under the sheets, which felt cool and fresh, like they'd just been laundered. I snuggled in next to Cole, who kissed my forehead. It was something that Uncle Chives used to do when I was a child. It made me feel secure somehow. I closed my eyes and snuggled closer as I breathed in.

The smell of sex, sweat and aftershave filled my nostrils as I drifted off to sleep.

# chapter twenty-six

Cole

I woke up, aware of a warm body tucked in next to mine. I nuzzled her neck, smelling the lavender scent of her hair. I wanted to tangle my hand up in her hair and pull her head back and kiss her awake. She moaned, and I froze; I felt her body go rigid.

"Good morning," I whispered. She opened an eye and looked at me.

"Morning," Shse replied, bestowing on me a breathtaking smile. How could a woman who looked so rough in the morning still look so damned sexy? My smile widened as I leaned in to kiss her. She put a hand over her mouth.

"Morning breath," she muttered. I laughed at her. It didn't worry me.

"Coffee?"

"That would be nice," she said as she rolled onto her back and stretched.

"I have mine white with one sugar," I told her. The back of her hand smacked onto my chest. I laughed as I pulled the sheets off me and padded to the bedroom door, grabbing my dressing gown and wrapping it around me.

"Same as you," she said, eyes closed as I opened the door. I couldn't help but fall even harder for this girl.

I wandered down the hallway and got the jug boiling and the coffee out, ready to pour. We hadn't talked after she got back into bed. She'd snuggled in, taken a big inhale, exhaled and was pretty much asleep. I had to admit that racing made me tired, too, but when I had such a warm body hard up against mine, it was difficult to sleep. I had to resist the urge to wake her up overnight and have my way with her again.

Coffees made, I headed back to my bedroom. The sight of Faith lying in my bed, naked, with the sheets pulled up to cover her, took my breath away. I put her coffee down on the coaster beside the bed and crawled in on my side.

"Thanks," she muttered, pulling the sheet higher.

"Don't need to be modest, you know. I've seen everything."

Her cheeks flushed red as she ducked her head down.

"You know, you look so sexy when you blush."

She tried not to smile, but she couldn't help herself."You know, you're annoying this early in the morning."

"Not a morning person?"

"Not a morning person," she agreed.Her smile was small, like an apology.

"Don't worry, I won't tease you." I paused. "Too much."

Her head swung around to glare at me, then she…she tickled me! I nearly spilled my coffee as I tried to put it down and defend myself. As soon as my cup got to the coaster, she stopped. I turned, but she had settled back onto her side of the bed.

"That wasn't fair," I grinned at her.

"Teasing isn't fair either," she said.

"Okay, truce."

"Truce." She picked up her phone and started scrolling through it. I leaned back against the headboard. The curtain was open, so I enjoyed the view of the sunlight on the tips of the trees as it rose over the horizon.

We sat in companionable silence for about three minutes before Faith threw back the blankets and started searching around for her clothes.

"I've got to go," she muttered.

"Something happened?"

"No, just have to get back to the track."

"Has someone said something?"

"No." She looked up at me, a panicked look on her face.

"What's wrong?" I asked, reaching out for her.

She sighed and sat down on the bed, allowing me to pull her into my arms. "I'm sorry…I just get nervous and anxious and awkward, and I don't know what to do."

"Relax," I said, smiling as I kissed her forehead.

"I can't. I feel…strange."

"I know."

"Do you?" Her hazel eyes penetrated my soul, trying to work out if I was telling the truth or not.

"I do. You're not used to being in a relationship. This"—I waved my hand between us—"awkwardness, is going to happen for a while. It's okay. We'll get up, have some breakfast, and then we'll head to the track. Racing doesn't start until ten, so we'll get there about nine. Okay?"

My words must have calmed her, because she stopped tensing in my arms and relaxed a little. Her face lit up with a little smile.

"Thank you." She kissed my nose, then pulled away and started dressing at a more sedate pace.

"Dress a little quicker if you don't want me to pounce on you," I said. This elicited a giggle as she stepped away from the bed. I couldn't help but smile at her. I got up and dressed, and we took our coffee down to the kitchen.

"Can I help?" she asked.

"Nope. I'm doing scrambled eggs for breakfast, you okay with that?"

She nodded vigorously at the suggestion, and I'm sure I saw her tongue flicker across her lips.

"The jug, coffee and sugar are all over there if you would like to make us another coffee," I suggested.

She drained her cup, grabbed mine and headed to the opposite side of the kitchen and set about making us new hot drinks.

We sat at the kitchen bench and ate breakfast. We said little as we ate. She appeared to look at her phone a lot, and when I sneaked a peek, she was reading news articles from the internet. Obviously, she liked to keep up with current affairs. She looked over at me, narrowing her eyes.

"What?" I asked.

"You spying on me?"

"No, just wondered what had your attention."

"I like to read the news while I have breakfast."

"Good to know." I grinned at her. Another piece of information that I didn't know before.

I checked my social media pages and emails, then got up and cleared away the dishes, putting them into the dishwasher.

"Okay, ready to go?" I asked.

"Ah." She ran a hand through her hair, making it flop over on top. I approached her and smoothed it down.

"Yeah, I guess," she said.

"You want to stay here all day?" I wiggled my eyebrows at her.

"No, I want to whip your butt on the racetrack."

"Bring it on!" I said, grabbing my keys.

I pulled her into a hug before we went out the door and kissed her forehead. She lifted her head, and I kissed her lips. The warmth that bubbled up inside me felt good.

"Just had to do that before you beat me on the track," I said. She laughed as she opened the door.

# chapter twenty-seven

Faith

We got to the track early, but Sara was already there, and she waved to Cole as he sauntered away.

"Good night?"

"You could say that," I said, feeling the heat crawl up my face.

"He looks good on you." She smiled. There was nothing teasing in her tone.

"I'm letting myself try," I replied.

"Good on you. Don't know what it's like until you try it." She hugged me, then went back to her laptop.

"Everything alright?"

"Yes, everything is running smooth. Checked over the stats from yesterday, made a few tweaks, she should fly like a bird." Sara said, making her hand move like it's gliding on the wind.

"I'd rather keep my tyres on the ground."

"You know what I mean," she said, giving me the side-eye. I did, and I was teasing her for a change.

My first race was at ten, so I didn't have to rush to get ready, but I put my racing kit on and jumped on the simulator instead. Nothing like preparing for a race like a racing simulation.

I focused and readied my mind, put on my helmet, and fired up my bike. I loved the sound she made and the vibration of her motor beneath my body. I did a few quick starts in pit lane, getting the tyres ready for the race, then headed off for the dummy grid. The wait wasn't long, and I pulled onto the track and got ready for the first race of the day.

A hand waved in front of my helmet as I focused on the distance. I looked over at a grinning Cole. He held up a fist, which I hit with my own, then went back to staring at the distance, waiting for the lights.

Bikes revved, spent fuel filled the air, I drew in a deep lungful, and the lights turned green. I pulled on the accelerator and leapt into the lead.

I loved riding so much, feeling the wind whip past me. At the front, I didn't have to smell everyone else's exhaust, only the fresh air, well as fresh as could be after two other races.

I pulled into corners, accelerated out, chicane, turns, twists. I loved every second, and it wasn't long until I pulled over the start-finish line in first place.

Our next race wasn't until midday, so we set the bike on its stand. Geoff tinkered with a couple of things, but everything was perfect. My bike purred.

Cole came over. "Going to grab something for lunch?"

"Yeah, we're heading that way now. Going to join us?"

"Sounds good." He took my hand. I looked at our linked fingers, feeling the heat rise into my face, but no one else noticed, or if they did, they said nothing. I squeezed his fingers, making him smile. We walked with Geoff, Sara and Mike to the food stalls. Halfway there, Cole pulled his phone out of his pocket. He paused, making me stop.

"Ah, bloody Dad. He wants me back. I'll see what the problem is, and I'll be right back," he said, kissing my forehead. I smiled at him and ran to catch up with my team.

We got to the food stall, and I watched as Geoff and Mike ordered hotdogs and fries. The thought of all that fat made my insides churn. Sara ordered a chicken and Camembert panini, which sounded nice, but I opted for a salmon bagel instead. Sometimes I hated not being able to eat fatty foods, but they really disagreed with my body.

I'd got a couple of bites into my bagel when Cole came up alongside me.

"Mmm, that looks good."

"Tastes good too," I said as he leaned in for a bite. I moved it before I lost a mouthful to him. "Get your own," I said. He grinned and was back in minutes with a chicken bagel. His hands were filthy, and he was eating it with a napkin around it.

"What did your dad want?" I asked.

"Oh, something about the tyres, but I couldn't work it out. My tyres are fine." He continued eating with gusto and finished his bagel in four bites.

"Are you hungry?" I asked.

"Need all the energy I can get to keep up with you."

Geoff laughed. "You'll need more than one bagel."

"Yip, probably should get another one."

He wandered off and came back with a hot dog and chips.

"Yuck, how can you eat that stuff?" I asked.

"I'll burn it off on the track." He grinned.

"You planning on running instead of riding?" Sara asked.

Cole kept grinning. "Maybe?"

We all laughed at him. Once we'd finished eating, we headed back to the pit area. Everything looked in order, and the bike was given a mechanical once-over while I headed in to ride the simulator. I probably shouldn't ride it so much, but it made my mind calmer and less time to overthink the upcoming races, because I knew what to expect. The simulator was programmed to react if it ran over ruts in the track, which helped me learn whether to hold on, or let go.

Five minutes before the race, I was on my bike, on the dummy grid, ready to go out on the track. The bike was humming; it had been running so well. I stroked my hand over the tank, thanking her for being such an awesome ride.

We got out and lined up on the starting line; I was in the middle this time, nothing like changing things up. I loved riding from the rear or the middle, which gave me a chance to improve my riding skills. Taking off and keeping the lead was a whole other set of skills.

The race started, and I took off, overtaking the two bikes in front of me by scooting through the middle of them. I hit the first corner and noted four bikes in front of me. I rode my bike to the best of its ability, but by the time I hit the start-finish line for the third time, something wasn't right. The bike slid a little when I turned the corner, and it threw my balance. I compensated, but knew that something was wrong. It was as if there weren't enough air in the tyres.

By the time the race finished, I'd come in third. I couldn't risk the bike skating out from underneath me, so had taken it quietly on the corners. I got into the pits and hopped off the bike.

"Something's not right. I slid on the corners," I said, squatting down to look at the tyres. They seemed fine.

Geoff got out the pressure gauge and checked them. The back tyre was lower in pressure.

"What the hell?" Geoff said. He tapped the dial to make sure it was reading right.

Mike looked at me with concern. "Don't look at me."

"I'm not blaming you. Is it a slow leak?" I asked, looking at Geoff and Mike. Sara came over and plugged the computer into my bike.

Geoff put the pressure gauge on the back tyre again, about to press down, and a small pebble popped out.

"That might have been your problem," he said.

"But how did that get in there? We checked the tyres this morning, and I had no problems in this morning's race," I said.

"It might have taken a bit to get into the pressure valve," he said, shrugging. His hands were scraping through what was left of his hair.

"Well, it's out now; let's hope that's the problem," Mike said, patting my shoulder.

My gut was churning. Cole had disappeared and come back with dirty hands at lunchtime and talked about tyres.

It wouldn't have been him.

No, it wouldn't be…

Could it?

# chapter twenty-eight

Cole

I'd won the lunchtime race, and Faith came in a distant third. She's normally right behind me, or I'm behind her.

"You okay?" I asked when I finally escaped my pit area.

"Yeah." Her shoulders slumped.

"What happened in the race?"

"I had a stone in my tyre, made it go flat during the race," she said, shrugging her shoulders. I reached out and touched her, hoping she would sense my empathy.

"You'll get me on the next one."

"Damned right!" she said, smiling at me.

I smiled back, because her smiles were contagious when she gave it. We had a coffee together, then we were back on the track for our last race of the day.

We were both mid-grid, and I reached out to fist-pump her. She did it back, then winked and pushed down her visor. I closed mine and waited for the light to change. When it did, she was off. Her reflexes were lightning fast, and I was behind her after a second, which when racing is a long time. She weaved through the front riders and made it out the front, where she put some distance between me and the other riders. I was stuck behind a newbie rider who was all over the track, and it took me a while to pass them, but once I did, it took no time to chew through the distance between me and Faith, but she beat me to the line.

It was a good win for her, and she needed it, as the third placing now had her in second place, with me. We had three more race meets in order to really decide the champion racer for the year.

While I loved racing, it wasn't the passion that it was for her. She lived for riding; she even had a simulator, for goodness' sake. I didn't; I just rode the tracks until I was familiar with them.

I circled the track and pulled into the pits.

"You lost again," Dad announced, his upper lip twisting in a snarl.

"I won the last race," I replied.

"You need to win more than one race to get yourself into the championship league," he said.

"It's my first year racing this class, give me a break."

"If I give you a break, you wouldn't win a single damned race."

"What's got into you? You're getting nasty and bitter with each round, and frankly, I don't like it."

"You don't like it. I don't like when my son is losing to a girl, who shouldn't even be racing."

"She's entitled to race like every other competitor. Get off her case."

"I'll get off her case when she gets off the track."

He glared at her as she cruised past our pit, fist pumping the air as she went. I'm sure I heard him growl.

"What the fuck, Dad, that's just…" I shook my head and took my helmet to the trailer. I changed out of my race gear and into shorts and a singlet top. It was bloody hot out there in racing leathers, but they're needed to prevent serious injury on the track. Just ask Faith.

I threw some sneakers on my feet and left, heading over to Faith's pit. She was getting changed in her trailer, so I helped Sara and Mike pack up the bike, ready to transport it back to Nelson. The next race was a month away and in Teretonga, just out of Invercargill.

"Hey, way to go." I high-fived her as she came out of the trailer. I pulled her hand to my chest and hugged her.

"Not around people," she mumbled into my ear.

"They know," I said and held her as Sara and Mike grinned at us.

"You've got all your gear packed?" Geoff asked Faith as he ambled back to the pit.

"Yip, all loaded and ready to go." She replied

"You off tonight?" I asked her.

"Yeah, I have a work meeting tomorrow, best to head off now and be ready for the meeting."

"How about you stay with me for the night and take the first flight back tomorrow?"

She looked at me with puppy-dog eyes. It was so cute! "I can't. It's an early morning meeting with the UK, so I will probably get home, shower, sleep, if I can, and attend the meeting at four a.m. on a Sunday." She pouted. "I'm sorry."

"Hey, it's okay."

"I would like to stay," she said.

"I'd have liked you to stay," I said, kissing her cheek.

"Alright kids, pack up into the truck; we gotta blow this popsicle stand," Geoff said.

I pulled her tight, and my lips met hers. She sighed silently, and opened her mouth, letting our tongues entwine.

"We have to go now," Sara said, poking her head out of the window of the truck. I laughed as I held onto Faith, who was trying to pull away.

"Text me when you get home," I said, knowing that calling wasn't her thing.

"I will." She tiptoed up, and kissed my lips once more, a brief but searing kiss. She ran and jumped into the back seat of the truck as it started to pull the trailer.

I walked back to my pit area and helped my mechanic pack up my bike.

"So, you fucking her too." A gruff voice said behind me.

"What does it matter to you?" I asked, turning to glare at the old man.

"She has you under her spell, doesn't she? You deliberately losing to let her win?"

"What? Listen to yourself; you sound delusional."

"No more delusional than you are, screwing the competition."

"Dad, for goodness' sake, drop it."

"I'm not going to drop it. Stop dating her, or stop racing."

"I'm not going to quit racing."

"Then stop dating her."

"I won't do that either."

"Then don't count on me for support any more."

"Sounds good to me," I said, as my father threw a rag on the ground and walked away. I stared after him, wondering what on earth had gotten into his underwear to make him so damned grumpy. What was it about Faith that seemed to really work him up the wrong way?

My mechanic was flushed red as he looked at me. I nodded and smiled. “That’s him gone then.”

Steve blew out a breath and smiled too. “Thank goodness. His negative vibes were killing my mojo.”

“I know what you mean.” I looked at Dad’s retreating back. Thank goodness I brought the ute to the track today; at least I could get the trailer back to work.

I headed over to the parking lot and got into my truck. It still smelled like Faith, her faint lavender essence. I inhaled through my nose, trying to soak up every molecule of the scent, then breathed out.

At least there was one good thing in my day, and I wouldn’t let Dad ruin that.

# chapter twenty-nine

Faith

Who sets a meeting for four o'clock on a Monday morning? The bloody marketing manager, that's who. Oh, that's right, *I'm* the marketing manager.

We got back to Nelson at about ten thirty in the evening. I was tired. The day had been a full-on race day, and the drive home was slow and laborious, as it is when you're towing a trailer full of race gear. We dropped the trailer and Mike off at his place, Sara at hers, then Geoff dropped me at mine, so it was close to midnight.

I got to my villa and fell-face first onto the bed. I wanted to close my eyes and sleep, but I had to text Cole and let him know I was home. I took a photo of myself pretending to be asleep on my bed and sent it to him. I set my alarm for three o'clock so I could shower and get organised for the meeting, then closed my eyes.

My alarm was a rude awakening. And I didn't appreciate it. I almost turned it off until I remembered the meeting. At least I could go back to bed once it was done. I shuffled off to shower and refresh myself. Since I hadn't showered since

I'd raced yesterday, the smell of sweat and leather clung to me until I washed it off. I washed my hair, too, and fluffed it up with the blow-dryer. Then got my black business blouse out, the one with the Hart Valley Vineyard logo on it, and put that on. I put my pyjama bottoms back on, as it was an internet meeting, and they wouldn't see that part of me. Heading to my kitchen, I turned turned on the kettle before returning to my office. I looked at the folder on my desk.

I'd organised everything so that I could look over my notes to refresh my mind before the meeting started. I was meeting with a new client in the UK, who was interested in investing in our brand and selling to their high-end clients. His name was Roger-someone. I looked at my notes.

Roger Hartley.

There was a photo of him in a business suit on top of the file. He looked vaguely familiar, but I couldn't place my finger on where I knew him from. Probably one of the many meetings I'd had over the last couple of years. I'd had to travel to the UK and France, Italy and Scandinavia to market our wines, with little success until last year, when the Racing Harts Red Wine became popular. It had been Grace's idea, and the sales of that wine allowed us to keep our racing dreams alive.

I made a coffee and sat down at my desk, with the blinds still drawn. There was no daylight, so it would be a good background for the call. Nothing personal on the blinds that could embarrass me or give away any clues about the type of person I was.

Nerves bunched in my stomach, and butterflies took flight as I started my computer up at three thirty. I needed to make sure that the internet room was secure before the meeting.

Not that there was going to be anything private to discuss, but we liked to ensure that all meetings were between us and our clients. I like to record them, too, because sometimes I miss things when trying to scrawl notes.

I was reading through my notes and drinking my coffee, when I looked up and noticed that Roger Hartley was already in the internet room, with his camera on. He was early.

"Hello, Mr Hartley," I said.

He looked up at his computer, but then desperately looked around the screen and keyboard. I could see everything he did because the camera was working, but he obviously couldn't see me. He was talking, but I couldn't hear him.

"Okay, Mr Hartley, you can hear me, but I can't hear you. You need to turn on the microphone, which is the little microphone icon on your screen. If you click it with your mouse, it should turn on the microphone. If it doesn't have a bar through it, then it is on."

The other thing could be the volume on his computer. I watched as he moved his mouse around the screen. I sighed inwardly. Mr Hartley was clearly a man in his sixties. Very distinguished with a mop of silver hair, which matched his well-trimmed beard. He had lines on his face, particularly around his eyes, which looked more like laughter lines than anything else.

"If you're looking for the volume, it is usually on the F8 button, at the top of the keyboard."

He looked about, then found it, and pressed it a few times. "Is that better?" His voice was rich and deep.

"Yes, hello," I said.

"Hello, Miss Hart."

"Please, call me Faith," I said. He was still looking around his screen.

"I can't see you, Faith."

"Okay, there should be a camera icon near the microphone. If you click on that…"

"Ah, there you are. Well, hello, Faith. You can call me Roger; all my friends do." His accent was definitely not English.

"Are you from New Zealand originally?" I asked.

"Very astute. I came to the UK about twenty years ago. I haven't got rid of my Kiwi accent."

"It's nice to talk to someone who understands our culture," I replied, smiling. Something about this man made me feel at ease, and the butterflies stopped flitting around my stomach.

"Alright, shall we get down to business?" Roger said.

"Okay, so we have set forth a proposal that I sent through to you on Friday."

"Yes, I have that, thank you. Our investors are interested in your plans and would like more information about the Racing Harts wine. Our investors have heard good things about it from its New Zealand agents, and we…well…we would like to support the racing team as well."

I sat back, floored. International money would help, but we really wanted our Hart Valley brand to be at the forefront, not our Racing Harts brand.

"Could we not start out with our Hart Valley branded wines first and gauge the interest before we start introducing the Racing Harts brand?"

"How about both? The investors believe both brands will be highly successful here. We have high-end clients in motels and private homes across the country and into Europe who believe that both of your brands will fit the bill."

"Look, I need to talk to the others before I can agree to this."

"Okay, set up a proposal for the Racing Harts brand, and we will start immediately on purchasing in bulk of the Hart Valley wines. We will sort out the import duty and get that underway."

I sat back once more, looking at the kind smiling face of the man in front of me. He'd accepted my proposal for the Hart Valley wine with no negotiation. And he wanted Racing Harts wine too. I would've jumped at the chance to say yes, but I really needed to discuss with Hope and Grace before we went any further.

"If that is all, I need to keep going. Thank you for your time, Faith. It was lovely to meet you after all this time."

I raised my eyebrows. What did he mean? We'd only corresponded twice by email in the last month, I wouldn't call a month 'all this time'.

"Thank you, Mr Hartley, nice to meet you too. Look forward to dealing with you in the future."

He clicked on the end-call button. He seemed to know where that was.

I looked at the clock. It was only four o'clock, the time the meeting was supposed to start. I finished my now-cold coffee and went back to bed, but I couldn't sleep. A part of me was excited about expanding into the UK and European markets, but a part of me wanted to keep Racing Harts just a local business. We hadn't set up the wine to be exported, in fact it wasn't even a popular wine like a cabernet sauvignon, or a pinot noir. It had been a blend that we had liked, a soft, smooth velvety mix of cabernet and pinot grapes.

It reminded me of long winter nights next to a blazing fire.

But what would that mean for our business? It would certainly get our brand of wine out there to new consumers. And that meant more money coming in, which we could funnel into more wine, more charity fundraisers, more money for our own racing ventures. Of course it would tie us all to the vineyard for a bit longer. I mean I had no plans to leave any time soon, but what if I wanted to get into professional motorcycle racing? I guess it was something that we would all have to sit down and discuss.

# chapter thirty

Cole

"How was your weekend?" Mum asked when I saw her at the office on Monday morning.

"I should ask you the same thing. Where did you disappear to last night?"

Mum's face reddened as she fidgeted with her hands, a smile hiding in the corners of her mouth.

"I might have gone out for dinner and a movie last night." She glanced at me out of the corner of her eye.

"And?"

"And I might have stayed the night at his place."

I smiled as I hugged Mum. "Well, that was obvious, since you weren't up for breakfast this morning. I even checked your room!" I planted my hands on my hips, mocking her like she used to do to when we were teenagers.

Mum blushed and lowered her head, hiding her grin. "Sorry."

"As long as you're happy."

"I am, and Faith is lovely."

"Pity Dad doesn't think the same."

"Why? What happened?"

"He's quit the team because of her. He doesn't want me dating her either."

"Cole, you can't let your father dictate your life. He did to me for long enough."

"I know; that is why I told him I wouldn't stop dating her. And he quit. Tell you what, the atmosphere changed immediately. Things felt calmer and brighter."

"Yes, I know what you mean. Your father is like a grumpy grey cloud on a beautiful sunny day. And how is Faith?"

"She's good. She didn't stay last night; she had a meeting at some ungodly hour this morning."

"Oh?"

"Business-wise, her family runs a vineyard."

"I see, so she has taste and a career." Mum smiled at me, and I smiled back.

"Yes, Mum, she isn't after me for my money." We laughed.

"Well, I better get back to the office and tidy up last week's invoices," she said.

"And I better get started on this week's jobs."

I got a text at lunchtime from Faith; her meeting had happened quickly and super early, and then she'd gone back to bed. She'd only just woken up. Oh, to live a life where I didn't have an eight-to-five job, or rather a seven-until-six or -seven job. This week was shaping up to be a busy one. I didn't know when I would fit in time with Steve to check on my bike and the computer data. My races had been good, and currently Faith and I were both on equal standings in the championship. We were still second equal. After her crash and the tyre incident yesterday, she hadn't made the first place she'd been hoping for, the points were still tight, and there was only about ten points between us and first place. And while I loved riding and racing, I didn't have that burning desire to win like Faith did. At least with Dad out of the picture, I could focus on racing my way now. I'd have to go to the gym more often though, and get up the stamina, because the last race of the season would be the big one, the twenty lap championship race, and that was the one that required endurance and strength, and I was determined to have a crack at making, at least, second place. I'd let Faith aim for first.

Late afternoon, Dad turned up. "What do you want?" I asked him, standing up and wiping my hands on the rag at my waist.

"To apologise. I shouldn't have gone off on you like that."

"Damn straight. Faith is my girlfriend, and I won't have you speaking about her like that."

I watched the redness rise in his face, the clenching of his teeth and the grinding of his jaw as he attempted to stop himself from saying something he shouldn't.

"Well, I would like to come back onto the team."

"I don't know if I want you back. We seem to have done alright without you." I stared at him, considering my options. There had been more peace and everything flowed nicely without his prickly nature around. But then I'd had to do all of the mechanicing with Steve, and hadn't had a lot of time to see Faith unless we were racing.

"Come on, son."

I sighed. "There are going to be rules. You do as I say."

"Unless you're racing."

"Especially when I'm racing. I will race my way."

Again, the grinding of the jaw. He closed his eyes and nodded.

"And no more comments about Faith or any other women riders."

Dad opened his mouth, but wisely shut it again. "Okay," he growled out between clenched teeth.

His jaw must have been aching from all the tightness I could see there.

"And no more negativeness. We don't need it." I might have been pushing it there. Dad's eyes flashed, and he blinked rapidly.

"Alright." I barely heard him say it. "Is your mum here?" he asked.

I blinked, the change of conversation confusing."I don't think so."

He nodded and headed towards the office. He peered through the sliding door window, shook his head, waved at me and headed off. Dad had agreed way too easily to my terms. He was up to something, and it worried me. But then, Dad was a hothead and would fly off the handle at anything. It took him a while to cool down. He rarely apologised, so I took it as a sign. Maybe he was going to change his ways, but deep down I knew he never would.

As long as there were women in the world, my dad would never see them as equals.

Faith prefers to text, whereas I prefer to talk. So, after she texted me tonight, I rang her.

"Hey, how you doing?"

"Hey yourself." I could hear the smile in her reply.

"What are you up to?"

"I'm just lying on my bed, wondering if I should go to bed, or watch a movie or something," Faith replied.

"Or, you could lie on your bed and we have phone sex."

There was silence on the other end of the phone, but I could almost see the blush on her cheeks.

"Or, we could just chat like normal people," she replied.

"I can hear you blushing!" I laughed.

"No, you can't!"

"I can, and I can feel the heat down the phone." Her laughter was light and airy. It was nice to talk to her without her getting all defensive. "It's going to be four weeks until I see you again."

"That's a long time," she agreed.

"What are we going to do about it?"

"I don't know. What do you suggest?"

"How about I come up to see you next weekend?"

"That sounds pretty damned good, actually, or I could come down and see you."

"You could do that the following weekend."

"I like the sound of that. How are you coming up? Driving?"

"And waste time I could be with you? No, I'll fly up."

"That'll cost you, being short notice." It sounded like she'd flopped down on her bed. I could imagine her lying there with her long legs crossed at the ankles, a hand behind her head.

"I don't care; you're worth the cost."

"That has to be the most romantic thing I've ever heard."

"Have you not read many romance novels or watched romantic movies?"

"Ah, no, I haven't. You know me; love…not my thing."

"Well, get interested, I'm coming up."

"Oh, big boy talk now."

I laughed as I heard her yawn. It wasn't very late, but then, she'd had that early morning meeting.

"Hey, best I let you get some rest; you'll need all the rest you can get. I'll book the ticket for Thursday night or Friday morning. And I'll fly back early on Monday morning."

"Okay." Her voice sounded dreamy. "Sounds good." Another yawn punctuated the sentence.

"Good-night, Faith."

"Good-night, Cole."

# chapter thirty-one

Faith

I stood at the airport, feeling strangely conspicuous. I knew I was fidgeting as I waited for the flight to arrive. Cole was coming to see me, and I was nervous. Knots tightened in my stomach, and I hadn't been able to eat all day. Even drinking water had been difficult. And I don't know why I feel like this; I should be excited. I guess because everything is still new, and I still had Hope and Grace to deal with and their teasing. I couldn't handle their teasing, but with Cole by my side, I hoped I would.

The plane had landed, and people were disembarking, but I couldn't see him. Passengers came in through the entrance, and people smiled, waved, hugged and kissed. I wondered how Cole would react? I didn't get the chance to think about it, because then he was there, and warmth flooded my body, my brain went fuzzy and I ran towards him, almost jumping into his arms. He kissed me and hugged me tight.

"I wasn't expecting that," he said. I just grinned like a child with a lolly, a big lolly and kissed him again.

"Nice to be greeted so enthusiastically," he continued after we'd finished kissing.

"You're welcome." I finally found my words, which had been locked up inside my brain. It seemed unreal that one minute I was nervous, and the next, I was acting like a puppy happy to see its owner.

Cole wrapped his arm around me and headed towards the exit.

"Have you got any bags?"

"Other than this, no. Only need a change of underwear." He winked at me, and I felt the heat rush up my neck.

We got out to my car and drove home, chattering the entire way about anything and everything. But the closer we got to home, the more I let him talk. He noticed.

"You okay?"

I nodded, but he knew.

"Nervous?"

I nodded again.

"It's going to be okay."

"You don't have to live with them," I grumbled.

"True, but then I'm your boyfriend, not theirs."

"Thank goodness." I said, parking my car and getting out. I took him to my villa first so he could drop off his bag.

"We could stay here for the rest of today," he suggested. I considered it, but then Grace would at least wonder where I'd got to.

"We could, but I can't put this off any longer," I said.

He nodded and took my hand as we headed over to the main building. We entered the main foyer and looked around. It was busy with people who had come in for their evening meal. The sun was setting on the horizon, and the sky was lit up orange and red.

"Wow," Cole breathed out.

"Stunning, isn't it? Have you eaten?"

"No," he replied, unable to tear his eyes from the vista.

I grabbed a couple of menus and found us a seat by the window so he could take in the scenery.

"You guys sure have the best spot," he sighed.

"I know, right?" I handed him a menu and waited as he continued to take in every piece of the view. I couldn't blame him; it was a view I often came to admire myself, and the sunset was proving stunning this evening.

Eventually, he turned back to me. "Sorry," he blushed as he looked down at the menu.

"Nothing to be sorry about. Why do you think we are so popular?"

"I get that now; I thought it was just the wine."

"That and the view."

"So, what do you recommend?"

"The steak, especially the carpetbag steak, our chef loves seafood. Other than that, the carbonara is pretty on point as well."

"Wine recommendations?"

"The house pinot noir with the steak, and the house pinot gris with the carbonara."

"A woman who knows her food and wine; we are so perfect together."

"Hmm," I said, feeling a little uncomfortable.

"Good evening, Faith. And this must be Cole. Welcome to our restaurant," Michel said.

"She's been talking about me?"

"Cole, this is Michel, our world-famous chef. Michel, this is Cole, the not as good as me fellow motorcycle competitor," I said, making Cole laugh.

"I knew she was picking you up tonight. So, what would you like to order?"

"Faith recommends the carpetbag steak," Cole told Michel. It was the right thing to say.

"She has excellent taste," Michel said. "Now, how would you like that steak?"

"Medium rare," Cole replied. Michel looked suitably impressed, pursing his lips and nodding.

"And you?" Michel asked me.

"I'll have the Chicken Kiev, thanks."

"Excellent choices. I'll send you your drinks." He turned and marched off back to the kitchen.

"But he hasn't taken our drinks order," Cole said.

"Don't worry about that; he knows what he's doing."

"I hope so," Cole said as a waitress brought a pinot noir to the table for him. He sniffed the wine and cocked an eyebrow at me. I grinned at his funny faces as he took a sip and swirled it around in his mouth. He swallowed, and his eyes popped open.

"That's really smooth and rich."

"Of course it is; it's one of our wines."

"Does the chef take all the orders for meals?" he asked, looking around the emptying restaurant.

"Only for special people." I smiled, leaning forwards and resting my chin on my hands. "So, what have you been up to?"

"Work, been a busy week for panel beating and spray painting."

"Catching up after the summer holidays?"

"Yeah, and those who wanted their cars repaired before then."

"That will keep you busy."

"It does, and what about you?"

"Putting together a proposal for a UK-based company that wants to import our wine. I spoke with the guy on Monday morning. He wants our Racing Harts wine over there too."

"Racing Harts wine? I didn't realise you had any."

"Grace thought it would be a great idea to help with the costs of our racing teams. Helps with the costs without having to pull money out of the winery all the time."

"Makes sense. So, have I had any of the Racing Harts wine?"

"I don't think so."

"Can I try some?"

"How about tomorrow?"

"That sounds good."

Michel arrived with two plates, and the steak was still sizzling as he put it down in front of Cole.

"Whoa, now that's cool." He smiled appreciatively at Michel.

"We do our best. Enjoy." He bowed and then left us to our meals.

# chapter thirty-two

Cole

I woke up and stretched, aware of a body in the bed with me. And it wasn't my bed. I snuggled in behind her, and she moaned. I kind of expected her to freak out that there was someone else in her bed, but she obviously didn't feel as scared about it as she once had.

"Morning, sunshine," I said, nuzzling her neck. Her hair smelt of lavender and something else; it was nice. I pulled her in tighter to me.

"Do you want sex?" she asked.

I stopped nuzzling her."If I wanted sex, I'd be more subtle about it. I just want snuggles."

"Guys don't normally like snuggles, do they?"

"Where did you hear that?"

She twisted around to face me."I didn't; it was just an assumption."

"I love snuggles. I love wrapping myself around my girlfriend and just getting lost in her scent."

"What? Sweat?" She grinned.

"You're a real mood killer, you know that?" I couldn't help grinning back at her.

"I'm not exactly a morning person." She'd told me that before, but I didn't mind teasing her a little about it. She swiped at her eyes, trying to remove the sleep in the corners, and she kept hiding her mouth behind her hand.

"Just lie still and let me snuggle you awake," I said.

"Okay." And she went totally still, and soon she was snoring again. I gently eased my arm out from underneath her and slipped out of the bed.

I headed to the kitchen to make a coffee, and then I'd head back and wait for her to wake up properly. I was an early riser. It didn't matter what time I went to bed, I was awake by seven every morning. Faith must have needed all the beauty sleep she could get, and I couldn't help but snicker at the thought. I wasn't being mean; she was beautiful and didn't really need any extra sleep.

Coffees made, I headed back to her room and placed one by her side of the bed and crept back under the sheets, careful not to disturb her. I picked up my phone and checked my email, messages and then my social media. There wasn't much going on. It was Friday, but work would happen soon. I fired off a couple of emails for work, just to make sure that things were going to happen when I returned on Monday.

"Tell me you aren't working?" the pile of sheets beside me muttered.

"I'm not now," I said as her head emerged, her hair all mussed up. I wanted to run my hands through it, to smooth it down, but then I liked it all mussed up too. There was something sexy about it.

"You made coffee?"

"Yeah, and I made some for you." I nodded towards her side of the bed. She looked over, then back at me, her face melting.

"You're a keeper," she said.

"Of course." She said the most adorable things. I had to remember that I was probably her first proper boyfriend, at least I thought I was. It wasn't something to discuss now, though.

She sat up in bed, pulling the sheets up with her as she did. It made her even more adorable because of her shyness.

"I've seen everything, you know," I said, and she flushed.

"I know. Just trying to keep warm."

"It's probably twenty degrees inside."

"Yeah, so?" She had a cute little grin on her face. She reached over and grabbed her coffee and took a sip, closed her eyes and sighed."That's nice."

"Pleased to be of service."

"I'll keep you on."

I laughed. "So, what's the plan for today?" I asked.

"Let me wake up! Gosh, I only just opened my eyes; let me have coffee and then I can think."

"Not a morning person?" I teased.

"Not a morning person." She lowered her eyebrows at me, and I chuckled.

"Oh."

"No, don't," she warned, but I couldn't help it. I leaned over and blew a raspberry on her cheek. She couldn't help but laugh.

"Laugh before breakfast, set up for the day."

"What kind of proverb is that?"

"It's not; it's wise words from Cole."

She laughed again, transforming her grumpy face into something beautiful and bright. Amazing what a smile can do.

"I thought we could go for a walk in the vineyard and have a picnic."

"And I want to try some of that Racing Harts wine."

She sighed. "Okay, I'll have some of that packed."

"How big is the vineyard?"

"As far as the eye can see."

"Really?"

"Pretty much, yeah. It goes over the hill and through that gully, and we own that native patch of bush at the end that way"—she pointed south—"and through to the neighbouring farms that way." She swung her arm west and east. It was quite a substantial piece of land they were sitting on.

"Hope you brought your walking shoes," she said.

"I certainly did."

# chapter thirty-three

Faith

The sun was high in the sky when we headed out with the picnic hamper. I took Cole up to the native bush because it was lovely up there, and above that was a lookout from which you could see out towards Tasman Bay and survey all the vineyard below. It showed how large the area was. The birds flitted around, fantails chirping, tui whistling and the low solitary call of the bellbird echoed around the gully. This had to be my most favourite place on Earth. The life within the patch of bush always comforted me.

We broke out above the bush and onto the plateau. The view to the south was of more hills and bush.

"Turn around," I told Cole.

His reaction was what I wanted to see, and I wasn't disappointed.

He drew in a breath, and then seemed to hold it, as his eyes scanned the horizon. To the west lay Tasman Bay and the Richmond Ranges; to the north was Tasman and Tasman Bay in the distance. To the east lay farmland and more bush. It felt like we were on top of the world up here.

"Wow." He finally breathed out. He turned towards me, pulled me into his arms and our lips met, crashing together.

"Ow," I said when we finished, but I was smiling.

"Sorry, but…this is…aw…it's amazing."

"I know. It's our family secret, really."

I pulled off the backpack and pulled out a blanket for us to sit on. Below, we could still hear the birds, and we could still see the view, which Cole seemed to struggle to keep his eyes off. I had to admit; it was hard to focus on anything else. Even though I'd been up here so many times, there were still things to see, new things to discover. Today, being late summer, people were making the most of the calm conditions, and boats filled the bay. Some were still, others had white trails behind them as they travelled. Sails dotted the bay, although the yachts were barely moving. There was little wind, especially where we were.

By the time Cole joined me on the blanket, I had the food out and the wine poured into the plastic glasses. It wasn't the best way to serve wine, but when we picnicked, plastic glasses were the best.

He took the glass I offered him and took a sip.

"Oh wow, you're rolling out the big guns, aren't you?" he asked as he sipped the wine. "That is superb."

"That is our Racing Hart wine."

"Wow, it's different, velvety, smooth and rich."

"We mix it ourselves for our own tastes. It isn't a traditional cabernet or cab sav, or syrah or pinot noir, a mix of all of them to make a full-bodied, flavourful drink."

"I like it a lot."

"The people in the UK want to stock it over there. I don't think they've even tasted it, only heard good things about it."

"That's awesome."

"Except it isn't really a wine made for that market."

"So, you all race?"

"Yes, Grace races rally cars and Hope, sprint cars."

"You're all adrenaline junkies, then."

"I wouldn't say that. We just like racing. I'm the most competitive, and I'm determined to win this year."

"You certainly deserve the win," Cole replied.

I looked at him sideways, wondering if he was trying to wind me up, but he seemed genuine in his comments.

"Thank you, I think," I said.

"How are your sisters doing, in their respective sports?"

"Grace does it for the fun of it. Hope, she likes fast. She'd race all year if she could, and I know she's talking about hitting the US circuit sometime. They race in our off-season, and there isn't much to be done here during the winter, except make sure the wine is maturing like it should. We keep encouraging her, but she hasn't done it yet."

"You girls are real go-getters."

"We had to be; our aunt and uncle encouraged us to follow our passions. Mine was motorcycles."

"Well, I'm pleased that you did; I'd never have met you otherwise."

Cole's eyes were warm, and I felt a jolt of that warmth flow through my body. He reached out his hand and touched my face, cupping my cheek. I leaned into it, feeling the peace and gentleness of his touch reach down inside my chest and untangle the knot of nerves that lived there, slowly easing them apart. I smiled at him before he leaned over and kissed me on the forehead. I loved when he did that. Something about the action made me feel—protected? That wasn't quite the right word, but it fit for now.

That evening, Grace and Hope wanted to catch up with us and have a meal. They also wanted to catch up at the restaurant. The closer the time came, the more butterflies appeared in my stomach. By the time we got there, I didn't feel like eating. They always teased me mercilessly, and with Cole there, it would be worse.

Cole and I arrived first, so we got a seat with my back to the restaurant. It was bad enough that Grace and Hope teased me; it would be even worse if I could see other people reacting to them and laughing at me behind my back. Hope arrived first in a swirl of pink cotton. Her summer dress floated around her like a goddess. Here I was in shorts and a tidy shirt. I immediately felt underdressed. Even Cole had a dress shirt on. He got up and kissed Hope on the cheek, and I was pleased to see she blushed, but she also fluttered her eyelashes at him. She was flirting with him. Grace arrived in her jeans and an almost see-through black blouse. Again, Cole stood and kissed Grace on the cheek. She didn't react other than to say hello.

"How was the walk?" she asked.

"It was amazing. I didn't realise you owned so much land."

"It's the vineyard that owns the land, not us," Grace said. She stared pointedly at me.

Cole caught the look. "Faith said that."

Grace nodded, even raising her eyebrows at me.

"I also introduced him to Racing Harts wine," I said.

Hope stared at me like I'd developed another hole in my head. "What?"

"You showed the opposition our main breadwinner?" Grace asked.

"I didn't realise it was a secret," I said, feeling my face get hot under their scrutiny.

Hope laughed, and I realised they were winding me up.

"That wasn't nice, girls. Your sister is taking a chance on me; don't fuck it up for us," Cole said in a lowered tone. Grace and Hope looked suitably abashed and apologised. I looked over at Cole and fell a little more in like with him. Because this wasn't love, was it?

We ate our meal in companionable conversation, with no more teasing or winding each other up. It was very pleasant for a change to behave like adults while eating. I enjoyed it.

At the end of the meal, Cole stood and kissed my sisters on the cheek as they excused themselves.

He was such a gentleman. And I couldn't help the warmth growing inside me get a little bit deeper into my soul.

# chapter thirty-four

Cole

We got back to her room, and she sighed. A happy sigh; there was a smile on her face.

"You okay?" I asked.

"That went better than I expected. Thank you for sticking up for me."

"It's the least I could do. Are they jealous?"

"I don't know, we all tease each other, but they tease me more because I react."

"I noticed." I pulled her into my arms and kissed her forehead. Her arms went around my waist, and she rested her head on my shoulder. We fit together so nicely.

"This is nice," I said.

"Hmm."

"Skin on skin is better." I felt her jerk slightly, and I pulled back to look at her."Do you not like snuggles?"

"Is that what you call it? Snuggles?"

"When you cuddle and are naked, yes."

"Oh, I thought it was your code word for sex."

"So, it's sex you don't like." I grinned at her.

She smiled shyly, dipping her head. "No, it's not that. I just like a little foreplay first."

"Like?"

She raised her hands and held my face. Her breath huffed onto my chin as she pulled my head down and her lips gently touched mine. I allowed her to take the lead, but my blood was coursing through my body, heating up skin with her touch. She deepened the kiss and opened her mouth, her tongue teasing mine. I cupped the back of her head and held her in place while we kissed. My other hand pulled her tighter in at her waist, and she wiggled against me. I groaned; it felt so good.

We stopped kissing; our lips were barely touching. "Like that," she said.

"Uh-huh," I agreed, then leaned down and claimed her lips again.

She leaned into me so much I thought our bodies would meld together. My hands wandered to her butt, and I picked her up. She wrapped her long legs around my waist and I walked to the bedroom, where we started removing clothes between bouts of kissing. With her shirt off, I kissed down her collarbone. She tipped her head back and made a purring sound before kissing the top of my head. Her hands reached up, and she curled her fingers into my hair, pulling my head closer to her chest. I removed my shirt, and one of her hands moved to curl through my chest hair. It felt nice to have it stroked and tugged. We removed our bottoms, her bra, and we climbed into the bed, curled up together, but still kissing and caressing each other, enjoying the feeling of our hands on each other's curves and valleys.

The gentle brush of her fingers over my body was building a unique sensation deep in my gut. I had pulled a condom out of my bag earlier, so I grabbed it from the bedside table and slipped it on.

I pulled her on top of me, and she took the hint. She sat down on my hardness, moaning as it filled her. She felt so tight and wet at the same time. I couldn't help but tell her. She giggled, but it didn't ruin the moment. It was a beautiful meeting of two souls entwining together. With my hands on her hips assisting her motion, it didn't take long for both of us to climax together; it almost blew the top off my head. She shuddered and lay down on top of me as we both struggled to capture our breath.

She snuggled up on top of me, and I looped my arms around her. Soon, I heard the steady breathing of her sleeping.

"Hey, sleeping beauty," I whispered to her.

"Huh?" she muttered.

"You need to get off so I can clean up."

"Don't want to," she said sleepily. "I like this sleeping platform."

I laughed, making her growl.

"Stop moving!" she grumbled.

"I need to get up."

"Urgh." She rolled off me and curled up on her side of the bed. "It's cold over here."

I got up and tidied myself up in the bathroom. I snuck back into the bed, where she was fast asleep. I turned out her lamp and snuggled up behind her.

It'd been a truly magical day, one I will remember for a long time. I think I could easily tell her I loved her, but I didn't want to scare her away. Our relationship was too new. She was learning to trust me, but it had been a great day. She'd coped with her sisters' teasing, we had viewed the world from the heavens, and had reached heaven tonight.

"You smell so delicious. Thank you for the wonderful day," I muttered into her hair as I drifted off to sleep.

"You're welcome."

I woke up with Faith's arm slung across my body. I snuggled in tighter to her. She stretched and then pulled me against her.

"Morning," she said, kissing the back of my head.

"Good morning." I twisted around in her arms to kiss her on the lips.

"Don't. Morning breath."

It was nice to wake up in a warm embrace. "How are you today?"

"Good, you?"

I laughed. "You're getting very comfortable in our relationship."

"It's a nice place to be," she admitted. I leaned up on an elbow and pulled her towards me so I was lying on my back.

"I'm pleased to hear that."

"I haven't felt this way before."

"I'm pleased to hear that too." I grinned. She lay in my arms for a few minutes before moving off me.

"I'll make coffee," I said, getting up.

"Okay."

After breakfast, we headed out to Mapua and walked along the precinct there, admiring the restaurants, bars and stores and a small maritime museum. It was an amazing little place, so busy at this time of the year. We had lunch at the Apple Shed, and then Faith took me to Rabbit Island for a walk. The tide was heading out, so we walked along the beach, enjoying the late summer breeze that came in off the sea. We explored various places on our way back to Hart Valley, and we slept well that night. I couldn't believe that the weekend had flown by so quickly. We had moments of quiet contemplation and lots of food and laughter. I remember patting my stomach and Faith commenting that we would both need to hit the gym before she came down the following weekend.

I couldn't wait for her to spend a weekend with me in Christchurch. I had to think of places I could take her and share my favourite foods with her.

All too quickly, the weekend ended, and on Monday morning, we were up before the sun in order for me to catch the first flight out to Christchurch.

"I've got my ticket. I fly in at seven thirty on Thursday night," she said.

"Right, eight thirty Friday morning."

She giggled, hitting me on the chest lightly. "No, silly. Thursday…"

"Night, seven thirty, I know."

"Don't tease me," she said, smiling. My arms were around her, and she seemed reluctant to let me go, even in the public space of the airport.

"Is it okay if I kiss you?"

"Of course it is," she said, getting up on tiptoes. I bent down and kissed her, my tongue flicking along her lips, tasting the lip balm she'd put on while still in the car.

"Mmm, that tastes nice," I said, looking around. No one was watching us. Faith didn't seem to care, which was a big step for her.

The call came through for my flight to leave. I held her and kissed her again.

"See you Thursday," I said.

"See you Thursday," she confirmed.

I waited until I got to the gate, then called out to her."Faith! I love you." I watched her go bright pink, but she didn't respond, just stood there, smiling and waving at me.

I didn't know what to expect, so I was rather pleased that she didn't turn and run from the airport.

# chapter thirty-five

Faith

Friday morning, I woke up in Cole's bed. His side was empty, but I could hear him in another part of the house. Well, at least I hoped it was him. I got up and dashed to the bathroom, relieving myself before climbing back into bed. He appeared just as I was pulling the sheets up.

"How many times do I have to tell you?" His smile was infectious.

"Well, I never know if your mother is going to come in or not."

"Do you think my mum is going to barrel in here without knocking first?"

"She might do," I said, grinning at him as he placed the coffee on my side of the bed.

"And isn't it my turn to make you coffee?"

"I was awake before you."

"I noticed."

"So, today, I thought I'd take you to see my car."

"I'd like that," I said, trying to picture what it would look like. I knew it was a gangster-type of car, but other than that,

I didn't know what make or model. I know he's already told me, but I'd forgotten the details. I'm a bike girl, not a petrol-head.

"It's partway through painting at the moment, so you won't get the full effect."

"That's okay," I said.

"Then maybe we'll head up the gondola and check out the view over the city."

"Okay," I said, looking at my hands.

"What? Don't do heights?"

"Not very well."

"Well, you won't even notice," he said, pulling me in and kissing my forehead.

"I hope not."

It was a beautiful Canterbury morning and promised to be a hot day. The Nor'wester was due this afternoon, so we had to get back to the house before that kicked in, because that would ratchet the temperature up to the low thirties. Cole took me to his shop first.

"Hello, Faith. Welcome back," Cindy said, coming around the counter to hug me.

"It's nice to be here," I said.

"Cole showing you his car?"

"Yes, that's the plan."

"He's very proud of that machine."

"Yes, I know; I can't wait to see it."

"I'll catch up with you guys tonight," Cindy said as the office phone rang. She dashed back around the counter to answer it.

"Follow me." Cole grabbed my hand, giving me little choice in the matter.

We walked past the workshops where cars were in various states of repair and painting. The last shed door was closed, but Cole stood me in front of it, then opened it. Inside the gloom, I saw parts of a car, soft curves of the panels resting on top of trestles, probably drying off from a coat of paint.

"Here she is," Cole said, pulling me into the workshop.

My eyes adjusted to the dim light, and I saw the rolling chassis with the motor in place. Some panels were attached, but I got the vague outline of what it would look like. The paint was deep maroon with an iridescent fleck through it. Even in the dull light of the shed, it sparkled.

"Watch this," Cole said, taking one of the smaller panels out into the daylight. The iridescence lit up and flashed as he moved the piece. The base of maroon shone a deep rich red.

"That colour is beautiful," I breathed.

"I know, right? I can't believe how well it came out."

"You've done all of this yourself?"

"Yes, three coats of the red, one of the glitter, and three clear coats, sanded in between."

"Wow, that must have taken you ages."

"It's taken me a while to get it to this stage, but she's not far from being finished."

"I can see it now. It will be a beautiful car when you're done."

"I hope so. Plan on using it as a wedding car, you know, renting it out."

"That's a great idea."

"Of course it will be our wedding car one day."

I took a step back, feeling my face go cold. "Let's not rush things, aye?"

Cole looked at me. "I said 'one day'."

"And 'our wedding' all in one sentence." I took another step back. I saw Cole's eyes widen as I crashed into someone standing behind me.

"Who's getting married?" I heard the gruff voice and felt myself cringe as I turned to face Nigel.

"No one," I replied, straightening up. Nigel wasn't overly tall, but we came eye to eye. I watched his face grow red, and his cheeks tighten.

"Thank the stars above, my son couldn't do any worse than you."

"I beg your pardon?" I said, planting my hands on my hips.

"Dad," I heard Cole's voice warning his father.

"You should be at home playing with your kitchen appliances rather than on the racetrack and away from my son."

"What is your problem, Nigel? Are you that insecure that you have to pick on people you think are weaker than you?"

"Ha, that's funny coming from the girl that fell off her bike earlier this season."

I opened my mouth, but nothing came out. I wasn't embarrassed, but I couldn't believe he would say that to me. I felt Cole move to my side as I glared at his father.

"Come on, you two."

"What? She started it. She should go back home and leave the racing to the men."

"I think you're jealous," I said.

"Jealous? Of you?" He tipped his head back and laughed. It was a nasty, vicious laugh. "I won the championship six years running. You only got second twice. You couldn't race your way out of a paper bag." Spittle flew from his mouth as he yelled.

"I'm a better racer than you any day. At least I didn't go whinging to the committee every time you won a race."

"I still won the championship. Six. Years. Running," Nigel said, getting up in my face.

"Enough!" Cole yelled. "Dad, go home. I'll talk to you later." Nigel glared at me for a moment longer before turning away and muttering as he walked off. As soon as he disappeared, I realised I was shaking. Cole must have noticed, too, because he pulled me into his arms.

"I'm sorry about that," he said.

"You have nothing to be sorry about," I replied, tucking my head into his shoulder. I felt safe here, the anger seeping away and the hurt rushing in.

"I don't know what I did to make him hate me," I said.

"I don't think you'd have had to do anything. He doesn't like women."

The tears were hot on my cheeks, and I hadn't been aware that I was crying until one hit my hand. I swiped at them before Cole could see.

"Hey"—he took my face in his hands—"don't let him get to you. You're a better competitor than he ever was."

"I know, but I don't do confrontation that well, and…"

Cole kissed my eyes, his thumbs swiping at the tears.

"You handled yourself beautifully." He smiled at me. I tried to smile back, but my mind kept replaying the words that he and I had said.

"Come on, let's go do the gondola," he said, closing the garage door. He tucked me under his arm and led me to his truck.

I appreciated his wanting to help me, but the whole encounter still shook me. Nigel had never been so spiteful at the track. He'd never really spoken to me either.

All I wanted was to shut the world out and spend time with Cole.

# chapter thirty-six

Cole

Faith's run-in with Dad put a real dampener on the weekend. She remained quiet and introspective. Mum tried to assure her it wasn't her; it was women he didn't like, but it didn't seem to make a difference.

When I got a chance, I rang Dad and bailed him up about it, but he didn't think he'd done anything wrong. I couldn't believe how he could brush it off without so much as an apology to me. I disliked what my father was becoming—a bitter and nasty man, and it wasn't a comfortable thing for me. I'd somehow sugarcoated what Dad said, but when he full-out attacks my girlfriend, it doesn't make me feel very compassionate towards him. I probably shouldn't have allowed him to come back onto the team, but I don't really have a lot of say in the matter; Dad is putting up the finance for the team this year. Next year I could do it on my own, but for now, I had to put up with him.

Saturday afternoon we did the gondola, and Faith really doesn't do heights, which I found amusing, but she burst into tears. I held her tight, and tried to comfort her, but I think it was more to do with Dad than the heights.

On Sunday, I'd planned to take her over to Lyttleton, but she said she wasn't feeling very well, so we stayed at home. We went for a walk around the neighbourhood, but she said little. No matter what jokes I cracked, I couldn't make her smile or laugh, which had me really worried.

"Look, Faith, I don't agree with Dad or believe anything he says."

"Uh-huh." Faith said, but she wouldn't look at me. I grabbed her chin, tilting it up so I could look into her eyes.

"Honestly, the sooner this season is over, the better. Then I can finance my team."

"You don't pay your way?"

"No, Dad does."

"So he can tell you not to race."

"No, he can't. He's already tried, and I told him where he could go. He's even quit, but came back."

"Can't he withdraw his funding?"

"He could. But I can afford to finance the rest of the championship."

"Why don't you?"

"Because…I kind of feel like I owe Dad."

"If I had a dad like him, I'd be walking away."

"Yeah, well, he's my Dad." I could feel my anger rising, that I was being put into this awkward position, having to choose between my father and my girlfriend.

"Look, let's just let it rest, okay?" I said a little too sharply, and I saw the pain in Faith's eyes."I know he isn't a nice person, but he's still my dad."

"I get it," she said, but I don't know if she did, because she didn't have a dad. But I wouldn't throw that back at her. Instead, I held her tight, and kissed the top of her head, while blowing out a sigh.

On Monday morning, I took her to the airport. She didn't leave until eight o'clock, so we didn't have to get up super early, but it was still a drive from my place to the airport. We drove mostly in silence, and the atmosphere in the truck felt a little tense.

"Hey, I'll see you next week," I said.

She smiled, although it looked a little sad."I know; I can't wait to get to Teretonga. It's my favourite racetrack."

Her eyes sparkled as she spoke, and I knew that I'd got her onto the right subject.

"I'm going to whip your butt this coming weekend."

"Bring it on," she said, crossing her arms over her chest.

"I intend to," I said. "And I'm bringing my A-game with me."

"Ha! You wish."

I grinned as I continued our drive through rush-hour traffic to the airport. When I got there, I found a park and came in with her. She suggeste I drop her off and leave again, but I didn't want to do that. I wanted to make it up to her for the shitty weekend we'd had.

I grabbed her bag out of the back seat and threw my arm around her shoulder.

"I can carry my bag," she said.

"You can? What have you got in here, anyway? The kitchen sink? It's bloody heavy."

She slapped me on my chest as I kissed the top of her head. We walked into the foyer and went up to the flight kiosk. She checked in at the computer and put her bag into the luggage. We still had about thirty minutes until her flight was being called, so we found a coffee cart and grabbed a coffee.

I continued to hold her hand the entire time because I didn't want to let her go, but I also wanted her to know how I felt. She already did. I'd told her at Nelson Airport that I loved her, but we hadn't talked about it since. She probably thought I was trying to embarrass her, which I was.

"Hey, I love you," I said. Faith stopped with her cup halfway to her mouth.

"I know."

"You do?"

"You made the declaration at Nelson Airport."

I grinned at her. "I wasn't sure if you'd think I was teasing you or not."

"I figured that in making such a public declaration, you meant it."

"I did." I rubbed my thumb over her knuckles, feeling the softness of her skin over the bumps of the bones.

She remained silent, and I let the silence stretch. She fidgeted with the cup, which was a sign that I'd made her uncomfortable.

"Look, I don't expect you to say it back to me. I know that it's difficult for you."

Her smile was beautiful as she looked at me. "Thank you for understanding." She gently squeezed my hand.

While I told her I didn't expect it, it hurt that she didn't say it back. I thought that perhaps she might have felt something for me. I mean, her being here went some way towards thinking that she felt the same.

The call for her flight came all too soon. She got up and waited for me to stand.

"Okay, I'll see you next weekend in Invercargill," she said.

"Try to keep me away."

"I hope you'll be there," she said, looking at me out of the corner of her eye. I grinned at her.

"Of course. Any excuse to see my girl." I pulled her into my arms and held her tight. She looked up at me, and I kissed her lips. I didn't want to let her go, but I couldn't make her stay with me.

"Alright, you better go."

"Alright," she said, standing within my arms and not moving.

"Come on, or you'll miss your flight."

"Okay, I guess." She pulled out of my arms and, grabbing her book and phone, tucking them under her arm. "See you Saturday."

"See you Saturday," I said as she walked off to the gate.

"I love you!" I called out when she was far enough away.

"Right back atcha," she called out.

My heart soared. It would be the closest to a declaration of love I would get from her.

# chapter thirty-seven

Faith

It's a long drive to Teretonga Park, in Invercargill, but it was my favourite racetrack. And during February, the weather was exceptionally nice in Invercargill. The championship coincided with the Burt Munro motorcycle rally held each year in and around Southland.

We arrived on the Thursday night after travelling all day. I had a practice run on Friday, ready for racing on Saturday. Cole and his team arrived on Friday. It's a six-hour drive for them. They'd left early Friday morning, and we got to catch up for dinner on Friday night.

Saturday, and my nerves were on edge. These last two race dates, here and at Hampton Downs, are the real championship deciders, and I needed to be on top of my game in order to win the championship.

"You'll be fine," Cole said, standing behind me and massaging my shoulders as we watched the other category riders in their races. The track was dry and fast, just how I liked it.

"I know," I said, crossing my arms. I was used to being on my own before a race, and I had a procedure I went through to calm my mind. Cole was helping, but I needed to go back to my process.

"I've gotta go get ready," I said, turning to look at him. He kissed my forehead, and I headed back to my pit area.

"You okay?" Sara asked.

"Getting ready," I said, grinning at her. I jumped on my practice bike, and without the screen going, I started leaning left and right, letting the movement of the bike soothe my nerves.

Soon enough, our race was called, and I got on my bike and headed to the dummy grid. I was in pole position, with Cole beside me. He held up his fist, and we fist bumped before I pulled down my visor and focused on the lights.

As soon as the green light lit up, I was off. I sprang ahead of the pack and I presume Cole was tight on my tail. I zipped around the corners and flew into the straights, twisting and turning on my bike. It was a five-lap race, and it was humming along nicely. I loved how the bike felt underneath me, and I knew I had this one in the bag. I crossed the start-finish line, taking the checkered flag.

I raised my fist in the air.

I pulled into my pit and got off the bike, high five-ing Jeff, Mike and Sara. The adrenaline rush and happiness were contagious, and I loved the high I got from racing.

Jeff checked over the bike; Sara ran diagnostics and found the bike was in perfect racing order. It was great.

"Let's go get something to eat, my treat," I said.

"I won't disagree with that," Mike said as he put his arm around my shoulders, and as a team, we headed out of the pit areas to find decent track food.

We found a kebab place, and after ordering and getting our food, we sat down to eat.

"Four more races like that and you'll wrap up the championship." Mike said.

"Let's just get through the two races today, okay?" I said. Even though I was confident in my bike, I didn't like to jinx the ride.

"Hey, congrats," Cole said as he turned up. His hands were black, and there was an oil smudge on his cheek.

"You mechanicing on your own?" Sara asked him.

Cole rolled his eyes. "Yeah, Steve called in sick, and it's only Dad and me. Dad wants to strip the bike after every race."

"That's over the top, isn't it?"

"Try telling Dad that." Cole squeezed in between Geoff and I and sat down. He looked tired.

"You okay?" I asked as I took a serviette and wiped the oil from his cheek.

He reached up and touched where I had touched. "Tired, but okay."

"We have racing tomorrow too."

"I know, will need an early night." He grinned at me, and the table laughed.

I felt my cheeks get hot, but laughed along with him. "No staying over then." I said.

Cole's eyes popped out at me, and he grinned."Look who's getting confident."

My blush only deepened, but I still smiled.

We sat and ate and laughed for a while before heading back to the pits. Cole kissed my cheek as he headed over to his own bike. The race was still half an hour from being called, so I jumped on my practice bike. I was finding I needed it more when Cole was around because he easily distracted me.

The call came through for the next round. I pulled my helmet on and jumped on my bike, starting it up. Feeling it thrum through my body, I could imagine my blood vibrating with the revs of the engine.

I headed to the dummy grid and waited there until we headed out onto the track. It was a reverse grid start, so I was at the back, with Cole beside me. We fist bumped and got prepared for the lights.

Green for Go!

I hit the throttle, dropped the clutch and took off. Head down over the handlebars I felt the bike surge with each pull on the throttle. I whipped my way through the crowd quickly and easily; Cole was no doubt behind me.

The bike was pulling hard and working fantastically. She was a real beast of a machine. But then I heard Sara in my earpiece.

"Faith, we have a problem."

"What?" I asked, trying to concentrate on the track.

"Your oil is dangerously low."

"What?" How could it be low? We'd just done diagnostics and checks on the bike before we left for lunch.

"The oil is low, so you might not finish the race."

"But I need to finish this race to be in the championship."

"Faith, come in."

I groaned. I knew the bike was more important than the win. If I seized the engine, I wouldn't have a bike to race on. I pulled into the pits and into my team. I took my helmet off and felt like throwing it. I thought we'd dealt with these issues.

"What's going on?"

"I don't know," Sara said, looking at her computer. She plugged it into the machine and confirmed that the oil was low.

"It wasn't like that before we went to lunch."

I looked at Mike, who shrugged, but he'd been with us at lunch, and he would've topped up the oil rather than let it out.

Geoff twisted the oil inlet screw and it came off in his hands."That was tight when we went to lunch, you know me, Faith. I check every nut and bolt after each race."

"We might have to start before each race too," I said, feeling a twisting in my gut. Cole had oil on his cheek when he came to lunch. It looked slightly blackened, like it had come out of an engine, but then he said he'd been working on his own bike. I tried to push down the feeling.

Cole wouldn't be trying to sabotage my bike, would he?

# chapter thirty-eight

Cole

I came in from our second race wondering where Faith had gone. She'd been ahead of me in the race, but not that far ahead. I saw her bike by her trailer when I pulled into the pits. I parked mine up, and before Dad could demand I do something to the bike, I headed over to see Faith.

"What happened?"

"Oil was low." She looked at me through narrowed eyes. The hair on the back of my neck raised.

"What? Your mechanic is better than that."

"Yes, he is. Someone emptied the reservoir before the race."

"Who would do such a thing?" I asked. Again, her eyes narrowed on me.

"You think *I* did it?"

She dragged me a distance from her crew and asked me in private. "Did you?"

I couldn't believe she was asking me this. "Why would I do that?"

"You had oil on you when you found us at lunchtime."

I realised why she might have thought it was me. I took her in my arms, but she remained rigid and kept her arms crossed.

"Faith, I was changing the oil on my bike. I wouldn't do anything like that to you or your bike. You deserve the championship."

"I don't want to think you did it, but you have to admit…"

Yes, I had to admit that it made me look bad. I pulled her in and kissed the top of her head. Then I moved my hands to cup her face, making her look me in the eye.

"I promise you, Faith, that it wasn't me. I didn't sabotage your bike." Her eyes moved between mine, trying to find the truth in them. I knew it wasn't me, but I didn't know how to prove it to her.

"Okay," she whispered and leaned her head on my chest. I held her close, kissing the top of her head again.

"We'll find out who did this," I said.

"Thanks," she said. "I'd better get back…" she pointed back at her team, who were carrying out diagnostics on the bike.

"We'll find them," I said again. She smiled, but it wasn't her full smile. I watched as she walked back to her team. When she got to them, she turned and looked back at me, and waved. I felt my gut turn, wondering who would try to stop her from racing. I think I already knew, but I also know that he wouldn't admit it. I would have to catch him red-handed.

I walked back to my pit, my head going through various scenarios. I went over my bike, checking that everything was alright on mine. The oil screw was intact and tight. I checked my brakes and tyre pressure. Being hot and racing meant that the tyre pressures needed to be slightly higher than usual. If it were wet, we'd have grippier tyres on, but when it was fine, we ran slicks.

"Everything alright?" Dad asked. He had a smug look on his face. "Pity about Faith's race."

"You had nothing to do with it, did you?"

"What?" He opened his eyes wide in mock innocence.

I let it go because, as I thought earlier, he'd deny it. Thinking about it now, he hadn't been here when I'd drained the oil from my bike and replaced it.

Had he done that so that I would look guilty? My face flushed as I realised what he was possibly trying to do. Not only make Faith lose the championship, but also bust up our relationship. I was even more determined to figure out what he was up to and catch him in the act.

In the last race of the day, I had pole position, but because Faith didn't finish the previous race, she was in the middle of the pack. I know they did full diagnostics on her bike before the race to ensure that there wasn't anything wrong. I was glad they did it, because now I knew Dad was the one behind it. It was so blatant that it had to be him. I had to focus on the race. I watched the lights and calmed my breathing.

Green, and we're off.

The bike beside me got the jump on me, but by the end of the first lap I'd passed him. I followed the track, followed my own lines, leaning the bike over, sticking my knee out for counterbalance, and off again. I barely braked, just used my clutch and gears to slow me down and speed me up. By the end of the fourth lap, I knew I had company. I also had a feeling it was Faith. I wouldn't make it easy for her, but I wouldn't throw a race just to let her win. I could see her livery out of the corner of my eye, confirming it was her. I smiled because I knew she would do it.

It was a photo finish; we both powered up for the start finish line. I think she got me by the merest of millimetres; it was that close. We slowed, and both sat up on our bikes at the same time. She pulled her visor up and gave me the biggest grin. I knew she liked those kinds of races better than being at the front, because if you have pole position, you only had to stay at the front. But running from the middle or the back of the pack, it gave you an opportunity to actually ride and use your skills to get to first place.

We got back to the pits just as they announced what I already knew, Faith had won the race.

I stopped my bike at her pit and yelled, "Wahoo!"

She turned and smiled at me.

"See you tonight," I yelled.

"Yip," she replied.

I headed back to my pit and put my bike on the stand. I was stoked with my second place, but I knew Dad was going to get onto me about it. I'd turned off the bike microphone system, because I didn't want his negativity inside my head through this race.

His surly face was on the gazebo. He was sitting on a folding chair at the back. If looks could kill…I got off the bike, took off my helmet and placed it on the ground. I went around the bike, giving it a cursory glance before stripping the top half of my leathers off.

Racing in the summer in leathers was bloody hot. There was no windchill factor while riding with leathers on. But I wouldn't trade them for anything. If I came off my bike, it would be messy if I wasn't adequately protected. And racing leathers had extra padding in the butt, back, shoulders and back of the legs, making them an armour that was difficult to get around in.

I ignored Dad and went into the RV and changed out of my racing gear. It was the last race of the day for our class, so I didn't need to stay in them. It took a while to pull them off; they're stiff and awkward, especially when you had boots to take off as well, and the leathers tucked into the boots.

By the time I'd changed, Dad had the bike inside the gazebo and had put the sides down. We had the RV for him to stay in. I wasn't staying here; I'd booked other accommodation. I wouldn't spend the night with him while he was in a foul mood.

"See ya," I called out as I left the RV with a bag of clothes.

I heard him grumbling, but I wouldn't let him spoil my mood.

# chapter thirty-nine

Faith

I walked into the Irish bar, and the noise of laughter, the smell of stale beer and hot roasted food assailed my senses. Cole had recommended this place, saying it was the best place for a meal in Invercargill. I didn't doubt him, but it was rowdy, and after three races today, I'd been looking forward to some quiet. I found him at the bar and headed over to him. He put his arm around my shoulders and kissed me on the cheek.

"This here is my girl that I was telling you about," he told the young bar staff. The young man looked at me, and back at Cole.

"She races motorcycles?"

"Yeah, and she's looking at the championship title this year."

The young guy's eyes nearly bugged out of his head.

"Her? But she doesn't look big enough to handle a bike."

"Believe me, she handles a bike better than anyone you ever met," Cole said. I felt my cheeks getting hot as he expounded on my virtues.

"You for real, miss?"

"Yes, I am," I said, turning and raising my eyebrows at Cole. He laughed and kissed my cheek again.

"She beat me by millimetres today. Millimetres!" He pinched his fingers together to show how small the gap was.

The guy pulled out a beer coaster and a pen. "Can I have your autographs? You might be world famous one day," he said. I smiled as I took the pen.

"I doubt that," I said as I scrawled my name across the Guinness coaster. Cole took the pen and put his on the other side.

"You betcha mate, this girl is going places."

The heat in my face was just about setting my hair on fire.

"Can we just find a table, please?" I asked. I was over all the attention and wanted some privacy. I wasn't used to having people in my face, except at the racetrack. I needed some downtime, and I'd had little of that since getting into Invercargill. I was at my wit's end.

A table was found in a quieter corner of the pub, but it felt like all eyes were on us. I couldn't wait to have our meal and get out. Cole picked up on my fidgetiness.

"You okay?"

"Feeling overwhelmed," I said.

"Why?"

"I need alone time, and I'm getting jittery because I haven't had any," I said, making out that I was sitting on a vibrating chair. He laughed, but he understood.

"Okay, eat, then we're out of here."

"Sounds good."

"Looking forward to some alone time with you," he said, smiling. His eyes sparkled, and his entire face lit up. It was surprising how much a smile could make a person look so different. I grinned back at him. He leaned over and kissed my cheek. Again, the heat seeped up my neck. It was one thing for him to kiss me; to do it in public…that made me nervous.

I ordered a steak with lots of mushrooms and a large coleslaw instead of fries. Cole got a steak with fries and a salad. We ate in companionable silence, even though the volume in the pub had increased since we had arrived. Apparently, Saturday nights were big nights at the pub.

We finished our meals, paid and headed out onto the street. The heat wasn't any different from being inside the pub, but it was not as humid, and didn't smell like sweat and stale beer. I breathed out a sigh of relief as we walked towards where I'd parked.

"You staying with me tonight?" Cole asked.

An icy chill spiked through my heart. "Yeah, that's what we agreed, isn't it?"

"I thought you wanted alone time."

"I can do that with you." I felt the tension ease, and my shoulders relaxed. "I need my own company, not with hundreds of other people packed in around me. I don't do crowds or parties very well."

"You did alright at the New Year's party."

"That is different. I can get into my zone and just dance. I'm in my happy place."

"And you can't do that in a pub or nightclub?"

"I can't escape if I want to. Outside, I can move off the dance floor and dance, can't really do that in a nightclub without looking like a dork."

"Then I'm constantly looking like a dork." He grinned at me.

"You go to nightclubs?" I was surprised. I believed he was like me and couldn't stand crowds, but I was wrong.

"Not as much as I used to, but I enjoy a good boogie now and then."

I couldn't help but giggle. "Boogie? You said Boogie!"

With Cole's hands planted firmly on his hips, a smile in the corner of his mouth, he tried to act offended. "Mum brought me up on seventies and eighties music, okay?"

"Okay," I said, laughing again. We reached my rental car, and I unlocked it.

"See you there? You've got the address?" Cole asked.

"Yes, and I have a map app." I held up my phone. He smiled and kissed my forehead. He closed the car door once I got in.

"I'm right behind you," he said, grinning at me.

"See you there." I started my car and headed off towards Otatara Street.

I sat and waited in the car. Being this far south in summer was great; the sky was still light at ten o'clock at night, which made for long days. Cole arrived within minutes, and I grabbed my bag and got out of the car, locking it, and waited while he did the same. With his spare hand, he took mine, and we walked to the door. He unlocked the door, and we walked into the small room. Being a rental accommodation, it had the basics; it was all we needed. A queen-sized bed with a cheap duvet sat in the middle of the room. We dropped our bags, and both charged at the bed. As we landed on it, it moved, making us both break out into giggles.

We looked at each other, and then we couldn't keep our hands still. Kissing, hugging, caressing, touching, removing clothing until they were strewn around the room. Our lovemaking was gentle and tender yet passionate and sometimes rough. I didn't mind; I instigated most of it. We moved together with the bed, which kept giving me giggles until a loud and painful smack on my arse brought me back to reality. I was making love to a drop-dead gorgeous guy. We aroused each other, tortured one another with touches and scratches until finally we orgasmed. I lay back on the bed, puffing like I'd run a marathon, while small thrills continued to echo through my body.

Lovemaking with Cole was a whole new experience, and every time it was different, and I still got a thrill from looking at him and knowing that he liked me, and wanted to be with me, as awkward as I was.

I went and showered to get the smell of stale beer, burnt rubber and hot sweaty leather off my skin, then snuggled up with Cole and fell into a deep sleep.

# chapter forty

Cole

Sunday was our final race day. We woke up and had a lazy start to the day, both knowing that our first race wasn't until ten. It was eight, but we had plenty of time. Teretonga was only a few minutes away. And we both had cars this time. It was nice to wake up with Faith in my arms, her hair under my nose, and I could smell the shampoo she'd used the night before. Her skin smelled of lavender, a scent I would always associate with her.

We got ready, said our farewells, and I dropped the key into the lockbox before heading back to the racetrack in my dinky smart car.

Dad had the bike set up on the stand. He was busy tinkering away when I arrived and looked over at me when I got there.

"Sleep well?" he asked.

"The best," I grinned.

He scowled and went back to tinkering with the bike. I got on the bus and got changed. The race suits can take a while to put on; they need to be tight to stop them from twisting. If you fell off the bike and it was loose, it could screw an arm or a leg off. After half an hour, I was out, ready to get on the bike.

"Any trouble overnight?" I asked.

"Nope," he said.

I started the bike up. She purred like a big cat. It didn't have the same sound as a V8 did, but it was still a pleasant sound. I rode over to the dummy grid, ready to take my place on the actual grid. With her impressive win yesterday, Faith was in pole position again. I was right beside her. We fist bumped and then got onto the track.

The wait for the lights is always the nerve-wracking part; your heart is pounding in your chest as you watch the red light, then flickering yellow. Your hand is on the accelerator, foot ready to drop off the clutch as soon as that light goes green. You don't want to miss that split second. Once it was green, the adrenaline dropped into your system and you were off, racing. I got the start on Faith, but she had me by the first corner, and didn't let up; in fact, she had quite a commanding lead by the time we finished the race.

"Great race," I called out to her as she pulled into her pit. She fist-pumped the air, and I continued on to my pit.

Dad was there, scowling at me.

"Don't want to hear it," I said as I took my helmet off. I heard him mumbling, but didn't take any notice of what he said.

I caught up with Faith at lunchtime. Even with all her crew around her, I kissed her cheek. She seemed to blush less, although, strangely, I kind of liked her awkwardness. I mean, I liked her cheeks going red whenever I did something with her in public, like I was slowly gaining her trust every time she blushed.

"How's your morning been?"

"Not too bad, some weird readings on the computer, but we can't find the problem." Faith said.

"It could be a problem with the program. I can't run diagnostics on the computer until we finish racing at the end of the day, or it might throw up even weirder numbers." Sara said.

"How do you check the motorbike through the computer?" I asked. I knew some machines had computers, but to do complete diagnostics was pretty much Formula One racing budget.

"Let's just say I'm a bit of a programming nerd." Sara grinned at him.

"How have you not sold this program to other racers?"

"And give them the advantage? Hell no! Though if you twisted my arm enough, I might just sell a copy of the program to you."

"Like hell you will," Faith said, laughing. "I'm barely beating him now!" Everyone at the table joined in with the good-natured ribbing.

"What's the odd number?" I asked Faith quietly.

She turned to talk to me, excluding everyone else at the table. "The program is saying that something isn't right, the brakes or something. We've physically checked them. Everything seems fine." She shrugged.

I couldn't shake it off like she did. "Have you checked everything totally?"

"Yes, yesterday and today. Geoff is happy with the bike."

"Are you?" I asked Faith.

"If Geoff says it's okay, then I'm okay with that. He's the professional here."

I felt really uneasy about this whole situation, that her tyre went flat, and the low oil yesterday. Her bike should be in pristine condition, these things shouldn't be happening.

Once we'd finished lunch, I pulled Faith aside.

"There are too many problems with your bike right now. Are you sure you should continue racing on it?"

She narrowed her eyes at me. "Of course, Geoff knows what he's doing, so I'm happy with his word."

"Are you sure he's not sabotaging your bike?"

"Geoff?" Her voice raised an octave as she thrust her hands on her hips. "I've known him since he worked on my karts. I have complete faith in him." She narrowed her eyes. "You're starting to sound like your dad, you know?"

"I'm just worried about you having a serious accident."

Faith blew out a breath, then looked at me. "I understand your concerns, but I'll be okay. I'll keep racing."

We started walking back to the pits. "Okay. I get it; I trust my mechanic, too, so if you have faith in him, then I will too." She glanced at me out of the corner of her eye. She wasn't sure about my motives, but I wanted her to be safe, not smashed up because her brakes weren't working properly.

My mind kept working overtime, wondering how I could help her out. I had a feeling that if the brakes weren't working, my dad was behind it.

I got back to my bike, and Dad was sitting at the back of the gazebo reading a newspaper.

"What have you done to her bike?"

"Who's bike?"

I put my hands on my hips, glaring at him. "Faith's." I dared him to deny it.

He dropped the newspaper down to look at me, and he shook his head, looking baffled."I don't know what you're talking about."

"Did you interfere with Faith's bike?"

"Why would I do that?" he growled.

I suddenly felt unsure of what I was accusing him of. It was the type of thing I would expect Dad to do, but he was denying it. Would Dad lie to me? Of course he bloody would.

"If anything happens to her because of any fault on her bike, I will hold you responsible."

"If there is anything wrong with her bike, it's because her team is incompetent." He shrugged and went back to reading the paper. His attitude was really winding me up, and I was over it.

I slapped the paper out of his hands. "Dad, you're fired."

"Suits me. Can think of more interesting things to do on the weekends than to pussyfoot around you and your girlfriend since you aren't out there trying to win. In fact, maybe I should talk to the race committee about you colluding with Faith to let her win the championship."

"You do that because there is no truth in the matter."

“They might not see it that way, especially if I talk to them.”

“Go ahead, do it. You’ll see that the truth will prevail.”

The old man screwed up the newspaper and stood up from the chair. I could feel the anger radiating from him. He got right up in my face. “You’ve ruined a perfectly good opportunity to be part of the Kinsey legacy, and you’re too far up her pussy to care.”

“How dare you speak of a fellow competitor like that? How dare you speak about any woman like that? You’re a misogynistic asshole and I’m really disappointed in you as a father, and I’m embarrassed that I’m your son.” My heart was pounding in my chest so hard. I clenched my fists, ready to swing, because the look on his face told me he wanted to.

He grunted and breathed out in my face. His face was red with exertion, and I had to keep my hands by my side. He backed away, mumbling as he grabbed his bag and walked away from the bus. I breathed out, feeling deflated and elated at the same time.

I’d finally stood up to my old man, and while it felt good, there was a deeper part of me that was sad because he was my father, and he would never change.

# chapter forty-one

Faith

At lunchtime, Cole didn't turn up to have something to eat with us. I wasn't worried; his dad had been making him do strange things since they were mechanicing on their own. We walked back to our gazebo, and I saw Cole turning from my bike as we got there.

"Everything okay?" I asked him.

His face split into a big grin. "Now I've seen my girl, everything is wonderful." He picked me up and swung me around as he hugged me tight. My cheeks felt hot as he put me down.

"Did you have something to eat?" I asked.

"Not yet, I guess you have."

"Yip."

"I'll go grab something now."

"Better be quick; our next race is coming up."

Cole kissed my cheek and ran off towards the concession stands.

Geoff gave the bike a once-over, and everything seemed fine. I got my leathers back up over my top half and grabbed my helmet, balancing it on the gas tank. I started the bike and let her run to warm up as I waited for the PA announcement. Minutes later, it came. I pulled on my helmet and half rode, half walked the bike to the dummy grid. I couldn't wait to get out and race. I was two wins away from taking the championship on points, three from the outright win. I could do this. This was my year.

Cole pulled up beside me. He looked puffed and red in the face as if he'd had to run. We fist bumped, as had become our tradition, and got ready to head out to the actual grid. We were first and second on the grid.

The anticipation heightened as I waited for the light to go green, slowing down my breathing to stop my heart from racing too hard, but that adrenaline drop, that was what I was racing for.

That and the win.

It was another easy race, and I won by a slight margin this time. I rode the track to the pits, once more raising my fist in the air as Cole rode past.

Sara looked at me seriously as I pulled my helmet off.

"How did the bike perform?" she asked me.

I tilted my head. "What do you mean? She ran fine, beautifully in fact."

"Okay, we have a problem."

"What is it now?" I got off the bike and went over to check out her screen.

"Did the brakes feel…off?"

"Nope, they were good as."

"The screen is showing that the brakes aren't right."

"What do you mean, aren't right?"

"We'll get Geoff to check them," Sara said, her eyebrows pulled down over her eyes as she studied the data from the bike.

Geoff checked the brake reservoir and then bled the brakes. Everything seemed to be fine.

"You sure the brakes were working?"

"Yes, I stopped in here, didn't I?"

"They didn't feel spongy?"

"No."

Sara shrugged. "The numbers must be off then; I can't explain it. It's showing that the brake fluid is low, but Geoff just confirmed that there is plenty of brake fluid. There might be an issue with the program."

"Do you think the program would put out false data?"

"I didn't think it could, but I might have got some coding wrong. I'll have to check."

"Everything else is alright with the bike?"

"Everything seems fine."

"Then we're good to race?"

"Yes, you are," Sara said, but she still looked concerned.

"You'll sort it," I said, clapping her on the shoulder.

The look she gave me didn't seem convinced.

The last race of the day was a reverse grid start, so Cole and I started from the rear. This was the type of racing I loved. The type of racing that really got my heart pumping, because there were obstacles between me and winning. A challenge.

The bikes were all revving heavily by the time the light turned green, and my bike did a little stutter, but I took off, finding a gap between the two opponents in front of me, and darting through. Cole must have been hot in pursuit, because I kept catching the colours of his bike in my peripheral vision. I came to a corner, changed down gears, and tapped the foot brake lightly, but I didn't slow down as I expected. I hauled her down another gear and then back up as I straightened the bike up.

"Sara, you're right; there's something up with the brakes," I said into my headset.

"Shit," I heard her say as I continued on through the race. The brake on the handlebars weren't much better. The first time I used it, it was fine, but after that, I had to drop the lever and pull again to slow down, effectively pumping the brakes.

"You'd better come in then. Before it get's any worse." Sara said in my earpiece.

"Nope, only one more win after this one." I said as I hauled the bike into another corner. I passed all but one bike as I crossed the start-finish line, but the points were enough. Only one more win, which I would have to achieve at Hampden Downs.

Once in the pits, Geoff stripped down the brakes and bled them out totally. There was nothing in the brake lines, the brake fluid looked fine, but the brakes had totally failed.

"What would have caused that?" I asked Geoff.

"I don't know," he replied, shaking his head. "I'll take her home and replace all the brake lines. Perhaps there was a problem with them."

I sighed. "Thanks, Geoff."

I turned to walk to the trailer when I heard someone call out behind me. I turned to see the last person I wanted to see, Nigel Kinsey.

"It was Cole; I saw him. He put water in your brake reservoir."

I glared at him."And why would Cole do that?" My heart was stuttering in my chest. It couldn't have been Cole; he promised me it wasn't him.

"He's sabotaging your races. He put the stone in your tyre, drained oil from your motor. He wants to win, and he knows the only way he can beat you is to stop you from racing."

I narrowed my eyes at him. I didn't trust him, but he knew exactly what had been happening with my bike. "And you're telling me this…because?"

"I didn't stoop to such low levels to beat you," he said, smirking. I didn't like the look on his face. He shrugged, turned and walked away.

Mike came up behind me. "What did he want?"

"He just said that Cole was sabotaging me."

"Seriously?" Mike looked incredulous.

"Yeah, but…Cole had that black smudge on his face last time we raced, and we had trouble with the tyres. Then he had oil on him, when the oil had been drained from my bike. And now the brakes?" My insides were quivering and my eyes were stinging with unshed tears.

"You can't seriously…" he looked at my face. "He wouldn't…"

"I don't know what to believe," I said. "Mike, he was hovering around my bike when we got back from lunch."

"And they are serious things to be mucking around with on a bike." Mike tapped his chin."We'll have to check this out fully and investigate."

My heart stopped in my chest, and pain settled in. I found it hard to breathe.

"I think we already know who the culprit is," I said.

It was too obvious, really.

It had to be Cole.

# chapter forty-two

Cole

I saw Faith coming over, but she didn't look happy. In fact, she was marching over; her fists clenched.

"You okay?" I asked.

As she got closer, she pulled back her hand, and *bang*!

I saw stars, and my jaw hurt. I looked at her, and she was shaking her hand.

"What was that for?" I asked.

"What was that for? Interfering with my racing, with my need to win. You're the one sabotaging my bike."

"What? Hang on a minute—"

"No, Cole…" Tears spilled down her cheeks. "I gave you a chance, and you proved to me why I don't do relationships. They hurt, and I can't handle the hurt."

"But…"

"No buts, Cole." She turned on her heel and strode off.

I reached up and held my jaw, testing it, and fortunately it still worked, but hell, that woman had a wicked hook. I ran after her.

"Faith. Faith, wait."

"Fuck off, Cole."

I grabbed her arm and turned her around. She whirled around and pushed me. I stumbled backwards and landed with my wrist taking the brunt of the fall, and I felt something snap.

"Faith, it wasn't me."

"Right, it was divine intervention. Your father told me it was you."

"And you'll believe him over me?" My voice pitched as the anger rose.

"You were covered in oil, with dark marks on your hands after each of my 'incidents'," she air quoted.

"I can't believe that you'd believe my father over me."

"Don't you twist this around."

My anger fired on all cylinders now. "I'm not. It was my father, not me, but you're too shortsighted to see that," I yelled. "I've had it with your insecurities and with my fucking father." I got up off the ground, bracing my wrist. "Goodbye, Faith."

I turned and walked away, not looking back. She was upset and angry. I knew better than to talk to her while she was this way, and my wrist hurt like buggery. I had to get it checked. If it was broken, I would be out for the rest of the season, which, to be honest, really didn't bother me. The way I felt right now, I didn't give a shit about winning or riding. I just wanted to stop the damned pain in my wrist and my heart.

I walked over to the ambulance and talked to the ambulance officer. He twisted my wrist, and I grunted in pain. He looked up at me.

"Mate, you're going to have to go to the hospital and get that looked at." The look of sympathy on his face wasn't what I wanted right then."I'll call you another ambulance. I can't leave while there's racing here."

"How long will that take?"

"About half an hour, an hour. Depends on how busy they are."

"I'll go get changed."

"Mate, that leather suit is probably the best thing for your wrist right now."

"I'm not having it cut off. These things don't grow on trees," I growled.

The ambulance officer's eyes opened wide. "Okay, look, what's your name and number?"

I gave those to him.

"Be back here in half an hour. I'll get it up in a splint and a sling, then you're off to the hospital to get it X-rayed."

I nodded as I walked off.

What a fucking day. Just what I didn't need, and I wouldn't call my father to see where he was because I really didn't want him anywhere near me. I would try to drive the truck home on my own.

As I got to the bus, I noticed an official waiting for me.

"What now?" I muttered as I got level with my bike.

"Mr Blythe?" he asked. He looked down at his clipboard and back at me.

"Yes."

"We've had reports that you and Faith Hart have been collaborating on getting her to win the championship this year."

"What?" I went to push the hair over my head, but it was the wrong hand, and it hurt. "We haven't been doing anything of the sort. Who's been saying this?" I asked.

"Nigel Kinsey made the allegations," the official said.

I rolled my eyes, my face heating up with the anger that seemed to be so close to the surface at the moment. "That would be about right. I just fired him, and he told Ms Hart that I interfered with her bike."

"And did you?"

"No! Look, I think I've broken my wrist. I want to get undressed and get this looked at. If it's broken, my season is over."

"Then we need to talk to Ms Hart about this matter."

"You realise that there is animosity between Ms Hart and Mr Kingsey, don't you?"

"Yes, we have received several complaints about Mr Kinsey over the years for his bad sportsmanlike behaviour."

"Let me tell you this, for free. He's an egotistical asshole. Ms Hart deserves this chance to prove that she's a better racer than Nigel, and I can guarantee that she is professional in all of her racing. We haven't been colluding; we have been dating until about fifteen minutes ago."

A look of pity flashed over the official's face.

"I'm in pain, and I still have to pack up this gear, and head back home, after I've been to the hospital, so I'd appreciate it if you would just let me get on with my shitty day and let me lick my wounds in peace."

The look on the official's face changed to something else. "I can get some people over here to pack this up for you."

"Much appreciated," I said as I got onto the bus and sat on the bed. I didn't see the official walk off, but I hoped I'd stopped him from accusing Faith of fixing the races, because all our races had been done fairly. She'd made me work for every win I'd had. I'm sure if they went through all the results, they would see that.

I braced my arm, and my head fell forwards. I couldn't cry; I didn't have time. I had to get myself out of this leather racing suit as soon as possible.

There was a knock on the door, and Mike, Faith's manager, put his head inside the bus.

"I swear to God that I did nothing to her bike."

"I know. I don't doubt you for a minute. Unless we get proof, she's going to think it was you."

"What do I do? I think our relationship has blown up as well." I tried to keep my voice from cracking, but it was hard. My chest heart, my heart was breaking, my eyes were close to tearing up, and my arm was starting to throb.

Mike patted my good shoulder with a sympathetic look on his face. A look I was sick of getting today. "Let's just get this sorted out, then she'll be back with you."

I looked at him, but I doubted that would happen. The hurt, the pain in her eyes and the way her face contorted, I doubt we would ever recover from this.

"Just make sure that you're at the next race in Hampden Downs. I have a plan."

"You're not going to let me in on this plan, are you?"

Mike shook his head. "Sorry, if you know, then it might not happen."

I put my head between my hands, and rested it there, until I felt my wrist twinge.

"I've gotta go deal with this," I said. I felt the tears prickling my eyes as the pain in my wrist pulsed with the shock wearing off.

"Do you need help?" Mike asked, indicating my arm.

"Yeah, please, if you don't mind." I knew it would be painful for me to do it alone. I also knew I'd need a hand to get out of the leathers.

Mike unzipped the cuff, allowing a bit more room for me to manoeuvre, but I still had to bend my arm to get it out of the suit. I puffed my cheeks out, trying to keep the pain at bay.

Next, Mike pulled the suit down my body. My cheeks grew hot as Mike eased the leathers down until I could step out of them.

"Anything else you need a hand with?"

"No, I'm all good." I wanted everyone to bugger off and leave me alone. My cheeks burned with humiliation and unchecked tears.

"Okay, well, don't worry. I'll look after Faith," Mike said.

I had to trust his word.

By the time I'd pulled some shorts on and wrangled a T-shirt over my head, all I wanted to do was cry. But a knock on the door of the bus kept me from my emotional breakdown.

"Yes?"

A young guy poked his face around the corner.

"Someone asked us to help you put your bike and gear away?"

"Yeah, thanks." I showed him where everything needed to be stowed before heading over to the ambulance.

# chapter forty-three

## Faith

It was a long, silent trip home. I refused to engage with anyone else in the truck. I couldn't wait to get home, but then when I got home, I couldn't settle.

I went straight to my villa and worked in the office for hours.

It wasn't like me not to go over and talk to Hope and Grace about my weekend, but I knew they'd ask questions. And even after sleep, I felt more confused than ever.

I honestly couldn't believe it was Cole who'd tampered with my bike, but Nigel had said he had, and every time something had happened to my bike, Cole had an excuse. His father had asked him to change the tyres; his father had told him to change the oil…too many coincidences for me. And I felt shattered because I had believed Cole when he said it wasn't him.

But was it? Nigel had told me it was, and had looked smug doing so, but would he be telling me his son had been causing the damage if he wasn't concerned about it?

The more I tried to process it, the more confused I got.

Grace finally called me over to the main building, which I couldn't put off any longer. I trudged over there and entered her office. Hope was there too.

They took one look at me, and crowded in for a hug. I loved these girls; I really did. They were of my blood. We argued, but they loved me at a deeper level, a DNA level. My eyes filled with tears as the pain from my broken heart poured out of them.

When they pulled back, I swiped at my eyes and grabbed a tissue from the box Grace kept on the coffee table in her office.

"What happened?" Hope asked. Both she and Grace sat with wide eyes, waiting for me to explain.

"Cole—" I couldn't get the words out.

"Cole cheated on you?" Hope said. I shook my head, pacing the small office.

"Cole dumped you?" Grace added.

"You decided you didn't want to be in a relationship with Cole and now you regret it?" Hope asked.

"No!" I shouted. "Cole was sabotaging my bike."

Both of them exploded. "*What*?"

Grace pulled me down to sit next to her on the couch. She put her arm around my shoulder and pulled me into a hug.

"My bike was playing up, and it turns out it was Cole."

"How do you know it was Cole?"

"I saw him."

"You saw him do what?"

"He was standing over my bike, and later that day, my brakes played up. He put stones in my tyre valve and drained my bike of oil."

"You saw him do all of this?"

"Yes, well, no, but the evidence stacks up. He came over covered in black marks, and then my tyre had low air pressure. He had oil on him, then my bike showed it was low in oil, and then he was standing over my bike and the brakes went weird."

"Did he do this over the weekend?" Hope asked.

"No, it's been happening over the last couple of races."

"And you're absolutely sure it was Cole?"

I glared at Grace as I pulled out of her arms.

"Who else would it be? Besides, Nigel told me."

"Nigel, as in Nigel Kinsey? Your rival, Nigel?" Hope asked.

"Yes, that Nigel."

"And you'd believe him over Cole?" Grace questioned.

"I saw Cole leaning over my bike! How could it not be him?"

"Are you listening to yourself? You're trusting the word of a guy who has always hated you racing, over the man of your dreams? Cole wouldn't come here, charm all of us just to pull one over on you. He didn't strike me as that kind of guy."

"I'm not; I'm trusting what I saw."

"Did you see him tamper with your brakes? Put a stone in your tyres and drain the oil out of your bike?"

"Well…no."

"But you still believe the man who prevented you from winning a championship for how many years?" Hope added.

My brain fog was just being compounded, and I didn't know what to believe any more. My bike had been tampered with. I'd experienced it. And they weren't little things either;

they could have caused serious harm to myself, let alone my bike.

"Look, I don't know; all I know is that someone was trying to stop me from racing."

"And you think Cole would do that?"

"Yes...No...I don't know." I started crying again because I was embarrassed, and with the hurt and anger burning in my gut, I felt like I wanted to be sick. "All I know is that I need to win one more race in order to win the championship. And the way I'm feeling, I don't know if I can do it."

"Is it that important to you?" Grace asked.

I glared at her, but then I realised she wasn't teasing me. She was genuinely concerned about me.

I thought for a moment, then blinked as I looked up at the two concerned faces. "Actually, no. It's not. I don't think that the championship is really worth the hassle any more."

Hope and Grace both sat back, shocked at my words, because I'd been so driven for the last four years to win the Superbike championships, because it would lead to more riding overseas, but right now, in this given moment, all of those dreams just didn't seem important any more. Nothing seemed important.

"Look, the race is a month away; give yourself some time. You might get your mojo back. Besides, Cole might be in touch to see how you are."

"I really don't think that Cole will contact me. I accused him of sabotage, and I really don't want him around. I'm not cut out for love. It hurts too much. I knew that from the beginning. It's easier to be on my own."

Grace raised an eyebrow, but said nothing, and I appreciated that. I didn't really feel like talking any more, so

I took more tissues, mopped up as best I could, then left her office and headed back out to my villa.

But there were memories there, especially in my bedroom. I needed some space, so I grabbed my earphones and went for a walk, but everywhere around the vineyard were more memories. The amphitheatre where Cole and I first kissed. The top of the hill where we picnicked as we gazed out at the view. No matter where I went, Cole haunted my thoughts.

I was so sure it was him. I'd seen him leaning over my bike before the brakes started playing up.

But Cole wasn't like that, was he?

My sisters told me he wasn't. Would he really try to stop me from racing? If he wanted me to stop racing, he was more likely to ask me point-blank that to try underhanded tactics.

My mind spun like motorcycle wheels but made no traction, and it hurt to listen to my thoughts. A deep ache had started in my chest, and I wondered if I was going to die of a broken heart.

"Hey, Faith." It was Uncle Chives. I hadn't realised that I had wandered down to their trailer.

"Hey, Uncle Chives," I said as I walked up to him. He pulled me into a bear hug and held me for a while. I felt safe in his arms, and I allowed him to squish all my broken pieces back together.

"Take a seat," he said, indicating the sun lounger beside his.

"Where's Aunt Dill?"

"She's gone to get her nails done," he said, smiling at me. I smiled back, albeit wearily.

"What's wrong, Chicken Little?" he asked. It was his pet name for me, because I was always the one running about thinking there was some disaster about to befall everyone.

"Life." I sighed.

He nodded sagely."It's pretty tough sometimes. Is it to do with that handsome young man I've seen you around here with?"

I couldn't speak. I knew if I opened my mouth, I would cry again. I nodded instead.

"Okay, let me make us a drink, aye." He got up from his chair, grumbling about aches and pains before heading inside the trailer and putting the jug on. He stayed in there as I composed myself and came out about five minutes later with a hot cup of tea.

"Tea fixes everything," he said as he placed mine on the small table beside the lounger.

"Thank you, but I don't think it does."

"We'll see about that, aye."

We sat in companionable silence, watching the world pass us by. I heard the gardeners in the shed beside us, but then the sounds of the birds filtered through and drew my attention. Piwakawaka and Tui flitted about in the native trees surrounding the gardener's compound. I could see why Aunt Dill and Uncle Chives enjoyed parking here. I thought it was so we wouldn't have to hear them arguing.

As if he read my mind, Uncle Chives started talking. "It's peaceful here. We love listening to the birds, especially first thing in the morning. It reminds us we are still above ground, and that there is promise in the day.

I wrapped my hands around my cup and took a sip. It had cooled sufficiently to drink. "I can see and hear that."

"We love being here with you girls. I know our bickering makes you uncomfortable, but I can assure you, your aunt and I love each other deeply."

"Then why are you arguing all the time?"

Uncle Chives tipped his head to the side. "It's our way of showing our love for each other."

I snorted. "Funny way to show it."

"It might be, but we still share a bed. And a little more than that," he said, but seeing the look on my face he changed the subject. "But you don't need to hear about that. We've been together for forty years."

"Forty years of always niggling each other. Doesn't that get on your nerves?"

"Sometimes, and I guess it's a weird way to show each other we care, but it works for us. When we get on each other's goat too much, we go separate ways and do our own things, then we get back together. We wouldn't travel in such a confined space together if we didn't care about each other."

I thought it through; I guess they were right. And people had an odd way of showing each other affection.

"Your aunt likes things done for her, so I make dinner, I bring her flowers, I cut up the wood, I will buy her a gift; that way I shower her with love. I like it when she touches me, a gentle touch to the elbow, a kiss, a cuddle. Everyone expresses themselves differently."

I nodded; I understood that. I liked it when I spent time with people I cared about. Cole was the same.

Thinking about Cole hurt. I closed my eyes as my chest exploded in pain again.

"Why did Dad leave us?" I asked.

Uncle Chives sat back. "That's an odd question to ask."

"No, it's not. Did Dad not love us enough to stay?"

"Oh, sweetie, your dad loves you all very much."

"Then why did he leave us?"

"He was heartbroken when your mum died. He loved her so much, and he couldn't handle the three of you and his grief, so we stepped in and said we would raise you."

"Where is Dad now? Why hasn't he contacted us?"

"Ah, now that's the hard part. You see, your dad travelled, and we heard periodically from him, but we have heard nothing in the last five years."

"So he's dead?"

Uncle Chives sighed. "I wouldn't say that. He's probably busy somewhere providing for you girls."

"What? Providing for us? What do you mean?"

"This vineyard, it's his. He put it into a trust for you girls and wanted the three of you to take it over when you were old enough. He spent a lot of time in Europe creating connections for the sale of the wine."

My heart leapt at the thought that although my father had abandoned us, he was still providing for us. There was still a part that was angry at him for not staying, or at least not contacting us, but there was a sliver of hope there. He still cared.

I put down my empty cup but stayed seated. The shade of the trees dulled the warmth of the day, and it was nice just sitting there.

"And how is that young man of yours?" Uncle Chives asked.

And the tears started.

# chapter forty-four

Cole

She hates me.

She thinks I sabotaged her bike.

How dare she.

Thoughts flitted through my mind as I slammed tools around in the workshop. My employees had distanced themselves from me for the last week as I vacillated between anger, hurt and missing Faith like crazy. It was like a pendulum swinging in my head, and I never knew which emotion I would wake up with each day. I either moped around like a lost puppy, threw tools across the shed when things didn't go my way, or sat in complete silence, staring off into space, wondering what I'd done that she thought I was capable of such things.

"You okay?" Mum asked as she came into the corner of the workshop I found myself isolated in.

"Yeah, I guess."

"There's a lot of noise here today. Working out your anger?"

I sighed. "Sorry."

"Don't be sorry; it's better than taking your anger out on Faith or me."

I looked over at mum who looked kind of meek. "Is that what Dad did with you?"

She took another step forwards and nodded. "Yes, he would yell at me, and everything was my fault."

My heart melted, and I reached out and pulled her into a hug. "I'm sorry." I tried not to pat her back with the cast on my right wrist.

"Don't be; it's not yours to apologise for."

I didn't know what to say. I barely remember Dad talking to Mum, let alone yelling at her, but it must have been something he did regularly for Mum to fear me in my anger.

"I'm sorry my anger scared you."

"It didn't. Your dad threw nothing; it was his words he threw, and they could be just as damaging. How's Faith?"

"I don't know."

"You haven't talked to her?"

"She won't answer her phone. I've messaged, I've emailed, but she isn't responding to me." I felt my eyes prickle as I spoke, and I blinked to keep the tears at bay.

Mum's face softened. She reached up a hand and cupped my face. "I'm sorry, Cole. She seemed so lovely."

"She is lovely," I said as I shook her hand away, trying to hide the tears that were filling my eyes. "But Dad fucked it up for me."

"Do you want me to talk to her?"

"She won't talk to you, Mum. Mike, her racing manager, told me to just hold fire. He'd sort things out."

"What does he know?"

"He knows I didn't do it. He knows Dad's a shit. God, I wish I'd never taken him up on the offer to manage me in Superbike racing."

"Then you would never have met Faith."

"And had my heart trampled all over."

"Unfortunately. But you know what love is; you will recognise it when you see it."

"I don't want to know what it feels like, or looks like. I want Faith."

"Then chase after her; let her know."

"But she thinks I did it."

"Then she isn't worthy of you."

I heaved a big sigh. "But she is, Mum. She's perfect."

"There's no such thing as perfect. We all have flaws. Mine is that I'm too kind-hearted." She smiled softly, her eyes gazing into the distance. I wondered what she was thinking about.

"Then she is as close to perfect as I want."

"You need to show her she's wrong about you, then. That you are worth fighting for. Is she worth fighting for?"

"Yes, but how? Dad convinced her I was damaging her bike."

"And we both know what your father is like. And so does she."

"Then why was it so easy for her to think I did it?"

"Your father convinced her you're stopping her from going after the one thing she desperately wants more than anything else. The championship."

And the lightbulb went on. Faith loved me, and she was running scared. As long as she was racing, she knew who she was, what she wanted. Loving me complicated things for her; she couldn't focus like she wanted to on the championship. She'd told me several times that she needed space to prepare for each race, but as we got closer, she didn't need that space any more.

Perhaps I had been overcrowding her.

And my father had so many opportunities to wreck her bike, which I'd handed to him on a platter. I was just as guilty as he was in not calling him out on it sooner.

I paced around the workshop, pulling at my hair as my mind whirled through so many ideas.

"I have to ring Mike," I said to Mum as I walked swiftly out of the workshop to my truck. I kept my phone in there so I wouldn't be interrupted while working, and Mike had given me his card so I could call him if I needed to.

As I jumped into my truck, my chest contracted, and my determination withered as I wondered what I would say to him. Did I ring him and tell him I needed to talk to Faith? Or did I need to talk to him just to clear the air? He knew I had done nothing, but there was an underlying guilt because it was my father that had been sabotaging her bike, and I'd done nothing to stop him. And Mike didn't want me telling Faith that. He wanted to catch my dad out.

But I needed Faith to know that it wasn't me.

But after such a lack of faith, I had to really think about whether I wanted to be with her. Because every time something happened, would she pull back, or blame me? I couldn't handle the swings in emotions. I was struggling now to deal with them.

I sat back in the seat and looked out the window of my ute, staring at the traffic beyond the workshop yard. No matter what, my season was over. I couldn't race with a cast on my arm.

Maybe I just let things be, lick my wounds, and try to get on with my life.

But the image of Faith's smiling face haunted me, her laughter the last thing I remembered at night before sleep claimed me, if it did.

I was beyond tired. I was exhausted.

# chapter forty-five

Faith

I wasn't expecting a video call from Roger Hartley, but it came the following evening.

"Hello, Faith, how are you?"

I swallowed back the lump that had permanently taken hold in the back of my throat. It had been two weeks since I'd seen or heard from Cole, and I was suffering from it. "I'm good."

He narrowed his eyes at me. "You don't look fine."

"I'm not sleeping well at the moment." I smiled, but knew it was fake.

"Are you sure you're okay? You have me worried about you now."

"Oh, please. Don't worry about me." I waved my hand at him, wondering why someone I barely knew would be concerned about me.

"Let's just talk business, shall we?" I pressed.

"I've got the clients all lined up. I'm sending you a list now. We want three lots of the Racing Harts wine, and two of the Harts Valley wine."

"Wow, three cases?"

"No, not cases, shipping containers."

"What? How did you manage that?"

"My contacts, darling."

I paused. It seemed arrogant of him to call me that. He interpreted the look on my face.

"Sorry, I shouldn't have said that. I apologise; it was very unprofessional of me." He put his hand on his heart and at least looked contrite.

"Apology accepted."

"So, business going okay at your end?"

"It is, yes, and thank you for your order, this will help keep us going for a while."

"And how is your racing going? You race motorcycles, right?"

His knowing that I raced, let alone bikes, was a little unsettling. "My season is just about finished."

"And you enjoy racing?"

"I do. It lets me blow off steam."

"I don't think you'd need to blow off much steam." He grinned.

"Wouldn't you believe it," I muttered.

"What was that?" he asked.

"Nothing, racing is going well."

He looked like he wanted to say something else, but then he stopped.

"Okay then, let us know when you can get that order under way, and I'll let my clients know."

"Thank you very much, Roger, much appreciated."

"You're welcome, oh, and Faith, chin up. It will get better." He ended the call before I could respond. What did he mean by things will get better? Has he been spying on me? On us? I guess he needed to do due diligence before placing a large order, but I didn't think that we'd been so transparent about our racing.

I brought up our vineyard website and looked around. It mentioned that we were into racing, but not what fields we were all in. Something felt weird about that.

I checked my email, and the order from Roger had arrived. I emailed it through to Grace and Hope before heading into the main building.

I arrived there in time to see Mike. He walked over and gave me a hug. "How are you holding up?" he asked.

My eyes stung, and I blinked them rapidly to stop the tears from forming.

"I'm okay, just had a large overseas order come through," I said, trying to put thoughts of Cole and racing behind me.

"Have you heard from the racing committee?" he asked.

I felt my face go cold as my heart thudded in my chest."No," I dragged out the vowel, wondering what was coming next.

"They've received a report of you colluding with Cole to set you up to win the races."

"That's a lie!" I cried out. Then remembered where we were. I pulled Mike into Grace's office, which was fortunately empty.

"What is going on?" My mouth felt like cotton wool had been stuffed in it, and I was struggling to get my words around it.

Mike indicated for me to sit and then sat on the couch opposite."They said that someone laid a complaint, but we suspect we know who it is."

"Who? Cole?" I asked, the last word tripping off my tongue slowly.

"No, more likely Nigel."

I put my head in my hands; my entire world was crumbling down around me. What was going on? First Cole, now Nigel was trying to stop me from racing again? I looked up at Mike. "He doesn't want me to win the championship."

"It looks like it. And we suspect he's the one sabotaging you, not Cole."

"But I saw Cole—"

"I know you did, we all did, but Cole isn't the type to do that, and you know it."

"Do I?" I felt my face heat as I glared at Mike.

"Yes, you do, you're just using it as an excuse because you're scared."

"What? You're attacking me now too?" I stood up and started pacing.

"No, I'm not. What I'm trying to say is that you're scared. It's okay to be scared. But it's not okay to accuse someone who has done nothing wrong."

"And how do you know that?"

"Because unlike you, I trust Cole."

I sat down. I thought I trusted Cole, too, so why did I jump to conclusions?

"What makes you think Nigel did it?"

"He's had more opportunities than Cole. Think about it, Faith. Cole was with us a lot of the times when these things happened. It would take longer than a couple of minutes to unscrew and let air out of your tyre, or to drain oil from your bike without us seeing any evidence."

I nodded, but still wasn't convinced."Right, okay, so what do I do about the colluding thing? Can we make it go away?"

"No, we have to present your case to the committee."

"When? Racing is in two weeks?"

"They're meeting next week, so we have to attend."

"In person?" My mind started to plan, booking tickets to wherever the meeting was taking place, making accommodation bookings.

"No, they will do an internet meeting. They'll send me the details, and I'll let you know."

"Okay." I nodded. "So, how do we fight this?"

"We have to convince them that Nigel has it in for you. We have to tell them about the previous seasons, and we'll need Cole on board too."

I shook my head. "We can't bring Cole into this."

"But he is the one they are suggesting you colluded with."

"But we didn't."

"We know that; we just need Cole to tell them that as well."

"But…I…" I swallowed hard, as pain clenched my heart. "I don't want to see Cole." I ducked my head, which felt foggy. My mind was swirling. Had I gotten it so wrong that I had stuffed up something so right? I clutched my hands together before I started wringing them. Mike put his hand over mine, holding them still.

"We'll win this, okay. They know there's been tension between you and Nigel for years. And if he laid the complaint, then it makes it easier to defend."

"How? He's not even racing any more."

"It plays into our hands, okay? You're going to have to trust us, your team."

"I do, I trust you every time I race with my life."

"I know, but you have to trust Cole too."

That was a little harder to swallow. But I nodded. I didn't know what else to do.

All I wanted to do was crawl into bed and sleep off this bad dream.

# chapter forty-six

Cole

When Mike contacted me about the racing committee meeting, it didn't surprise me. Dad said he was going to report us, and I'd spoken to a race official in Invercargill, though I'd been in so much pain, I remember little of the conversation.

Mike asked me if I could prove that we hadn't colluded, but I didn't have any proof. We'd been sleeping together, but how did you establish that we hadn't tried to fix the races so that she'd win? Faith didn't deserve to lose the championship because we'd gotten together.

And as for Dad sabotaging her bike, it was my word against his because he would just say that he did nothing. And it was words spoken, not actions captured on video…or was there?

Our bus had a camera on the outside to film comings and goings. I wondered if it had been active while we were racing? I had to find out. The problem was the campervan was at Dad's. It was technically his, and chances were, he'd already wiped the video. My excitement deflated like a balloon.

But I had to check.

I waited until I knew Dad was out, and then sneaked into his yard. The trailer was locked, but I had my own set of keys for it. I walked around the outside, and the camera was still there, looking out to the doorway of where the awning would be when we set it up. I unlocked the door and climbed inside. There wasn't a lot of room when we had it packed with my motorbike and gear, but the cupboard was accessible, and I pulled out the memory stick. I wasn't sure how long it would have recorded, or if it had already been recorded over, so I put it in my pocket. I pulled my cell phone out and hit record to view around the trailer. There might be something I missed that could be used; I didn't know. There wasn't anything else there that was of any interest, so I climbed out and locked the door behind me.

"Find anything?"

I screamed like a girl, dropped my phone and fell backwards, kicking my feet out. My father laughed as he reached out a hand to help me to my feet. Fortunately, I hadn't landed on my broken wrist, but that now thrummed with pain from being jolted. I took his hand.

"Thought I'd left my book in here, but I couldn't find it. Probably left it at the motel," I said, trying to sound as natural as I could.

"Didn't see any books in there, and you could have rung and asked."

"We had a fight when you left, didn't think you'd be talking to me."

"We're family; we always talk." He nodded towards my wrist. "Are you alright for racing in two weeks?"

"Probably not," I muttered, looking at my wrist, encased in a blue cast. "Snapped the bone."

At least my father winced."Oh well, no worries, we'll get them next year."

"Look, Dad, I don't think I'll be racing next year." The look on his face was pure thunder. Surprising just how quickly his emotions could change. "I'm not into this racing game, and I certainly don't like the underhanded tactics you've pulled this year."

"I have done nothing that didn't need to be done. And I did it to get that girl out of the race. Championship races aren't made for them. They should have their own class and race on scooters."

"Dad, how can you say that?"

"Very easily."

"Is it because she's a better racer than you?" I knew it would provoke him.

Dad's face went red, and his fists clenched. "I won the championship three years in a row. I did it all by racing hard."

I took a step back. "And she proved herself each time by placing in the top three. And you couldn't let her have her moment in the sun."

"Hell no, why do you think I plotted against her. It was ever so easy to make it look like an accident with the pebble in the tyre valve, but draining the oil, and putting water in the brake reservoir, they were strokes of genuis! I had to do something to stop her racing. She's a hazard out there, waiting to take someone out."

"It was you!" Suddenly, all I could see was red. She had dumped me because of him. Before he could flinch, I swung a punch and caught him on the left cheek. His head snapped sideways, blood spilling from his mouth.

He gaped at me, holding his cheek. "How dare you hit me!"

"I've seriously had enough of you and your narcissistic ways. Keep away from me and Mum. And Faith." With all my strength, I turned and walked away before realising that I'd left my phone on the ground. I went back, and keeping an eye on Dad, who was glaring at me, picked it up, before stalking off again. He was my Dad, my flesh and blood, but he was an idiot. Unfortunately, I was related to him. But I wasn't anything like him, and I hoped I never would be.

As I got to my car, I opened the door and sat down, putting my phone on the seat beside me. I blew out a breath, my head swimming and my heart pounding. I had to get away from here as quickly as possible. I started my car and drove off. Glancing in the rear view mirror, Dad was standing by the trailer, waving his fist at me, but that was all he would do. I'd punched him and he hadn't retaliated, because he was more scared of me.

I blew out a breath and smiled to myself.

My father was afraid of me.

# chapter forty-seven

Faith

The race committee held it's meeting a week before the last races in Hampton Downs. My hands fidgeted, and there was a burning sensation at the back of my throat. Mike sat down, patting me on the shoulder as he did so. We were in my office, sitting in front of my computer. We were both called into the meeting, and I understood Cole would be there too.

I didn't know if my nerves were from the meeting or from seeing him again. My heart ached for him, but there was the pain of betrayal as well. I know everyone told me he wouldn't do it, but I couldn't help that a small part of me thought he could of, and that was what made me sick.

The video flickered on, and we saw six other faces. There was a blank spot. I gazed around the screen and realised that it must be for Cole. The screen flickered again and then there he was. My heart leapt in my chest as I saw him. He looked good, though he seemed to be tense and ill at ease.. The blood thundering through my ears increased, and my vision blurred. I gripped the desk, and Mike passed me a glass of water. I gulped down a few mouthfuls and felt a little more alert.

"Alright. Good afternoon, everyone. My name is Cliff Newman. I'm the chairman of the race committee. I called this special committee meeting because we have received information that you, Cole Blythe, and you, Faith Hart, have been colluding to win the championship."

"Hello, my name is Mike Mason. I'm Faith's manager, and I would also like to introduce charges of interference with Faith's motorcycle prior to races in Christchurch and Invercargill."

"You have proof?" Cliff asked, his gruff voice showing his annoyance at being interrupted.

"We have proof it was interfered with," Mike said. I turned my head to look at him. I touched his arm, but he shook his head at me.

"Hello, I'm Cole, my father was sabotaging Faith's bike."

There was an intake of breath, and I felt my heart seize in my chest. What?

"I have some video surveillance of my father heading out from our trailer in the middle of the night when we were at Invercargill. I can't confirm that he was sabotaging Faith's bike, but I have audio proof he did.

He hit play on his phone, and a grainy conversation came through.

"Look, Dad, I don't think I'll be racing next year. I'm not into this racing game, and I certainly don't like the underhanded tactics you've pulled this year."

"I have done nothing that didn't need to be done. And I did it to get that girl out of the race. Championship races aren't made for them. They should have their own class and race on scooters."

"Dad, how can you say that?"

"Very easily."

"Is it because she's a better racer than you?"

"I won the championship three years in a row. I did it all by racing hard."

"And she proved herself each time by placing in the top three. And you couldn't let her have her moment in the sun."

"Hell no, why do you think I plotted against her. It was ever so easy to make it look like an accident with the pebble in the tyre valve, but draining the oil, and putting water in the brake reservoir, they were strokes of genius! I had to do something to stop her racing. She's a hazard out there, waiting to take someone out."

"It was you!"

He stopped the recording.

Cole's voice had sounded angry at his father's words. I sat in stunned silence. The throbbing in my ears had gone, and I released my breath, not realising that I'd been holding it.

"Sir, with all due respect, I won't be racing at Hampton Downs." He held up his wrist, which was wrapped in a blue cast. "Faith and I started a relationship while we were racing, but it had nothing to do with the championship. She's an amazing rider, and I can't ride like she does. And next year I won't be racing at all. She won those races of her own volition, and I'm sure if you look at the video footage, you'd be able to tell that. I don't think that you should deduct points or remove her from the championship. I've forwarded the audio clip to the committee for their consideration because I think it is Nigel Kinsey who needs to be sanctioned and not Faith."

There was silence on the other end of the video call as all the members started using their keyboards on their computers.

"Well, this puts a different slant on things. Thank you for your co-operation, Mr Blythe, Mr Mason and Ms Hart. We will continue our discussions in private and let you know the outcome. Thank you."

Cliff disconnected the video call, and we stared at a blank screen, unable to see even Cole.

I put my head in my hands. How could I have thought that Cole was responsible? Tears stung my eyes. He'd stood up for me, even after I'd accused him, and had proven that his Dad had been tampering with my bike. He'd also told them we hadn't been colluding, not that I got to have a say at all. But how would I tell them that I rode every single race to win?

How would I ever repay him after this?

I felt Mike's hand rub across my shoulders.

"I hate to say it," he said, "but I said he wouldn't do something like that."

"I know, I know, I was just so angry. I…I…" I couldn't say anything else. It was Cole I needed to apologise to."When will they tell us the results of their meeting?"

Mike shrugged. "Hopefully soon." He stood up and looked down at me.

"Faith, Cole's a good one." The look of pity in his eyes really drained my heart of the last of my hope.

I nodded as tears filled my eyes. I didn't show him out; he knew the way, and I needed some time.

But first, I needed to do something.

I picked up my phone, swallowed over the lump in my throat and rang Cole's number. He didn't answer, but I kind of figured he wouldn't. I hadn't answered my phone when he rang me.

But I would leave him a message anyway.

# chapter forty-eight

Cole

"That was intense," I said to Mum as I got off the computer. She'd stood beside me as I'd provided the evidence to the committee. As soon as the computer screen had blanked off, she placed her hand on my shoulder and squeezed.

"She looks terrible."

"You would too if your dreams were about to come crashing down."

"No, I meant she looked miserable, as in emotionally. She misses you."

"Hmm," I replied, not really wanting to talk about it. My emotions still swung between hurt and anger, but lately they'd been more angry. My phone rang on the desk, and Mum and I looked at it.

Faith's name and face showed up on the screen.

"I'll leave you to it," Mum said as she slipped out the door. I picked up the phone and stared at the face that I'd saved as the avatar. It was one I'd taken on the picnic up on the hill. Faith has her eyes closed, her head tilted back, and she's laughing. Her entire face lit up when she laughed, and

I could hear it echo through my memory. I wanted to answer the phone, but I didn't have the emotional energy within me. I disconnected and put my phone down, instantly regretting my decision.

Why was I feeling like I was riding an emotional rollercoaster?

At least I'd done my part. I'd confirmed my father's part in all of this, and I could put the entire season behind me. Besides, we lived in different towns; I don't see how we could make this work.

I just had to move on.

It wasn't until later in the day that I realised that she'd left a message. I was at home making dinner when a text message came through from Rueben. When I opened up my messaging app, it said I had missed a call from Faith and she'd left a voicemail. I stared at the notification, trying to decide if it was worth putting myself through that pain.

Maybe she was apologising. Yes, she owed me that much.

Selfish, I know, but I needed that closure.

I replied to Rueben about his car needing paintwork and went back to making dinner. But the fact Faith had left a message haunted me throughout the evening. I couldn't concentrate on any of the TV programs I normally watched, or focus on the conversation that Mum seemed determined to have with me. I eventually called it a night and went to bed.

I lay there, looking at the phone, at the message that Faith had left a voicemail. It was unusual for her; she preferred to text rather than call. It had always been me who called her. I keyed in the number for my messenger service and took a deep breath, at the same time as my heart started pounding in my chest.

"Hey, Cole, Faith here. Um…look, thank you for today. I appreciate what you did. I, ah…I'm sorry that I doubted you. I can't apologise enough. Um…Your dad told me you'd been interfering with my bike, and I was stupid enough to believe him. Yeah, stupid, stupid. I shouldn't have, but hey, I'm an idiot.

"I don't expect you to forgive me; I can't forgive myself. But…ah…I'm sorry, so sorry I hurt you. I shouldn't have.

"Anyway…You're an awesome guy…I just wanted you to know that."

There was a long pause. "Yeah, okay." Another pause. "Bye." The word was whispered, and I could imagine her closing her eyes as tears fell.

Then I heard the phone disconnect.

My heart skipped a beat as I replayed her words. I listened to the message twice more.

I could tell that she was genuinely sorry. There had been the occasional hiccup in there, so she was trying to hold back tears.

I closed my eyes, imagining her crying, and holding her in my arms, comforting her.

Did I really hate her?

No, I didn't.

I loved her so deeply that it hurt so much even to think about her. But the fact that she didn't trust me really blew me away. Perhaps it was to do with her dad's abandonment? Trusting someone is hard when you've been abandoned.

My head ached, and I closed my eyes as I put one hand on my forehead, the other holding the phone, a tenuous connection to Faith.

Do I ring her back?

Do I text her back?

Do I let her know I got the message?

I put my phone on charge and turned my light out.

And lay awake.

Faith's smiling face haunted my thoughts.

Her lack of trust disturbed my troubled dreams when I did manage to sleep.

I didn't know what to do.

Except toss and turn in my bed.

Damn it, I picked up my phone and sent a text.

# chapter forty-nine

Faith

We hadn't heard from the race committee, but took our chances and packed everything up and headed up to Hamilton to Hampden Downs for the last chance at the championship. If I didn't race, then at least I was there to cheer on the other contenders and congratulate the winner.

Leaving home at two in the morning was a killer.

The drive up was rough. I hadn't heard from Cole. Part of me hoped he'd ring or text, to at least let me know he got my message, but he didn't. I felt better for having apologised, but not knowing if he had listened was hard. I hoped he did and realised that it was heartfelt. I knew I didn't deserve him back, and my heart constantly ached, but it was getting easier to bear. Still hurt like hell.

I was staring out the window, lost in my world of thought and grief when I heard my name called.

"Yes?" I looked around to see who had spoken.

"You with us?" Mike asked.

"Yeah," I replied.

Sara, sitting beside me, took my hand and squeezed it. I looked over at her and then leaned my head onto her shoulder.

"You'll be okay."

"I know," I said. I'd told her all about the unanswered phone call and my bumbling apology.

"You never know, he might actually be there."

I sighed. "I don't think so. He broke his wrist; he's not riding."

"Would you have let a broken wrist stop your chance of racing?"

I smiled sadly; she knew me so well. "Only if I were in pain," I replied.

Sara nodded. "Okay, I get it."

"I just wish he'd let me know he was okay."

"He'll be hurting as much as you are."

"You think? Or is he pleased to have escaped a hellish lifetime with a woman who can't trust a fly?"

"You trust me, and Mike and Geoff."

"You guys are different; you're like family."

"Cole could've been like family."

"Except I accused him of doing really horrible things."

"I get it, Faith, but you need to just let it go."

"I can't let it go. I felt crushed when I thought he had damaged my bike. I wanted him to feel that way too."

"Look, you jumped to the wrong conclusion. Just learn from the lesson, and don't let it happen again."

"Oh, I won't. I gave him a chance to prove that love isn't painful, and look where I am. It hurts so badly." I felt tears well up, and I buried my head in Sara's T-shirt to hide them. Her arm came around my shoulders, and I felt comfort and love from her as she kissed the top of my head. I knew that no matter what, I had her friendship to guide me through the rest of my old, spinster life.

I must have fallen asleep, because I woke up to find we'd parked in the grounds of Hampden Downs.

"Wake up, sleepyhead." Mike said.,

I was still leaning against Sara, who must have been terribly uncomfortable during the trip.

"Sorry," I said, wiping my mouth with the back of my hand. Drool sometimes pooled in the corner of my mouth.

"It's alright, I have another shirt." She grinned.

I rubbed my eyes and stretched, feeling every muscle in my body pull and move. I sat up and waited for Sara to get out before I climbed out too.

It was overcast, and the forecast was for rain, which would make for messy racing, but we had the slicks for the wet track, so we should be good. Racing wasn't until the following day anyway, but we set up, got scruntineered and then Mike went off to find Cliff or someone from the race committee. At least the bike was up to scratch. Geoff had stripped it down, drained every fluid from it, and put it all back together again in the three weeks since we last raced, making sure there were no foreign objects in it anywhere.

Once we'd set up the bike, I was worried that someone would interfere with it. Call it paranoia, I felt uneasy about leaving it.

"It'll be fine," Mike said, slinging his arm around my shoulder and directing me towards the truck. "Security will monitor it."

"I thought that last time, and look what happened." Pain seared my chest. I couldn't believe it was almost a month since I'd accused Cole…

"Believe me, it's fine." The gazebo had walls, which were all let down, and the trailer sat behind it with my practice bike.

"I have a funny feeling…"

"It will be alright. You need to rest, and we need to find out if you're racing tomorrow."

In all the commotion of setting up, I'd forgotten that I might not even be able get out on the track.

"Have you tracked down Cliff?"

"No, but one of the committee members said he would be in touch." His phone rang, the old Nokia ringtone. Everyone groaned except me.

"And speak of the devil," Mike said as he took out his phone.

I stood beside him, my hands fidgeting and I paced back and forth as he spoke on the phone. None of it sounded positive, and my heart sank to my stomach. I felt like I wanted to throw up.

"Okay, I'll let her know." He hung up and looked at me. I couldn't determine what the look was, one of pain or happiness, he had such a poker face.

"You're in," he said, then grinned broadly.

The words took a while to soak in. It wasn't until Mike, Geoff and Sara all crowded around me cheering that I knew what it meant. Some of the other racers came over to clap me on the back.

"They're deducting five points, but it still gives you a chance for the championship."

"Why are they deducting points?" I asked. My gut churned as I tried to mull over the words.

"For collusion. They think that you and Cole were working together to stop other riders from getting first or second position."

"But—"

"Don't complain. You're racing."

I put on a brave smile and accepted everyone's congratulations.

But my heart wasn't in it.

I was happy to race, and that the championship was still on the table, but I realised I didn't want it.

I didn't want the win. I wanted Cole.

# chapter fifty

Cole

Mike asked me to attend the last race meet in Hamilton. I don't know why. I couldn't ride with my wrist broken. It didn't bother me; I wasn't planning on racing any more. Mike told me that Faith could race but had points deducted. I was pleased that she could have her shot at the championship; it was what she wanted after all.

The smell of burning rubber and high-octane gas filled the air as I headed towards the stadium. I wouldn't see much of the race from there, only the start-finish line, but there was a large screen showing the action on the rest of the track.

Being the end of the season, it was a big weekend. Lots of championships were on the line; only the Superbikes had been settled prior to this weekend, because of points. Faith would have had the points in her class if she hadn't been stripped of five of them. For collusion. For goodness' sake. But it was hard to prove we weren't, I guess. It was our word against Dad's. I figured Faith would've been furious.

My phone vibrated. I picked it up, a call from Mike.

"Hey, Cole."

"Hey, Mike, how's Faith?"

"She's good. Where are you?"

"In the stadium at the start-finish line."

"Good, keep an eye out for your dad."

"He's here?"

"Yip, got footage of him tampering with Faith's bike overnight."

I felt heat rise in my face, and my stomach tighten as I clenched my fist.

"We got it on surveillance," Mike continued.

"How's Faith coping?"

"She doesn't know. We locked her race bike away last night and used a decoy, but he doesn't know that, and neither does Faith."

"She'll be pissed when she finds out."

"I know. I'm going to call the police. Just keep an eye out for him, okay?"

"Yeah, I will," I said.

"Come down to the pits during Faith's race. She doesn't know you're here."

"Right, okay."

They had footage of Dad tampering with her bike overnight.

I sighed. I knew it would happen.

I wonder how he knew she would race? Or had he come up here on the chance that she would?

My heart was heavy and cold in my chest. My own father. And he still wouldn't let her be. I don't know what he'd done this time, but the video and the bike would be the evidence. Mike must have damn good video coverage. Especially to pick out Dad.

I watched the races with varying degrees of interest. I wanted to watch Faith's race, but I guess I would have to wait until later in the day.

As they called for her race, I made my way to Mike, and he showed me the video. It was high quality, and it clearly showed Dad putting something into the petrol tank.

"Sorry to have to show you this," Mike said.

"It's okay. I figured out he wasn't a nice person a long time ago."

"Still, it's hard to see it in person."

"Yes, it is." I hung my head. "How's Faith been?"

"Sadly, she's given up."

"Yeah? I thought she would've been going strong."

"No, she misses you and knows how badly she screwed up."

A glimmer of hope lit up my heart. "She's going to win this championship."

Mike shook his head. "Her heart isn't in it."

"It isn't?" My mouth fell open. For as long as I knew Faith, she wanted this win so badly. But now? Why wouldn't she want the win? It was everything to her.

I took off running towards the dummy grid, but they'd already placed them onto the track and shut off the gate. I couldn't follow her out, but I could try to get her attention on the start-finish line. I went to the front, but she wasn't in pole position. I glanced back; she was at the back of the pack.

I waved furiously at her, trying to get her attention, but she was too focused on the lights. I prayed as hard as I could that she would turn her head, but nothing would sever her attention from those lights. It was pointless, but I prayed again that she would know I was there and supporting her and wanting her to win.

The light went green, and she had a smooth takeoff. She wound her way through the first three racers in front of her before I lost sight of them on the first corner. I ran back to the pits and stood with Mike, Geoff and Sara as they watched the surrounding screens, taking in every aspect of the track.

"Come on, girl," I muttered as I stood there watching her duck and weave through the fellow riders. She was in third position and chasing down the front runners. They were in her sights, and I was relieved when she shot around one and cruised through the corner in front of the first-place getter. Then she settled in and rode like the champion she was. It was like her body relaxed, and she just went with the flow, at one with the bike. I'd never watched her race before. She had such a smooth action, I couldn't help but admire her.

We all high-fived when she hit the checkered flag, taking out the win and more championship points. I laughed and clapped, jumping up and down as I waited for her to come into the pits. She pulled up the bike and was taking her helmet off when she saw me. The helmet came off in slow motion, and her face broke out into a smile. It was small at first, almost disbelieving, but then I came in and swept her off her bike.

"You're here."

"And you're racing."

"I'm sorry."

"I know."

I stopped her from talking more by kissing her hard on the mouth. Her lips opened, and her tongue tentatively licked my lips. I deepened the kiss, and her arms came around me, holding me close. When we came up for breath, she was giggling.

"You're here," she kept saying.

"I am."

She ducked her head into my chest, and I felt the helmet hit the back of my head.

"Okay, we need to put that down before you give me a concussion."

"Oh, sorry," she said, putting her helmet on the table at the back of the gazebo.

"So that means you forgive me?"

"Well…"

Her eyes darkened, and I saw the deep, profound sorrow that she'd been carrying with her, and I realised what Mum meant when she said she looked sad.

"Of course. How could I not? You were going to dump the championship over me."

"I was."

"Why?"

"Because my heart wasn't in it. I thought I wasn't even going to be racing."

"But racing is everything to you."

"Not without you. I missed you so much, and it was you I wanted, not racing."

I couldn't help but pull her against me again. I didn't want to let her go, but I knew I had to.

"I'm here now. Let's get you ready for your next race," I said and took her hand and led her into the gazebo. Instead of putting her on her practice bike, I led her through some yoga moves, which isn't easy with leather overalls on, but it helped to calm her down and get her focused on the races.

"Go out there and win them for me."

Her smile radiated into the world, and I was stunned by it. "That I can do."

"I love you," I whispered into her ear. She ducked her head and pushed a strand of hair behind her ear.

"Right back atcha," she said with a grin.

Within an hour, her race was called again, and she prepared to get on her bike and head to the dummy grid.

"You got this," I yelled at her over the roar of the bike, and fist bumped her. She nodded, then turned to focus on the move through to the real grid.

"You two make a great team," Mike said.

"I know."

"I'm looking at retiring at the end of this year…"

I turned to look at him.

He grinned widely. "She'll need a decent manager."

"You're offering me the job?"

"I reckon you could handle her."

"It's up to her, really."

"I don't think she'll mind." Mike slapped my back as he walked away. I couldn't help but smile as I looked over the pits to the starting line.

Then I glimpsed something that made my heart go cold.

"No!" I yelled.

# chapter fifty-one

Faith

The bike thrummed underneath me; my heart was pumping fiercely, matching the vibrations of the bike. Adrenaline was kicking in, and my fingers were ready to let go of the clutch on one side and wind on the accelerator on the other. The lights flashed red, then orange, then green. The takeoff was almost at Mach 2, and my head snapped back before I pulled it down behind the minuscule screen to provide me with the most streamlined figure I could get. I needed to win all these races. I had Cole back; I had to win them for him.

I wove my bike in and out of the other competitors and got to the front. Now I had to stay there and complete the race.

Thankfully, my bike was running perfect. No one had interfered with it, and it was at its performance best. I loved riding my bike when it was like this. I twisted and turned in my seat, throwing out my knee on the corners. It felt so nice to be on it again. The last race, while I won, felt like I was going through the motions. Now, I was actually riding, and the competitive nature came out. Cole was here, so all was forgiven, although we still needed to talk. I held onto the guilt that I'd accused him of trying to disrupt my championship. How cold-hearted was that!

Race, focus on the race.

"You're doing great," Mike came through my headset.

"I am now."

"You're always great, kid."

"No, I'm not, but with Cole by my side…"

It happened in a split second.

One minute I was riding free, then it was like slow motion.

The bike jolted and tumbled onto its side, skidding across the tarmac. I flew over the handlebars, my gloved hands out to cushion the blow as I landed and tucked into a somersault, then I slid along the track. The racer behind me hit my bike and tumbled over; the next two missed, but the fourth bike didn't see me, and hit my ribs as I rolled down the racetrack, causing him to fall off his bike.

The pain was immense; I thought I was going to die. I was vaguely aware of a red light flashing, and moments of gasps and murmurs. Two riders ran up to me and rolled me onto my back. I groaned as I looked up into their faces.

"Don't take her helmet off; she could have spinal injuries," someone yelled. I couldn't see who it was. My body was stiff and spasming horribly. I couldn't take a breath.

I tried to reach up to lift the visor, but someone lifted it for me.

"Ow," I said, making the two men laugh. "No, seriously, it hurts."

"I'm Noel," said one of them, kneeling down next to me. "It's okay; the ambulance is on it's way."

"Where's Cole?" I asked. I thought he would've been here by now.

"Cole? He's here? I thought he'd withdrawn from the championship?"

"I want Cole," I muttered between painful breaths. The tears were hot as my chest spasmed again. I didn't want to die like this.

"Shh, it's okay, Cole will get here," Noel said as he placed an arm on my shoulder. I gasped, and he gingerly lifted it away.

"Faith!" Mike skidded in beside me, puffing.

"Where does it hurt?"

"All over."

"Can you move your legs?"

"I can barely breathe, and you want me to move my legs?" I clutched at my side, feeling the raw leather underneath my gloved hands.

Two more men bustled in, and leaned over me.

"Faith, are you okay?"

"No! I fucking hurt!" I yelled. There was a smattering of laughter around me. "It's not fucking funny!"

"My name is Matthew," he said, putting on latex gloves, his eyes roving over my body. "And you're, Faith?" I nodded. "Where does it hurt?"

"My side," I pointed with my hand. He pulled my gloved hand away and gently touched down my left side.

"Yow!" I howled.

"Yip, I think you have broken ribs. Can you move your legs?"

"What is it with the legs?"

"Do you have any pain in your neck?"

"No."

I wriggled my toes. "Is that good enough?" Matthew looked at me baffled. My boots were still on.

I lifted my left leg, and then my right, grimacing with each movement.

"They work. My neck works; everything is fine unless I breathe. And where is Cole?" I looked around for Mike, but the ambulance guys had pushed him back.

"Where is Cole?" I called out, trying to get Mike's attention, but he was busy talking to a race official. The tears spilled again.

"Can I take this damned thing off?" I asked, trying to unbuckle my helmet, but my gloves impeded my actions. I pulled off the first glove, but the second one pulled on my shoulder, and I cried out.

"Lie still, please, Faith," Matthew admonished. "We need to cut these leathers off. Do you wear anything underneath?"

"I have a bra and singlet top on, but only knickers on the bottom."

"We'll only need to remove the top. You don't appear to have any broken legs, but we need you to stay still. You might have a neck injury.

"My neck is fine," I grumbled.

"We don't know that until we've done X-rays."

I sighed heavily.

I felt the scissors cut through the leather as if it were paper. They cut along my shoulders and then down the front, carefully peeling back the leather like the second skin it was.

"Okay, I can see a broken collarbone." He lifted the singlet top to my bra line and carefully felt down my ribs. About halfway down, I felt a searing pain. I groaned and nearly passed out.

"Okay, broken ribs as well." He pulled the leather scraps back over my body to give me some dignity.

"I'm just going to reach underneath your head, and feel along your neck to see what I can feel, okay?"

"Yes, please, hurry."

"We can't hurry this, sorry, Faith."

The overuse of my name sounded weird. "Mike?"

"Yes, Faith."

"Where is Cole?"

"I don't know; he took off just after your race started. Sara and Geoff are trying to find him. You don't think he did this, do you?"

"Did what? I fell off my bike!"

The look on Mike's face told me something different.

"What happened?"

"We don't know," he said.

I tried to push myself up, but the pain in my shoulder made me groan. "What the fuck is going on?"

"Please lie down." Matthew placed his hand on my good shoulder and pushed me firmly onto the ground.

"I want this damned helmet off." I yelled at him.

"We will take it off when we know you don't have an issue with your neck or back."

"I can move everything," I said, wriggly, uncomfortably, on the ground.

"Please don't do that. You could have an injury that will only become apparent if you get up and walk. We need you to stay still for now."

"I need to find Cole."

"Cole will find you," Matthew growled. The tone of his voice told me he wouldn't put up with my fidgeting, so I stopped moving and blew out a loud, annoyed sigh.

"We're going to slide this backboard underneath you. It's going to be uncomfortable, but we need to stabilise your neck, just in case," he added hastily. Mike moved in beside them as they rolled me onto my side, while keeping me extremely still. They pushed a large wooden board underneath and then settled me onto it. With the leather padding it wasn't too bad, but it was still hard, and my helmet amplified the noise whenever the board moved. They transferred the board onto the stretcher and into the ambulance.

"I'll come with you," Mike said, reaching out to hold my hand.

I would rather it had been Cole, but he was nowhere to be found.

# chapter fifty-two

Cole

I rushed to the other side of the track before the gate closed. I'd seen my father, and I knew that seeing him by the track wasn't a good thing. I needed to get to him before he did anything. I ran around the grandstand, looking for the position where I'd seen him. He wasn't there, but he couldn't be too far away. I kept my eyes open as I heard the race start. Faith's livery flashed past me. Mentally, I sent up a cheer for her, but I needed to find my father.

I made my way around the track, the crowd thinning out. I knew that high-traffic areas wouldn't be where my father was; he'd be somewhere secluded. Where that was, I didn't know, but I had to find him before he did anything.

My heart pounded in my chest as I brushed past people, most giving me a glare as I offered a pathetic sorry in return.

Where was he?

I spotted him on a corner, near the start-finish line. He had a high-powered slingshot in hand and was aiming down the race lanes.

"Stop him!" I screamed at the top of my voice, but there were few people around, and they looked around like I was a crazy man, even though I was pointing in his direction.

I ran forwards, my dad the only thing in my focus. I heard the bikes approaching and saw him take aim. The rubber band stretched, then relaxed, and I heard a bike rev, then crunch and skid along the road. I got to him as I saw him grinning.

He turned and saw me, still grinning like a madman. I looked over at the racetrack and saw Faith lying on the tarmac, just as another bike hit her in her side.

The red haze that bubbled up inside me made me turn and glare at my father. His shit-eating grin was still on his face, and didn't fade as he saw me come at him. He took off.

I ran after him, growling. My heart was in my mouth. I wanted to go to Faith, but I had to get my father. I needed to stop him. I needed to make sure that he never harmed Faith again, even if that was by my own hands around his throat. The heat inside me pushed me on, and I leapt through the air and tackled him to the ground.

A crowd filled in around us, roaring in disapproval. I expected to be pulled off him and he would escape again, but I wouldn't let go of him this time.

"You're a class-A asshole, you know that?" I hissed into his ear. I wanted to punch him so hard, I wanted to knock the life out of him, but I couldn't. It wasn't who I was, but God help me, I wanted to really make him pay for what he did.

A race official ran up to us and knelt down on Dad's legs, holding him still, while talking into a walkie-talkie.

"She deserved it; she doesn't deserve to win."

Some of the crowd heard him and booed. One tried to kick him, but I fended off the blow with my cast, which reverberated through my wrist.

"This is for the cops to deal with," I growled, glaring at the man from where I sat on Dad's back. The offender backed away.

I turned to the official. "How's Faith?"

"She's alive."

"Barely?"

The official laughed. "She's giving the paramedics hell, apparently," he said. I wanted to laugh.

"You hear that? You can't knock a good racer down and get away with it." I grabbed a fistful of his hair and pushed his head down into the ground. I didn't want to hear his response.

"She's in the ambulance; her manager is with her."

I leaned down into Dad's ear. "I should be the one with her, not sitting on top of you, you bastard. You don't deserve to be called a father."

All the years of bitterness and anger spilled out as I told my father exactly what I thought of him. How dare he try to take it upon himself to ruin someone else's career?

"We have plenty of evidence to lock you away for a very long time," I muttered into his ear, refusing to listen to his mumbling as he tried to push back against me.

"We'll take over now," a gruff voice said from above me. I turned to see two police officers as the crowd parted for them.

"Happily. Take him away and lock him up," I spat at my father. I actually spat at him. The cop beside me looked at me, like I'd grown another head.

"This lowlife is my father, but not any more," I said. The cop nodded as he helped me to my feet. The other cop had crouched down and was talking to my father.

"Arrest him for assault. I did nothing wrong," my dad yelled.

"Sorry, sir, but we have video evidence of what you did, and more evidence besides. You are under arrest for the attempted murder of a racer, along with interfering with her bike." The cop wrestled with my father to pull one of his arms from underneath him. "You have the right to remain silent. You have the right to an attorney, or to have one appointed to you." The cops both hauled my father to his feet and dragged him away. I could hear his voice as he yelled and screamed at the cops.

I looked around as the crowd dispersed. I grabbed the official by the elbow before he disappeared into the throng.

"The ambulance, has it left?"

"Yes," he said.

I ran, pushing my way back to the pits to see if I could find Sara or Geoff. Mike was with Faith, but the others would be at the pits, surely, but they weren't.

I grabbed my phone out of my pocket and dialled Mike.

He answered on the second ring.

"Cole," he said.

I heard Faith in the background. "Is that Cole? Can I talk to him?"

"I'll put you on speaker," Mike said.

"Cole? Where did you go?" Faith said, her voice faint as she spoke.

"I had to stop him. I'm sorry I didn't get there in time."

"Stop him? Stop who?"

"Dad," I said, feeling the hot bile rise in my throat again.

"Nigel did this?" I heard Faith ask; her voice was muffled.

"Is Faith okay?"

"She'll be fine. Meet you at the hospital."

"Which one?"

I heard Mike talking to someone in the background, but road noise, and the occasional groan, covered it.

"Waikato, but she may be medevacked to Auckland."

"I'm on my way."

# chapter fifty-three

Faith

Triage and the ED were strangely quiet, but then, it was the middle of the day on a Saturday. They rushed me through pretty quickly, and they finally removed my helmet once they realised I didn't have any broken vertebrae. It felt weird having the helmet off, and everything seemed extra loud, but my hearing soon became accustomed to it. As soon as the helmet came off, an oxygen mask went on, because there was the possibility I had damaged my lungs. I lay on a stretcher, Mike beside me, busy texting on his phone. He had to let my sisters know I was okay, and the officials at the raceway. Sara had the bike back, and Geoff was checking it out.

A dark-haired doctor arrived with a stethoscope draped around his neck, his hands in his pockets. His face lit up with a smile when he came through the curtain.

"Hi, my name is Kevin. How are you doing today?" he asked. I looked at him as if he were insane.

"I'm fine, ready to go home," I said, trying to take off the mask. Mike glared at me, but I wasn't in the mood for this pretentious behaviour.

"Okay, so sweetness won't win you over. I must insist that you keep the oxygen mask on, please. I understand from the paramedic that you came off your motorbike."

"Yes."

"How did that happen?"

I opened my mouth to talk, but then, I couldn't remember what had happened. I remember riding my bike, then going over the handlebars, hitting the ground, lying there, and then being hit again. "I'm not sure."

The doctor looked at me sideways. "You might have a concussion."

"I had my helmet on."

"It doesn't stop concussion; it cushions your head, but doesn't stop your brain from rattling around in there," he announced. "I'm going to shine a light in your eyes, okay?" He took out a penlight. "Can you look at a fixed point and not move your eyes, please?"

I picked a spot on the curtain rail. He flashed the light in my right eye, then my left eye. "There doesn't seem to be any problems there, but we will require you to stay here for the night. We think you have a collapsed lung."

"How do you fix that?" I asked.

"It's not pretty. Let's just discuss that once you've been and had an X-ray. We can confirm that you have no spinal injury at the same time."

I rolled my eyes. I wanted out of here; I wanted Cole.

"We know you have a broken clavicle"—he pointed to his collarbone—"but the paramedic said you took a hit to your side, and suspects that you have some cracked or broken ribs."

"Broken ribs?" I felt the hair rise on the back of my neck and crawl over my head. "What does that mean?"

"It means that you won't be racing for the rest of the weekend." The doctor smiled.

"Well, that's pretty obvious."

"Okay, I'll get onto the X-rays, then we can make a plan."

He disappeared back through the curtain, and I was alone with my thoughts.

What had happened? I remember being on my bike, feeling great, and then, I went over the handlebars, which is unusual in racing. Normally you slide off your bike because you leaned too far one way. Did the bike stop?

"Did you see what happened?" I asked Mike.

"No, but Cole probably did."

"It was his dad, oh man, that's gutting."

"You're feeling sympathy for Nigel?"

"Hell no, I feel for Cole."

"Yeah, well Nigel tried to sabotage your bike again last night, but we caught it all on camera."

"Is that why the bike stopped? But I'd had a good race the one before."

"No. We swapped the bikes out. That bike is now being held by the police as evidence."

"When the hell did you organise all this? And why wasn't I told about what was going on?"

"Because you thought it was Cole. I knew it wasn't."

"Then why is Cole here?"

“I thought you might need some inspiration. To race. You’ve been so down, and you’d lost your fire. I thought that having him here might get you racing again.”

I looked down at my hands. “Yeah, well, it worked.”

“I know. He deserves an apology.”

“I have already. I called and left a message after our meeting with the race officials.”

“I’m pleased to hear that.”

“I won’t doubt him any more.” I fiddled with the starched blanket that covered my legs. Why, it was there, I don’t know. I still had my racing leathers on my bottom half. Someone took off my boots, though. I really didn’t care. I just wanted Cole here with me.

A rustle and commotion came from the Emergency Department door before someone threw back the curtain. Cole, his hair dishevelled, appeared.

“Found her,” he growled over his shoulder. He came into the room and looked me over..

“What’s wrong?” he asked, his head moving between me and Mike.

“Broken collarbone and suspected broken ribs,” Mike said. Cole winced and looked at me, his eyes brimming with unshed tears.

“Shit, he made a mess of you, didn’t he?”

“What happened?” I asked.

“Nigel had a slingshot; I saw him draw it back, then heard you crash. I don’t know what he fired at you, but you came off your bike. What do you remember?”

“Not a lot. It’s like photographs. I’m going over the handlebars, hitting the ground with my hands and feeling something crunch in my shoulder, then skidding along the road, and another bike slamming into my side."

Cole winced again, then gingerly sat on the bed beside me.

"Have you had X-rays yet?"

"They're being organised," I said.

He picked up my hand and held it as if it were a piece of porcelain china. My hand actually looked so pale in his, and so small. I glanced at it as he rubbed his thumb over my knuckles. The sensation was soothing, and I relaxed a little.

"That's the end of your championship this year then."

"Yes," I replied. "But I'm not worried. There's always next year."

"You sure you want to race after this?"

"I've been racing for four years; this is the first major accident, and it had nothing to do with my skills," I said. Mike and Cole stared at me.

"What? I enjoy riding," I said. "Besides, I don't need to win a championship now; I won my reward." I squeezed Cole's hand, and the smile he gave me was blinding.

The curtain moved back, and a young orderly stood at the foot of the bed.

"X-ray for Faith Hart?"

"That would be me," I said. He smiled as he undid the brakes on the gurney and pulled it out. Cole walked beside me.

"I'll wait here," Mike said.

"See you soon," I said as I took Cole's hand and was wheeled down the corridor to the X-ray machine.

# chapter fifty-four

Cole

"Stop fussing," I said to Faith as I tucked her into bed.

"I don't need to be in bed," she argued.

"The doctor said to rest."

"I can rest sitting up."

"No, you can't," Grace said as she fluffed up the pillow behind Faith.

X-rays confirmed the cracked ribs. They hadn't broken, only by the grace of God.

"Will you all stop it, please?" Faith said through gritted teeth. Hope took a step back from the bed..

"Well, the accident certainly didn't help her humour," Hope muttered.

"Being fussed around by my family doesn't help my humour," Faith said between clenched teeth.

"If it were one of us, you'd be there to fuss over us too," Grace said.

"If it were one of you, I'd say, serves you right."

"Huh," said Hope. "Really? Well, serves you right! You're the one who dicked off her bike."

"With help!"

"Hey!" I had to raise my voice to stop the girls from their bickering. "How about you guys leave Faith with me? I'll take care of her," I said.

Grace and Hope looked at me, mouths gaping open.

"Please leave," Faith said as she slumped back on the pillows. Just getting her out of the car, her sisters surrounding her and then arguing with her had tired her out. Grace and Hope muttered as they left Faith's villa, slamming the door behind them. Faith closed her eyes and leaned back.

"You sore? Need more painkillers?"

"No, I'm good. I just didn't need them annoying me."

"They were only showing they cared."

"Hmm," she said. She settled down a little more in the bed. I sat and watched her as her breathing slowed, and she fell asleep with a little jerk and twitches as her muscles relaxed.

The doctors kept Faith in hospital for four days, because her lung had collapsed. They put a drain in, which was particularly difficult to watch. Her lung came up after the second day, and they took the drain out, stitching up the hole in her side. They released her from hospital on Thursday afternoon.

It was an epic trip back. Fortunately, the air ambulance brought us back to Nelson, and her sisters met us there. I don't know if she would have been able to fly a normal domestic flight home. Mike and the team were bringing the rest of the gear back via the road, but there was no way that Faith would've handled the long road trip back. We would have had to put her in a special suspension trailer to remove as many of the jolts as possible. There was still the possibility that the ribs could crack and dislodge, piercing her lung. The fact that hadn't happened was a minor miracle in itself.

She had lost the championship for the year, but she seemed keen to take it up next year, although I wasn't sure that was a good idea. It's hard watching her come off her bike, and a massage wouldn't help her this time. Only rest.

I rolled my eyes. How did one keep a whirlwind from doing anything? A smile pulled at my face.

My whirlwind.

The pain that had filled my body when she'd yelled at me and accused me of messing with her bike had gone. I'd forgiven her and understood why she'd said those things. It had looked like it was me, thanks to my dad. He'd manipulated it so that I had dirt on my hands and oil on my suit when he'd been the one doing it all along. Still, it hurt a little that she'd thought that I could do that.

We'd talked a lot in the last two days. She told me how Nigel would say things about her in front of the other racers, which made her more determined to win. Nigel had seriously underestimated Faith, and so he'd had to resort to desperate measures. I explained that he'd had to quit racing because of his diabetes; he was blacking out.

A hand reached out and touched my arm. "Stop ruminating," she whispered.

I laughed."I'm only making sure that you're being restful."

"I can hear you thinking. The cogs are noisy." She cracked one of her eyes open and looked at me.

"Well, look at you, getting to know me better."

"I know. I'm so sorry I ever doubted you. I shouldn't have, but I was so angry, and I just reverted to my old ways."

"We all do that when we're tired and angry."

"Well, I'll try not to from now on."

"And I will remind you of that."

"I know you will. Now, come here and kiss me."

I couldn't help but grin. I moved up the bed as quietly as I could and sat beside her. She leaned her head on my shoulder, grunting a little in the process.

"Is that uncomfortable?"

"It's okay," she said, wincing as she tried to twist herself around. I kissed her forehead, because that was the only part of her I could reach, and I felt her settle more into my shoulder and her body relaxed.

"Thank you," she whispered.

"What for?"

"Everything, getting me home, looking after me."

"I love you," I said, settling in gently beside her.

She looked up at me, and grinned..

"Right back atcha."

And I knew she meant I love you too.

Read on for the first chapter of Gaining Grace

# gaining grace

A Racing Harts Novel

It's taken Grace Hart three years to get back on her feet and have the confidence to take part in the Rally of New Zealand. But her past is about to come back and disrupt her plans.

When Lachlan Ngawhika left for France chasing a rugby contract, he broke Grace's heart. He's underestimated the bitterness Grace holds onto.

But fate wants them together.

Even keeping Lachlan at arm's length can't stop the feelings they have for each other. But when Lachlan has to return to France, old wounds resurface. Is history destined to repeat itself?

In this Second Chance Romance, Grace and Lachlan must navigate their way through their love, where every turn could lead to victory… or heartbreak.

# chapter one

Grace

I sat in my Mazda 323, affectionately nicknamed Sally Rally Car. I had my helmet on, waiting for the go-ahead from the race official. This was the rally sprint, one of my favourite types of rally racing. Jordan, my co-driver, sat next to me, except her visor was darker than usual.

"You okay?" I asked. Jordan nodded, but remained silent. She indicated to move forward, just as the official did.

"Ready?" the official asked. I nodded back, pulled my visor down and waited for the go signal.

When I got it, I slipped one foot off the clutch and planted my boot onto the accelerator and took off. My car spewed a stream of dust and grit behind us, but I didn't care.

Jordan indicated left or right depending on the map that she carried. Words often accompanied her directions, but Jordan remained strangely silent. It worried me and disrupted my focus.

We rounded the corner at the top and clocked past the finish line.

"What's wrong?" I turned on her as soon as I stopped the car.

"No…nothing."

That voice was too deep for Jordan. What the hell was going on?

I got out of the car and walked around to the passenger side, opening the door and pulling Jordan's visor up.

But it wasn't Jordan looking back at me; it was Lachlan, my ex, who was supposed to be in France.

I stood there stunned. Pain tore through my chest as I gazed upon the handsome guy, but tears stung my eyes.

"What the fuck?" I asked, straightening up and walking away.

Lachlan was supposed to be somewhere in France. He'd broken up with me prior to going 'so that I could find a decent guy if I wanted to'. He'd broken my heart because I loved him so damned much. I angrily removed the straps from my helmet and dumped it in the driver's seat.

"Hey, Grace," he called out.

I turned and walked back to him, pushing him in the chest.

"Fuck off."

Turning on my heel, I went to leave, but he grabbed my wrist and spun me towards him.

"That's no way to greet a friend?"

"You gave up that right when you dumped me and left New Zealand without a word."

"I sent you messages."

"I deleted them all."

"I sent word; you chose not to read them."

I harrumphed. I could see the red blaze filling my vision. I clenched my fists and my teeth. The anger rising inside was about to come surging out, and I couldn't stop it. I punched him as hard as I could in his jaw. Not only did I feel the crack, but I heard it too, and realised that I'd broken a knuckle, probably two. I flexed my hand, still encased in gloves, knowing that I'd made a big mistake, yet feeling so much better for letting that anger go, and laying it on Lachlan. How many times had I dreamed of doing such a thing to him?

"Fuck, Grace, that hurt."

Clutching my sore right hand, I looked up. He was holding the left side of his jaw, glaring at me.

"Now you know how it feels," I said and stalked off. I had to get my hand out of the glove because my fingers were aching so badly. Rushing to the ambulance, I finally shook the glove off.

"How did you break your fingers?" the ambulance attendant asked.

I'm not normally a violent person, and I didn't want to tell him I had hit my ex-boyfriend.

"I smacked the steering wheel," I replied. It could have happened. I'd seen others do it when the time trial didn't go their way.

"You're the third one today. You guys need to learn to cope with your frustration better."

I nodded, knowing that he was right. I needed to learn to deal with my anger better, and the farther away Lachlan was from me, the better I could cope with it.

"And what happened to you?" I heard as the attendant smothered my hand in a large towel with ice. I glanced over and saw Lachlan behind me. "I'm the steering wheel," he replied, a glimmer of mischief in his eye. The attendant dealing with me looked at me sideways. I shrugged. He was trying to be funny. How he had a sense of humour at this moment I didn't know, but I wasn't feeling in a mood to laugh. In fact, my fingers were aching so much I wanted to smack him again to make the pain go away.

The other attendant sat him on the bench next to me, and I shuffled over so that we wouldn't touch. The farther away I was from him, the better.

Over the smell of the leather overalls, I could smell his familiar scent of sandalwood and pine. His nearness to me made my nerves tingle with remembered feelings, and I moved again to put more space between us so I couldn't smell him, or see him.

Then I remembered. "So where's Jordan?"

"Down at the bottom of the hill."

"Did you bribe her?"

"I didn't need to bribe anyone. She thought you'd be happy to see me."

I mumbled a response, but my brain was thinking of ways to murder my best friend when I saw her again. How dare she assume I'd be happy to see Lachlan? The man broke my heart, crushed it, jumped up and down on it and then mushed it into the ground. How could I find another man who would measure up to him when he did that to my fragile heart?

I focused on the ice, on the cooling effect on my fingers. The pain of the broken bones was barely perceptible under the numbing coldness of the ice, but it was there, and I knew it was going to really hurt later on.

"We've called another ambulance to take you to the hospital," my attendant said.

"Please don't put him in there with me," I said.

He leaned in to me. "Why not? Is he an abuser?"

I heard Lachlan snort as he must have overheard his words.

"Yes," I replied, glaring at Lachlan. "I was defending myself against his unwanted advances."

Another snort of derision, but I didn't care.

"That's okay, there's someone at the bottom with a broken arm, so you'll be in the same ambulance as him," the male attendant said. "He"—he nodded towards Lachlan—"doesn't need an X-ray because his jaw isn't broken. She hit you in the strongest part of your jaw."

I breathed out a little, relieved, then realised that I was holding my breath so that even in breathing, I wouldn't touch him.

"Can I go now? I can walk down to the bottom," I replied.

"The ambulance is on its way up," my attendant advised. "It should be here in about three minutes."

"Is he doing the time trial too?" Lachlan asked, smirking. I itched to wipe that bloody smile off his face. But I already had broken fingers. I wanted to take part in the Rally of New Zealand championship this year. Breaking all the fingers on my hand would only delay it for another year. I wouldn't do that. I wanted to race it this year. Racing through the dirt, mud and rain to hone my skills for the last two years, only to have Lachlan delay my driving again…I was second on the Nelson Car Club's rally board. I had a good chance of making headway in the national rally.

"Here it is," the attendant said, pointing to the ambulance that pulled up beside us. I got out and waited as they opened the back door. I climbed in as the two ambulance attendants spoke about my hand and the suspected broken fingers.

"Do you need him to meet you at the hospital?" she asked, nodding over towards Lachlan.

"Nope, I'll ring my sisters," I replied, then sat back. The other guy in the ambulance leaned forward and offered to shake my left hand with his left hand.

"Jason," he said. "First rally, rolled my car."

"Bugger," I said. I awkwardly shook his hand. "Grace, punched my ex-boyfriend in the face." I held up my fingers wrapped up in an icy blanket.

"Remind me not to annoy you," Jason said, leaning back in his seat, looking at me out of the corner of his eyes.

"I don't think I'll need to." I said, sitting back as well.

I had to bite my cheeks as I watched Jason blanch at my words. It was mean, I know, but I was still trying to get the last of the aggression out of my system, and he was the poor sucker who was nearest to me.

## Behind the Story

This story was originally devised about ten years ago when I was grass karting, and it was becoming a popular sport. I wanted to have a mother and daughter racing team, who meet a father–son team, and while the parents clashed, the daughter and son hit it off.

But I couldn't seem to get past the thinking about the idea phase of story development.

Then about three years ago, I started thinking about doing a trilogy, and for some reason, this story came to mind, and I thought, I could develop this to three sisters, and the rest is history.

Racing Harts has stayed, but now I have three very independent sisters who race different machines. Faith, the youngest, races motorcycles and has had her eye on the championship for a few years.

Faith doesn't believe in love because of what she sees going on around her, so she's resistant to falling in love, instead focusing all of her attention on winning.

Her older sister Grace races rally cars, and Hope, the eldest, races sprint cars.

I wanted to write the stories consecutively, so that they had some flow to them, however I started Hope's after I wrote Faith's, because Hope was going to be the middle sister, but I decided to change tack and make her the eldest, so I wrote Faith's, Hope's then Grace's.

Each sister works at the family vineyard, and family is important to them, because their mother died when they were young, and their father left them. The thread through all of the stories is their father's return to the family.

I really enjoyed writing all of these stories, and developing the girls and the guys that would win their hearts. While I love each story on their own, I think it was Hope and her hulking American that I loved writing the most. But you'll have to wait to see that story.

Thank you for taking the time to read this book. If you enjoyed it, please leave a review on Goodreads and wherever you purchased this book from.

**Gratitude and Beatitudes**

Thank you for reading this story. If you enjoyed it, please consider writing a review or sharing your thoughts on your social media page. I love connecting with my readers, so feel free to email me direct. Or join my newsletter here.

**Carole** and **Janet** – for your encouragement and the cheerleading from the sidelines.

**Serena** and **Barbara** – for the catch ups, write in's and general chitchat and encouragement to keep going when things get tough

**LaVerne Clark** – I love you! Thank you for being my editor and making my stories shine.

To all my fans – (especially **Nicola, Michelle, Brenda, Jeanette, Joan, Estelle** and **Viv**) thank you for buying my books. I really appreciate it.

And always –

To **Mum, my son,** and **Sheri** – Thank you for your support and encouragement. It means the world to me that you guys believe in me.

My **Mr H** – who boasts to everyone that I write, and for telling me I'm a good girl when I get writing or editing done. That small amount of praise is enough to keep me going. You are my heart, thank you so very much for accepting me as I am.

**Bobba and Beth** – My guardian angels. From the bottom of my heart, thank you for being there for me when I needed you guys most.

YOU GUYS ROCK.

**Who is Catherine Mede?**

Catherine Mede lives in Motropolis, in the South Island of New Zealand with her handsome hero, her tall and lanky son and a rescue cat called Lunar. When not writing, Catherine likes to read, be crafty and work in her garden.

Although having developed a love for writing when she was at high school, it wasn't until she was in her thirties she decided to really get down and dirty with the words in her head.

Romance and speculative fiction are the genres Catherine likes to dabble in, because hey, why not? And adding fantasy elements fulfils her need to create fanciful worlds.

When she was younger, she wrote to escape reality, now she writes it to allow others to enter a world where love has a happily-ever-after ending.

**Stalk Catherine Mede on:**

Facebook: www.facebook.com/Catherine Mede
Pinterest: www.pinterest.com/Catherine Mede
Instagram: @CatherineMede
Website: www.catherinemede.com
Email admin@catherinemede.com

www.ingramcontent.com/pod-product-compliance
Lightning Source LLC
LaVergne TN
LVHW091108080826
845145LV00008B/1851

* 9 7 8 1 0 6 7 0 9 0 1 7 3 *